PRAISE FOR And Still W

Genocide in Bosnia

"A powerful story that needs to be heard and known. It puts a face on hatred and intolerance in Bosnia during the genocide in 1992 but it also portrays the human capacity to surmount that hate with bravery that gives you hope for a better tomorrow." Jasmina Dervisevic-Cesic, survivor and author of *The River Runs Salt, Runs Sweet*

"Sher's characters are fictional, but the events in the book, described with great skill and attention to detail, aren't. This a fascinating tale dealing with personal stories both during and in the aftermath of the Bosnian genocide, while still confidently delivering a strong message of peace and hope." Eldin Hadzovic, freelance journalist, Sarajevo, Bosnia and Herzegovina

And Still We Rise

A NOVEL ABOUT THE GENOCIDE IN BOSNIA

JORDAN
STEVEN
SHER

Jordan
7/10/22

atmosphere press

Published by Atmosphere Press

Cover design by Josep Lledo

Atmospherepress.com

GLOSSARY

Prijedor (pron. Pri-eh-dor)
A municipality in Northwestern Bosnia that contains many villages, towns and cities with Prijedor (city) being the largest; population 54,000.

Kozarac (pron. Ko-za-rahtz)
The second largest city in Prijedor municipality; population 27,000

Omarska (pron. O-mar-ska)
A town with former iron ore mining company referred to with same name, turned concentration camp in Prijedor municipality.

Trnopolje (pron. Turn-o-poll-yay)
A village where a primary school and sports fields were turned into concentration camp in Prijedor municipality.

Keraterm (pron. Ker-a-term)
A former ceramics factory in Prijedor city turned into a concentration camp.

Manjaca (pron. Man-ya-cha)
A Prisoner of War (POW) camp used to imprison mostly civilian Bosniak and Croat civilians

Bosniak (Baz-knee-ak)
An historically acceptable term used to refer to Bosnian Muslims

Croat (pron. Crow-aht)
Bosnians who consider themselves as part of the wider Croat ethos

Karlovac (pron. Kar-lo-vahtz)
City in central Croatia

TABLE OF CONTENTS

Foreword		i
The Path to Genocide		iii
Disclaimer		ix
1.	An Unease Arises	3
2.	Elvir and Hajra	11
3.	The Beginning of the End	16
4.	The Spiral Downward	24
5.	The Fall of Kozarac	32
6.	Omarska	42
7.	Trnopolje	51
8.	The Camp Visitor	66
9.	Just Before Summer	70
10.	The White House	82
11.	Dysentery	88
12.	The White House Redux	92

13.	Keraterm	98
14.	The List	105
15.	Trnopolje	111
16.	New Lists Revealed	115
17.	Ride to Manjaca	122
18.	Last Days in Omarska	127
19.	Open Reception Center	130
20.	Manjaca	134
21.	Father and Son	140
22.	Leaving Trnopolje	150
23.	The Lost and the Found	159
24.	More Truths	168
25.	Merjem's Walk Backwards	176
26.	The Snow is Upon Us	183
27.	Karlovac	189
28.	"Finding My Way"	195
29.	Leaving Manjaca	201
30.	Hajra and Merjem	213

31. Germany 219

32. New Lives 227

33. America: 1996 240

34. Danis' Reckoning 254

35. A Somber Return 267

Epilogue 275

Data from ICTY on genocide in Prijedor II

Resources III

Bosnian Alphabet VI

For the millions who were displaced, the many thousands who returned, and those who remain part of the diaspora—never forget the past, but always look to the future.

Foreword

By Satko Mujagic, survivor of Omarska and Manjaca concentration camps and human rights activist

Ed Vuillamy, one of the British reporters who discovered the concentration camps in Prijedor on August 5th 1992, once told me, "People I later met at the Holocaust Museum in Washington, D.C. said that Omarska was an echo of Auschwitz." Of course, nothing can be compared to Auschwitz, but his statement stayed with me. He referred to Omarska as an echo of such a horrific place 50 years later. I was detained in Omarska with my father for three months in 1992 where 700 civilians were killed, probably more, five of them women. Many others, including my mother and younger brothers and sister were sent to Trnopolje camp.

Torture and dehumanization were more regular than the meals in Omarska. I was there the same year at the Olympics in Barcelona that America's Dream Team with Michael Jordan, Magic Johnson, Larry Bird, and other NBA superstars competed. I love basketball, and I wanted to watch them very much playing against the country where I was born, Yugoslavia. Instead of being home in front of the television, I was in a real concentration camp watching my home town Kozarac burning. The TV and furniture stolen, and many of my neighbors and friends shot by the same weapons they also paid for to be protected by the Yugoslav People's Army, which in 1992 was transformed into the Bosnian Serb Army under General Ratko Mladic in their attempt to create an 'ethnically clean Serbian state'.

When I first read the manuscript for this book, I told Jordan that I would only associate myself with it if it stayed true to what really happened in the camps. At first reading, it wasn't. There were many gaps, illogical scenes, and it didn't really align with my experiences. How could it? He was not in the camps. He is not even from the Balkans. How can I expect him to write from that perspective? That was the moment I decided that I would help him. And, he listened. Jordan Sher did not just want to write a fictional book full of horrors, but it was also crucial that the events described were as close as possible to the facts and reality of the war in Bosnia. He heard how neighbors put their non-Serb neighbors into the camps. He listened to my stories of how I almost died, how my father saved my life twice, how I saw first-hand the beatings and killings, and lived in the most dismal conditions one can imagine. And he wrote. He wrote about families, which could have existed, divided and imprisoned, not only in Omarska, but also in other camps run by Bosnian Serb authorities: Keraterm, Trnopolje and Manjaca.

My father once told me that there is no point of explaining what happened in the camps. It is too hard to portray. "Those who have been there don't need any stories about it because they know. Those who haven't will not be able to understand the true horror of it because it is impossible to explain." He said this after the war. In Omarska, he always tried to stay optimistic and would often repeat: "My son, every war has a beginning and an end. And after every war someone survives and writes about it."

Well, the time has come that not only survivors write about the camps in Northern Bosnia.

With this book Jordan Sher managed to capture the 'echo of Omarska' almost 30 years later and it deserves to be remembered as one of the best truth-based fiction works about the concentration camps in Prijedor that has been written. By reading it, you will learn to see it what Vuillamy was saying to me, with Jordan's book now being an echo of Omarska.

(For an historical context)

The Path to Genocide

By Hikmet Karcic

With the fall of Communism in Eastern Europe and the rise of nationalism in Serbia under Serbian President Slobodan Miloševic, Slovenia and Croatia decided to separate and form their own independent states in 1991.

Both Slovenia and Croatia were now internationally recognized independent states. Bosnia and Herzegovina (BiH), not wanting to stay left by itself in Serb-dominant Yugoslavia, following their examples, voted a referendum for independence on 29 February 1992, and declared independence on 1 March 1992. The Serb nationalist parties declined independence of BiH and pledged loyalty to Belgrade. With the help of Yugoslavia, the Serb Democratic Party (SDS) - a leading Serb nationalist party - decided to form its own Serb Republic in BiH.

The Serb Democratic Party, with overwhelming support of the Serb people, started forming parallel institutions throughout BiH. On 9 January 1992, the Serb Republic of Bosnia and Herzegovina was declared. The Parliament of the Serb Republic of Bosnia and Herzegovina was composed of democratically elected Serb Democratic Party members from municipalities and state institutions.

On 6 April 1992, the Yugoslav Peoples' Army along with local Serb extremists and members of the Serb Democratic Party started an all-out attack on non-Serbs throughout Bosnia and Herzegovina. The aggression lasted for three and a half years, resulting in ethnic cleansing and genocide of Bosniaks in Eastern and Northern parts of Bosnia, now known as *Republika Srpska (RS)*.

The plans to establish their own new Serb state were already underway in 1991. They constituted their own assembly made up of Serb politicians, established the Autonomous Region of Krajina—a semi-state consisting of municipalities in the Krajina region of Bosnia, as well as the Serb Autonomous Regions of Bosanska Krajina (including Prijedor), Romanije, Birač and Herzegovina.

The Serbs demanded the separation of municipalities, the creation of parallel institutions and that these Autonomous Regions remain in Yugoslavia. In April, Serb militias, named "The Tigers" and "The White Eagles" attacked, along with the regular Yugoslav People's Army, the border towns of Zvornik, Bijelina and Višegrad. The war had officially started.

The intellectuals and elites were targeted first. Hundreds were executed, and thousands expelled from their homes, left to seek refuge in Bosnian Government-controlled areas. The Bosnian Serbs were shocked by the amount of unexpected resistance, especially after the Bosnian Serb Army's failure to take control of the Presidency building in Sarajevo on 2 May 1992.

As the war already seemed to be lasting longer than had previously been assumed, on 12 May, the 16th session of the assembly of what was then 'Serbian Republic of BiH' was held in Banja Luka, the largest city in the *Republika Srpska*. There was a long discussion on how and what should be done to bring about a Serb victory.

The President of the *Republika Srpska*, Radovan Karadžić, then announced the strategic goals of the Serb people in Bosnia and Herzegovina. These goals were adopted by the Serb Assembly and became the official policy of *Republika Srpska* throughout the war:

The Six Strategic Goals of the Serbian Nation

1. State delineation from the other two national communities.
2. The establishment of a corridor between Semberia and Krajina.
3. The establishment of a corridor in the valley of the Drina River, meaning the elimination of the Drina as a border between the two Serb states.
4. The Establishment of a border on the rivers of the Una and Neretva.
5. The Division of the city of Sarajevo into Serb and Muslim parts, and the establishment of a state authority in each part.
6. Creation of an outlet for Republika Srpska to the sea.

The first strategic goal was the separation of the Serb communities from the Muslim and Croats communities, leading to the creation of an ethnically 'clean' Serb state on Bosnian territory. The second strategic goal would create a territorial connection between the *Republika Srpska Krajina* (the Serb republic in Croatia which was militarily defeated in 1995) and Yugoslavia (which by then, was comprised only of Serbia, Macedonia and Montenegro)

The third strategic goal, was well defined by Radovan Karadžić during his speech in assembly:

> "*We are on both sides of the Drina and our strategic interest and our living space are there. We now see a possibility for some Muslim municipalities to be set up along the Drina as enclaves, in order for them to achieve their rights, but that belt along the Drina must basically belong to Serbian Bosnia and Herzegovina. As much as it is strategically useful for us in a positive way, it helps us by damaging the interests of our enemy in establishing a corridor which would connect them to the 'Muslim International' [Official Serb*

propaganda portrayed Bosniaks as fundamentalists who wish to establish a Muslim state and connect with the other Muslims in the Balkans' so-called "Green Transversal"] and render this area permanently unstable."

The Six Strategic Objectives were the starting points which shaped the rest of the war. The most horrible crimes were committed after these objectives were adopted by the Serb Assembly. They were later further elaborated upon and 'upgraded' by Directive 4 and finally Directive 7, issued by *Republika Srpska* President Radovan Karadžić to the Bosnian Serb Army several weeks before both Srebrenica and Žepa fell. Directive 7 of 8 March 1995 issued the following commands to the Drina Corps of the *Republika Srpska* Army.

In the same regard, the Una and Sava rivers were also a strategic goal for the Serbs. Karadžić stated in the Bosnian Serb Assembly that "It is our vital interest that the Una and the Sava become our borders, that the Drina {River} be ours, for it is ours. It has been ours for 19 centuries."

This idea became institutionalized. On 25 July 1992, the Bosnian Serb Assembly brought a unanimous decision "on establishing disputable and indisputable borders of its territory in the following ways: The indisputable borders are: the western border is the Una River; the northern border is the Sava River; the eastern border is the border with the Federal Republic of Yugoslavia; the southern border is just one part of the border with Croatia; and the south-west border is partly the border with Croatia and partly with the Republic of Serb Krajina."

In other words, all Bosniaks and Bosnian Croats were to be moved from the left banks of the Una river. Thus, the towns of Bosanski Novi, Bosanska Otoka, Bosanska Krupa and other towns along the Una were strategically targeted by the Serbian army.

Hikmet Karcic, PhD, genocide scholar at the Institute for Islamic Tradition of Bosniaks in Sarajevo, Bosnia-Herzegovina. Senior Fellow with the Center for Global Policy in Washington, DC.

Disclaimer

The names of the perpetrators of violence within this book are fictionalized. Their deeds are not. I have tried to base all of what you are about to read on true events. I have gathered this information from interviews, articles, books, documentaries, short video clips, ITN (Independent Television News in the UK) reports, news stories, testimonies at both the International Criminal Tribunal for the former Yugoslavia (ICTY) trials at the Hague of the convicted war criminals, and smaller trials in other parts of Bosnia and the world. The atrocities committed by the nationalist Bosnian Serbs led to 35,000 Bosnian Muslims being killed, according to ICTY date, and mostly men and boys being primary targets. Upwards of 50,000 women and girls were raped and victims of sexual violence (according to some statistics). The numbers for those injured and those who sustained post-traumatic stress syndrome, depression and anxiety are unknown statistically, but if you read about the genocide, my preferred reference to what the entire campaign actually was, various studies bear out the enormity of the problems.

As for the victims and survivors within this book, the names are fictionalized, but if you read up on the genocide you will find that how these characters are depicted are quite accurate.

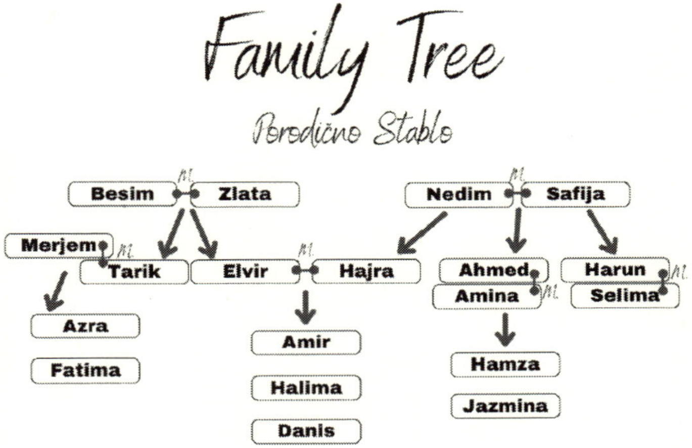
Family Tree
Porodično Stablo
Besim
M.
Zlata
Nedim
M.
Safija
Merjem
M.
Tarik
Elvir
M.
Hajra
Ahmed
M.
Amina
Harun
M.
Selima
Azra
Fatima
Amir
Halima
Danis
Hamza
Jazmina

Chapter 1
An Unease Arises

It was early spring in 1992 when fifteen-year-old Amir Kovacevic came home with sweat caked on his forehead, hair slicked down, and grass stains on his team jersey.

"We won again," he proudly shared. "One more victory and we're going to the regional tournament in Prijedor."

Unfortunately, various chores got in the way of the family going to his game. But they promised to attend the tournament if his team got in. His younger brother, Danis, was especially unhappy not to attend, but he hadn't done his homework, which was the toll he needed to pay in order to watch Amir play.

Amir had a zest for life, especially sports. Aside from soccer, he loved basketball and followed the great Yugoslav National Team. His favorite was the Croatian star, Toni Kukoc. In the late 1980s and early 1990s, in both world championships and the Olympics, the national team dominated every country, including the United States. He followed the NBA, too, and was hungry for any information he could find. Magic Johnson was his hero in the U.S., and he loved the Los Angeles Lakers, watching videotaped games of them whenever they were on TV in Bosnia, which was not very often, but a treat nonetheless.

Thirty-four-year-old Hajra had just begun to warm the burek, her delicious ground lamb pie, for a picnic planned for later that day when her son burst through the front door of their modest home with his good news.

"I'm proud of you, "sefe." She would tease calling him the "chief" being the older brother, and because as captain he led his soccer team with pride and leadership.

She gave him a warm hug and kiss on top of his head. She marveled at his thick and wavy black hair that black reminded her of pictures she'd seen of her father when he was younger. Amir, too, had the dark complexion and deep brown eyes of Roma, once called Gypsies, which in fact he was.

Just then, Halima entered the kitchen to see what the fuss was about. The twelve-year-old was lighter skinned with blue-green eyes and light brown hair that was more in line with Bosnia's Muslims, Croats, and Serbs who, other than affiliating with different religions that began centuries before, came from the same Balkan genetic make-up. She looked more like her father's side of the family. A small girl, she could pass for nine or ten-years-old, and that disturbed her. She was ready to be a teenager. Halima was the most curious of the children, often asking questions.

"Are you guys moving on in the tournament? No surprise there. You and Nikola don't mess around on the pitch!" she exclaimed.

Whenever she heard herself or someone else mention Nikola's name a slight flush appeared on her cheeks. Amir never failed to pick up on it, and he'd slap her knowingly on the shoulder. He never told his friend, recognizing that it would embarrass his sister. Still, she'd practically run away as if she had something very important to attend to elsewhere not wanting to acknowledge his playful teasing. Since she was very studious, it was easy to excuse herself to head back to her studies, which made perfect sense. Of all three children, she loved school the most. Actually, she had told her parents she wanted to be a lawyer someday. And they never ceased to encourage her to follow her dreams.

Danis, the nine-year-old, had his radar tracking his older brother's location. He was especially attuned to when Amir returned from a soccer game that he was not allowed to attend. He was listening for the front door to open.

Like a stone hurled from a slingshot, Danis bolted from his room and yelled to his brother even before he was in his presence.

"I knew you'd win. I knew it! How many goals did you score? Two, three?"

"Hang on. Slow down. OK, well I did get one. A header from Nikola's cross. The keeper had no clue where I was going to direct it. And we won 3-0. We're going on to the big tournament!"

Danis' gangly body didn't always have control over itself. When he came into a room the energy level rose. He idolized his older brother and wanted to be a soccer star like him. He looked like a younger version of Amir, displaying the Roma features of their mother. He often had a serious look on his face, but when prompted, he could break out some great impersonations of British rock stars like David Bowie. And he was a bit spoiled as the youngest often was, a point that Amir and Halima never failed to remind him of.

"Kids, go get ready please. Your dad is coming home early and we're going to meet Uncle Tarik and Aunt Merjem and your cousins down by the river. We're going to picnic with Emir and Amela."

"Can we invite Nikola with us?" asked Amir.

Halima's ears perked up at hearing this, even from her bedroom.

Nikola was a Serbian boy who was practically Amir's brother. They went everywhere together. In school they were inseparable, meeting up with other friends, most of whom had been on their soccer team since it formed five years earlier.

On some weekends, either Nikola slept over at Amir's house, or vice versa. Nikola's mother often sent over some of her homemade baked goods like bundevara, a a kind of pumpkin pie, and if you didn't pay attention, it would be devoured by the boys before anyone got a chance to sample. Or, she might send over some fried dough sprinkled with powdered sugar, which was usually closely guarded by Danis to ensure that everyone would get some for dessert.

Hajra knew that her husband, Elvir, loved Nikola, too. He was a respectful boy with a wry sense of humor. Halima's crush on him was a more recent development. His shoulder-length blonde hair and blue eyes attracted her attention, though she only had a burgeoning notion that this was the beginning of an infatuation. And he did not seem to pay much attention to her anyway. After all, though she was twelve-years-old, she looked younger, and she was sure that would be a no-go for him.

It was an unusually mild day in March, and the buds of the native flowers were just beginning to reveal themselves. It was mid-afternoon and Elvir had just come home. Although some vague rumors of nationalist activity were making the rounds in nearby Prijedor where his brother lived, they were not so disconcerting to prevent an enjoyable family gathering.

"Good idea to have a picnic at my cousin's house. I love the river this time of year. And I'm glad Tarik and his family will be joining us."

The nearby Sana River was where the family often went to sit under its sprawling beech trees. The water always provided them with a place of respite, a place of calm. But Elvir was not comfortable with picnicking at the river's edge with concerns about what was going on in Prijedor. Besides, it was still wet from the winter snow melt. So, rather than going to their usual spot, he had suggested to Hajra that they go to Emir's house, which sat 500 meters from the river's banks and only a few kilometers further from their usual spot.

The six of them squeezed into the Russian-made Lada station wagon, and wound their way to Emir's house.

When they arrived, his brother Tarik's car was already out front. They were just about to enter the house when they saw the Lada pull up. Tarik, a year younger than Elvir, and Merjem's two young daughters, Azra and Fatima, made a quick U-turn toward the new arrivals. How they loved their cousins from Kozarac.

The two families greeted each other warmly as Emir stepped out of the house. He beckoned them all to come in, that the food was ready.

Amela knew the children loved her version of dolma, delicious stuffed green peppers. The luscious aroma greeted the guests at the door along with hugs. Accompanying Hajra's burek, and Merjem's djuvec, her delectable vegetables and rice, was a loaf of hard-crusted bread fresh from the bakery that Elvir had stopped at before heading home. Hajra and Amela dished out the food on plastic flowered plates while Merjem delivered them to the table. The others complimented the chefs as they dug in. The bundevara that Nikola's mother sent was the perfect ending to a lovely late afternoon meal.

Before exploring the riverbank after they ate, Elvir told the children to be back before dark. He was not comfortable having them wander too far for too long. Being close to the house, their laughter echoed from where they played.

The adults settled down for some coffee outside on a small, concrete patio surrounded by trees, facing the river. They were all acutely aware of the stirrings within some of the Serb Orthodox Christian communities in both Prijedor and Kozarac. This was unusual for those in Yugoslavia, and now the independent Bosnia. True, they were of different religions, but that often meant little to the people of the Balkans. However, nationalist Serb rhetoric was beginning to cultivate ethnic divisiveness in the Municipality and all over Bosnia and Herzegovina.

"How's the import/export business these days?" Emir asked Elvir.

"Not bad. It seems to be a little more difficult getting some fabrics in from Asia lately. But otherwise, OK."

"Although our new independence from Yugoslavia is a wonderful thing, I don't know that many of our Serb neighbors think so," Tarik said, almost not paying attention to the previous question.

"Tarik," Merjem interjected, "we're just talking about your brother's business. Can't we wait to speak about politics till later? Or not all?"

"I'm sorry, Elvir. I guess my mind is elsewhere. Um... delicious meal. Thank you for preparing it, you three," he said quickly, veering from his real worries of the present-day.

"No, no, Tarik is right, Merjem. We have concerns that supersede talking about my work," Elvir responded. "I know that we'd all like to just talk about our daily lives. That would truly be the most pleasant, but maybe we need to take a look at what's happening around here and not pretend it isn't. I'm hearing there's some tension now between politicians of both parties, SDS and SDA."

"You know," added Tarik, "I've been talking to Merjem about what I've seen at my precinct in the past few days. I love my new job as inspector, but after that damned Stevanovic from the Serbian Democratic Party was appointed to be their leader in our city government, some new Serb reservists have joined our ranks. I don't know how they bypassed regular police training, or maybe they had some secretly somewhere, but they are starting to show up."

"The other day, I overheard something in Prijedor when I went in to pick up some tools to fix the leaky sink faucet. I heard two guys talking. I am sure they're Serb and part of the SDS. I've seen them go in and out of the government building. They were speaking somewhat quietly, but I got the gist of it. From what I could gather, they were saying that any Muslim extremists in the municipality who showed their faces should be arrested on the spot. They stopped talking when they saw me walk past. Have you ever heard of such a thing? I can't say that I know any extremists or have heard of any activity, to be honest," said Emir.

"I'm hearing some of that talk, too," replied Tarik.

"Why would they tell these lies? Why stir up the local Serbs against their friends and neighbors? We've even spoken with our Serb friends and have gotten assurances that they didn't buy into these lies." Merjem said.

"It's absurd," said Hajra. "I can't believe that anyone in Prijedor Municipality would buy into this, including Serbs. I mean, it's 1992. This is not the Ottoman Empire, or even the 1940s for God's sake. We all should be well past that."

Hajra was referring to notable periods of violence between the three major ethnicities in the region. But all nodded in agreement with her assessment.

"I hope you're right," Tarik said. "It just feels a little strange since we became our own country."

"We all saw the results of the voting. Most of us Muslims and the Croats in Bosnia wanted independence, with a minority of Serbs doing the same. But even with that, we all will benefit from a new prosperity being a sovereign state," said Amela.

"True, and we've been nothing but good neighbors to everyone no matter what religion. We're Yugoslavs first. Well, now we're Muslims from Bosnia is a better way to put it," replied Merjem with a smile.

"Don't know if you are aware, but the Yugoslav constitution entitles republics to vote for independence, so we're just following suit after Slovenia and Croatia. And, many of the world's governments have wanted us to verify our desire to be independent since last year," added Amela.

"Maybe we're jumping the gun here," said Elvir. "Maybe what you overheard, Emir, was the minority. I want to believe that this is the case. And maybe we should finish our coffee and the delicious dessert that our dear Nikola's mother sent over. It's getting dark, so we'll need to round up the kids soon and get on our way."

The others agreed and shifted the conversation back to the mundane. As they all cleaned up, the children came to the house from the river bank laughing and teasing each other. The men smoked one last cigarette before the families said their goodbyes.

Before the two brothers and their families got in their cars, and while the cousins and Nikola were still horsing around in the front of the house, the four adults quietly entered into one more brief conversation.

"I don't believe that anything will happen here, you'll see," Hajra said. "We are a young country now. We get along well with all of our neighbors, Croat and Serb. In Bosnia, there is always a place for us all. Look at the beauty surrounding us. Perhaps we are being overly concerned.

"You're right. But with the invasion of Slovenia and Croatia by the Yugoslav People's Army after they voted for independence last year, and the restlessness in Prijedor, I guess I'm a bit wary," said Tarik.

"Those Kozarac committees I'm on, with all our residents represented, are still pointing toward improving our city. I have faith that that's how we'll proceed. Anyway," Elvir concluded, "let's make sure our cities and the municipality move forward, not backwards."

"Kids," yelled Merjem, "time to go. Say goodnight to your cousins."

They all hugged one more time and then each car sped off as they headed for their homes.

Elvir peered into the rear-view mirror. He saw how his children and Nikola seemed so content with one another. Nikola's family could never feel bitterness toward Amir and his family. Or for Muslims in general. Look at the fine son they've produced.

While the children chatted away Elvir and Hajra stared silently at the road in front of them, each lost in their own deep thoughts.

Chapter 2
Elvir and Hajra

Elvir and his brother Tarik grew up in the village of Trnopolje. It was there they went to primary school, but because there was no middle and high school in town, they had to take a school bus to Prijedor. When they were old enough, before the school day began, the boys tended to the dairy cows.

There were usually no more than two head of cattle at a time. Still, the milk, cream and butter their livestock produced was enough to sustain the family while selling the rest of it to a small distributor in Kozarac. Additionally, a small plot of land grew the tomatoes, lettuce, corn, potatoes, and beans that provided for them year-round.

Tending to the farm, their mother, Zlata, could be seen tilling the soil and ensuring that the produce was healthy. She also cooked and took care of the household chores. Besim, their father, worked at the sawmill in Kozarac, but he, too, got up early with his sons to take care of the cows.

This was a close, hard-working family typical of others in the small villages in Bosnia. They were Muslim, but other than Zlata who was more observant, they only went to the mosque during the holy days. The boys did what most boys all over the world did. They talked about their favorite soccer stars, and how they would someday want to be part of a great European team. And they talked about girls.

The brothers loved to play soccer when they had time. After school and chores were completed, they would wander over to the small soccer field next to the primary school to meet up with other teens to play pick-up games. The games got rough, and it was not unusual for Elvir or Tarik to come home with a few bruises or cuts.

It was a particularly beautiful early summer day, he liked to recall, when Elvir saw Hajra from afar walking into the village's small central square, and he pointed her out to Tarik.

The two had been acquaintances in high school, but had been talking to each other more and more of late. Elvir found himself attracted to her beyond friendship.

"I'm going to marry that girl someday," he told his brother, while draping his arm around his shoulder.

"Aren't you the confident one," said Tarik. "And why would she want to even go out with you?"

"Because I am handsome, a hard worker, smart, and I only brag a little," replied Elvir, mussing up his younger brother's hair.

Hajra had tuberculosis as a child, and her mother home-schooled her for the first few years of her education. There was no need to expose her to anything that would stress her lungs as might happen in their small community primary school. She was the third child of three, born to Safija and Nedim, and the only girl. Her brothers, Ahmed and Harun were each just a year, and two years older than her. Protective as they were, they knew Elvir quite well, and approved of his infatuation with their sister.

Elvir was a healthy, strong sixteen-year-old boy. He approached fifteen-year-old Hajra more seriously than his usual jovial self after school one day. Following some small talk, he told her that he knew he would marry her someday, that this destiny was marked upon meeting her.

Though she was a bit taken aback, she too liked him much more than just friends, and she didn't brush off his bold statement.

Their relationship blossomed, and Elvir visited Hajra frequently. For Elvir it had been 'love at first sight'. Her long, wavy, jet-black hair nearly reached her lower back. Her big brown eyes, set brilliantly like obsidian against her rich olive-colored skin, held him in their power. That is, when she was able to meet his gaze. She was timid, having been home-schooled, with very few friends even after her illness dissipated and she entered fourth grade.

She was shy and had little in the way of confidence, but she did have a sharp mind that she occasionally revealed by coming up with answers to questions that never ceased to amaze Elvir. She had a penchant for geography.

He'd ask, "How long is the Una River?"

Without hesitation she'd respond.

"214 kilometers."

"Ok, then name the three highest peaks in Bosnia."

She'd immediately rattle off, "Maglic, 2,388 meters; Volujak, 2,314 meters; and Cvrsica, 2,228 meters."

Her specificity would always impress him. She was quite bright, and he wouldn't hesitate to compliment her.

Of course, then she would crawl back into the shy young woman that she was known to be.

He could be a clown who enjoyed silly, but harmless pranks that amused her, but mostly, she loved it when he'd sing a sevdalinka to her, which was an old-fashioned love song. He was surely serenading her, she thought. His shoulder-length light brownish-blonde hair, clear blue eyes, loosely fitting jeans, and his outgoing nature was the antidote to her shyness. His quirky sense of humor would trigger her sweet laughter. Their connection grew stronger every day. He could see that she had, at her core, a silent strength that he admired. They remained friends for the next year, and began officially dating the following year. And when Elvir was nineteen and Hajra eighteen, they got married.

Elvir spent a brief time in the Yugoslav People's Army, the JNA, as was required at the time. But a complication with a fractured foot forced him to return to their small apartment in Trnopolje; a studio really, situated on Hajra's parents' land. He helped out on his own parents' farm bringing the dairy products to the distributor, and picked up small jobs with builders. But his foot was in constant pain with all of the movement he was doing. Meanwhile, a year after their marriage, Amir was born. Needing to earn more money for his new family, Elvir turned to his uncle in Prijedor.

"Uncle Safet," he asked one day, "do you think you can give me a try in your import/export company? I'm good with people, and will work hard to grow the business."

In the mid-1980s, his uncle, who had moved to Germany in the 1970's to open his first import/export business, had recently opened his company in Prijedor upon his return to Bosnia.

"I can even apprentice for a while if you want me to, so I can learn the business. You don't have to pay me much."

"Sure, my boy. You can apprentice with me. But I'll pay you more than apprentice wages. You're starting a new family, and I can't have a nephew of mine eating rice and a few beans every day."

So, Elvir eagerly joined his uncle and voraciously learned the ins and outs of import/export.

He loved his work and the customers who visited the store. Safet taught him to see the world as a great, connected network. He trained Elvir to seek "treasures," as he called fabrics, from places that he may never get to visit, but that he should get to know.

Elvir was a fast learner, and soon he was even picking up some other languages aside from his native Bosnian. He learned Arabic when dealing with sellers in Iraq, Libya, Egypt, and Emirates. He learned to speak passable English, which he had some rudimentary knowledge of from high school classes. This came in handy when dealing with other European countries, as well.

When Safet suddenly died of a heart attack in 1988, having

no children of his own, he left the business to Elvir. Within a year, he moved the company to a larger space in Kozarac. He hired a couple of buyers to help him, and the business continued to grow.

By 1992, the couple was content with their lives. After six years of marriage, they had three children who they adored. And Elvir had a thriving business.

Their marriage was solid, and family life equally so. They loved to walk the streets in their city with one of the children in-between so they could swing him or her high into the air, and feel the joyous laughter reverberate straight through to their hearts.

He had bought a nice piece of property, and with the help of his father and Tarik, built a beautiful, though modest house. His children were raised the right way. Out of respect for his parents, they celebrated the Muslim holidays with all of their family members in the municipality.

The day after their picnic at Emir and Amela's house, all seemed calm. Perhaps their discussion during dinner was unnecessarily bleak. After all, they had built solid lives, and there was nothing but a bright future ahead.

"You know what, my husband?" I guess we Bosnians don't say it a lot even if we feel it. But I love you. And I love what we have here. Nothing can take that away. Nothing."

Elvir put his arm around Hajra's waist. The kids were all outside, so he didn't mind so openly showing his affection for her. It wasn't their custom to do so. He kissed her on the lips, which surprised her. She looked out of the window, seeing the children kicking a ball out front. She returned the kiss.

"You are an amazing man."

"And you are the true glue that keeps this family going."

They kissed once more, and parted just as Danis burst through the door asking for a band aid for his scraped knee. They both were thinking the same thing: what could possibly shatter such a glorious existence?

Chapter 3
The Beginning of the End

On April 30th, Elvir came racing home from his office in the middle of the morning. Hajra was just straightening up the kitchen when he came through the door. His face was pale, but his cheeks reddened from news he had just learned.

"The Serbs just took over Prijedor!" he stated breathlessly. "Tarik just called me and said that early this morning the SDS party assumed political and police power. They took over the courts, banks, and post office, too. We had all worried about this after seeing on the news what began earlier in the month with the shelling in Sarajevo and incursions in Visegrad and Foca, and even Bosanska Krupa, but I'm afraid we let our guard down. How naïve!"

He paused to catch his breath.

"Tarik had even seen police reports by non-Serb residents that they were being harassed by local Serbs in their homes to give up their weapons. They were told if they didn't, they would be arrested. As for this takeover, not a single bullet was fired. It was almost like a bloodless coup. All Muslims and Catholics were sent home and not allowed to enter the police station. In fact, all of those who worked in city services were sent home."

Barely catching his breath, Elvir continued.

"The police and government officials were replaced by Serb nationalists. He told me that the Bosnian Serb military are establishing check points with armed soldiers so they're cutting off the exits from Prijedor as we speak. And he saw that local Serb civilians were wearing the Serbian tricolors. I was almost unable to respond. But I managed to tell him that I was going home to continue our conversation."

"Oh, my God. Yes...yes, call him right away."

Elvir, who had been pacing while explaining this to Hajra, picked up the phone and dialed.

As soon as he answered, Tarik began with a warning.

"Let's be careful in what we say. Remember, there might be other ears on the phone, if you know what I mean?" he said.

"I understand. I wanted to be here to continue our call so I wouldn't be as distracted as I might have been at the office. Busy time of year, you know," said Elvir.

"A police colleague of mine said that the Serbian flag was erected at the local police stations, and that all Muslim police officers coming into work had to turn in their guns. I guess I'm out of a job," he said with a muted chuckle.

"I now have 1,500 Serbian brothers who were made reserve police officers. Oh, actually, since I'm no longer employed, I guess we're not brothers after all."

"Interesting development," said Elvir.

Without saying it out loud, and with the grim news in Prijedor, Elvir and Tarik realized that this was a very dangerous time to be Muslim, or Croat for that matter. Neither had expected it would come to such a precipice for non-Serbs.

Tarik continued.

"I'm worried about my family—our family. We have a lot to think about going forward. A lot."

"It sounds troublesome," said Elvir, suppressing any shrill in his voice. "What's happening with you guys and the kids?"

"I am not sure what to do? With the situation here, we are figuring out our best option. If they hadn't blown up the bridges, maybe we'd take a holiday," Tarik said sarcastically.

"Truly, I don't think anyone can leave. The checkpoints are being set up as we speak. I did hear that there is a little group of locals forming to try to prevent the activities around us from getting out of hand, but the Bosnian Serb Army is very well organized."

"I'm sure. How are Merjem and the kids holding up?"

"For now. I haven't said anything to the kids, but Merjem has already started biting her nails again."

"I can't say I blame her. This is a precarious development. Things are quiet in Kozarac, but I'll bet it's just a matter of time. We've heard rumors."

"Listen, let's just keep as calm as we can. There is no violence here, more like a changing of the guard with the SDS," Tarik said while clearing his throat obviously, signaling that he was downplaying his concerns.

"I think we just need to see what happens? I'll call Mom and Dad. I'll let you know what's going on in Trnopolje," he concluded before saying goodbye.

"OK, let's talk later then. Bye."

Elvir stared out the window as if searching for some unknown creature stalking them. He looked out at the street and houses out front; there was nothing unusual about the scene.

Hajra came up next to him and gently touched his arm. Elvir jumped ever-so-slightly, and turned around. He asked her to step outside so that he could relay what his brother had just said in case the kids, who were getting ready for the second shift at school, were nearby.

"It's not good. All non-Serbs in government services are out of a job. My brother and his family are just laying low at home. He indicated that there is some meager resistance forming, but the Bosnian Serb army is very powerful and won't find it too difficult to suppress it."

"I wonder if any of this is beginning to happen here?

"Nothing is happening here as far as I know. Let's hope it doesn't. Maybe their mission is done with Prijedor, but this development is worrisome. The kids should go to school. I'll go into the office, but we need to get ourselves prepared in case the same thing happens here."

"What do you mean? How do we get ourselves prepared?" she asked. "And what about our parents?"

"We'll figure this out," he told her as he walked out of the door to get into his car.

As he drove back to his office, he tried to grasp what figuring this out might actually mean. They were still in Kozarac, a primarily Muslim city insulated by many Muslim villages surrounding them. *How could the Serbs destabilize us? And they know we are not their enemies. Yet, with Prijedor's government taken over, what could be next?*

Tarik called Elvir later that evening. He took a deep breath and tried to sound relaxed.

"So far, Mom and Dad are alright. They heard about what happened here. I told them to stay vigilant, and to mostly stay inside. Mom says Dad can't believe anything like that will happen in Trnopolje because he's friends with all his Serb neighbors, and they won't turn on their neighbors. I'm not so sure. For now, we are going about our business as if nothing has changed."

"Thanks for letting me know. I need to find a way to see you and speak in person, so we don't have to worry about those other ears."

"Sounds good. I'll think about that, too. We'll talk soon."

A few days later, a solution to the brothers seeing each other emerged. Danis had injured his foot while playing in their basement. He stepped on a rusty nail that was hidden in the corner on the floor. It went right through his sneaker and into his foot. He hobbled in to show his father.

Elvir called his brother.

"Danis stepped on a rusty nail. His foot is bleeding and I'll bet he needs a tetanus shot. Meet me at the emergency room at the hospital near you. I'll be there in about a half hour."

Though the new Bosnian Serb police force was patrolling the area, travel was permitted between Kozarac and Prijedor.

It didn't feel quite normal, but a boy's bleeding foot that required medical attention would still not be thwarted by the new local authorities.

Tarik was waiting with his daughter, Azra, outside the ER when his brother and nephew arrived. They all hugged, a little tighter than usual, and went inside.

They exchanged small talk as Danis got his shot and had his foot dressed and wrapped up in a bandage.

"Let's go get a cup of coffee, and some cake for Danis and Azra," suggested Tarik.

"Good idea."

"Cake? I like that plan, Uncle Tarik. That's better than any bandage they put on my foot."

The two men laughed as the four of them got into Elvir's car and made their way to the nearest café.

The server quickly brought over two coffees, and fruit juice and cake for the children, who were already chatting about a cartoon character they both enjoyed on TV.

Elvir began, speaking in hushed tones.

"I'm not feeling so confident about the new guy in charge here in Prijedor. We have formed a committee that wants to meet with him and the others to smooth out any misunderstandings or misconceptions that the SDS might have about Kozarac. Just a feeling, but we've sent a few appeals for a meeting, and our requests have been met with silence."

"Are you on the committee?"

"Peripherally. I helped plan it, but I'm not with the group that would sit down with the SDS. Still, they don't seem to be interested."

"No doubt. I don't know that a meeting will happen, to be honest. From what I've seen here in town, they seem to have taken pretty complete control. Even being at this café, it feels strange. See that cop across the street? New guy on the force. He knows me, and is giving me a good stare."

Elvir dropped his napkin, so that he could pick it up to see what his brother was talking about. He turned back around, and nodded his head toward Tarik.

"It's becoming a serious concern in Prijedor, and pretty quickly. In fact, we should get out of here so we don't raise any more eyebrows."

"OK. But before we go, what do you suggest we do?"

"Nothing. Stay inside your home. But if you have to go to the office, keep it short. And hope that this is it: that they leave us alone. If they want to take over Prijedor, maybe they'll all come to the conclusion that we're not the lethal enemy that their propaganda has been pandering. If not, it's all-out war. Not that our own side won't fight back, but it's not there yet. I know that a network of resistance throughout Bosnia is forming, and with some, already established. We have our own group that is organizing as I mentioned. But Bosnia's Serbs have the JNA doing their dirty work all over the country, and they've been supplying their own military with men and equipment, so it will take some time to counter that. In the meantime, we wait. That's all I can think of for now."

Elvir could say nothing in response. Waiting and hoping was all they could do.

He interrupted the children's conversation. They had long before finished their treats.

They all stood up and hugged each other once more. For the brothers, there was an ominous air hanging, and an unspoken realization that they would not be seeing each other for quite some time.

***

At the outset of April, a month before the takeover of Prijedor, Hajra's parents took their annual bus trip to Banja Luka, about an hour away, to be with her brothers, their wives, and the grandchildren.

Her brother, Ahmed and wife, Amina had a boy, Hamza,

age seventeen, and a girl, Jasmina, who was fifteen. Harun and his wife, Selima, had no children. The brothers had good jobs as did Selima, and Amina worked part-time as a librarian in an elementary school, which she loved. They all liked the bustling city life there, and it was a well-regarded place to reside.

But Hajra was getting disturbing phone calls from Ahmed that the children were being harassed in their school. They even had to list their nationality on a document circulated by the principal. Hamza wrote "Yugoslav," not knowing what else to put. He was confronted by a school administrator who told him that there was no longer that category, that he should put Muslim. She had not heard from any of them in the past two weeks.

***

There was no way Elvir and his family could resume a normal life right now. Events were happening too fast. Elvir was speaking to his brother and parents regularly. Food was running short for everyone in the municipality. Schools were closed. And it was feeling like a noose tightening around their necks.

The family tried to act like everything was going to be alright. However, there was an air of fear-fraught anticipation that seemed to permeate Kozarac. The children, who usually got along quite well, argued more. And they all watched TV news almost religiously now for any indication that their world would be turned further upside down.

Hajra was cooking lots of food. She had pickled and jarred vegetables and fruits. Her thinking was that with a food shortage, she should take the few fruits and vegetables they had and store them so they wouldn't spoil. She told the children that she was going a little stir crazy and this was a good way to keep busy. But they were not naïve, and though unspoken, they understood what their mother was doing.

Elvir continued to check in on his parents.

"Dad, how are you?"

"Well, I'm fine. But they closed the school. No explanation given. I still think our friends here will not betray us. They're good people, and so are we. Still, your mother got nervous seeing what's going on in the municipality. I can't go into details, but she's not here now. She's fine, but she's gone somewhere. I won't tell you more than that. I'm staying just to make sure the house is fine, and to take care of some things around here."

Elvir was taken aback by this news.

"What are you saying? Mom's not there? I know you can't tell me details, but I wish you could tell me more. No. no. I know you can't. Do you think she'll be safer where she is, or where she's going?"

"She wanted to do this and wanted me to go, too. I told her I'll send for her when things settle down here. I know they will."

"Sure. I hope you're right." Elvir pondered what to say to warn his father that they were entering a dangerous period.

"Listen, this is Trnopolje. I've lived here practically my whole life. I'll be alright. You'll see. Let's talk in a day or so. I will have heard from your mother by then."

"OK. I'll call you soon," Elvir responded, dumbfounded by what he'd just learned.

When he hung up, he had an almost queasy feeling. Where had his mother gone? She was not typically the adventurous type. He was sure she'd tried to convince his father to leave, but he was a stubborn man. Talking to him sometimes was like going up against a brick wall--you just couldn't get through.

Elvir called Tarik as soon as he hung up. The brothers were consumed with worry for both their parents, but they were in no position to do anything.

Chapter 4
The Spiral Downward

"Mom," asked an almost breathless Amir, "did you hear that on the TV this morning? Belgrade is saying all this stuff about us."

"Yes. Unfortunately, I did."

"They've been saying the same type of thing over and over again. And they're telling lies that Muslims are organizing units to slaughter Serbs in Bosnia."

Amir turned up the volume, so his mother, who had stopped putting away the breakfast dishes, could listen.

"We tried very hard to live with them as human beings and brothers, but they thought they could create an Islamic State. Again, it's Muslim extremists we will be identifying. The rest of you will be safe."

Amir turned off the TV. Hajra shrugged in disgust. They didn't notice that the two younger children were quietly standing at the entry way to the kitchen.

"Who was that? What are they talking about?" Halima asked.

"I think it was the regional police chief, Stojan Ilic. I heard him on the radio the other day, but he wasn't as...as..."

"Ominous?" said Halima, finishing her mom's sentence.

"Big word, Halima," said Danis. "What does that mean?"

"It means not so good," interjected Amir.

"Listen kids, with school still closed, I think today you'll just continue to keep up on your studies from home," said Hajra, trying to sound as calm as she could.

There was no argument from any of them.

The stories used to foment hate against Muslims and Catholic Croats were certainly working. Though the minority, Serbs who the Kovacevic family knew in Kozarac, some they knew quite well, seemed to pull away. Even Nikola kept his distance from Amir. The locals no longer displayed the friendly greetings of just weeks before that were part of the fabric of this community.

This was only the beginning.

Elvir couldn't focus at work. He was worried about his brother and family, his parents, his extended family, and his own. When he got home late morning Hajra told him about what they'd seen on TV news.

"It's getting worse. I need to call my father. I don't know whether he's heard from my mother yet."

"Of course," Hajra replied, although Elvir had already finished dialing the phone.

"Hi Dad. It's Elvir. Have you heard from Mom?"

"Yes. She called from the road to tell me that she was headed in the right direction, was all she could say. But I took that to mean she's closer to her destination. She was speaking quickly from a pay phone, and didn't have many coins for the call. She said she'll call when she gets to where she's going. I guess she's alright. At least I hope so."

Elvir breathed a little easier hearing this. But he knew that Bosnia was a dangerous place now, so his worry about his mother could only ease to a point.

"Dad. How are you holding up?"

"I'm fine. Mom left me with food. I have rice, beans, some burek she cooked before she left for me to heat up. And there are a few things left in the garden. I'm OK."

Elvir sensed his father was trying to give the impression that he was managing well. He was not so convincing this time.

"I wish I could come over and bring you back here, but it's

not possible, as you know. I don't know what to do for you, Dad. I'm worried, to be honest."

"You know that I was in the JNA for a couple of years. I was willing to die for Yugoslavia. My friends here know how loyal I have always been to them whether they want to say they're Yugoslavs, Bosnians, or Serbs. I don't care. We'll get through this."

Elvir's shoulders slumped as he realized that his father continued to believe that nothing had essentially changed. He understood that for him, Yugoslavia was in his blood. He was living in the past. There was just no way he could fathom that being Muslim was like wearing a bullseye on his back. It was with great sadness that he ended the call, telling his father to be careful. He sat with the phone in his hand after disconnecting the call, staring into the void of an unlit room, as the sun had just sunk below the horizon.

***

It was over a week since Prijedor had been taken over. Elvir had contacts on the committee trying to meet with the SDS in Prijedor about Kozarac.

"I didn't want to alarm you," he told Hajra, "but the committee has been trying to get meetings with the Serb authorities who have recently been telling the mayor and others here that they need to sign some kind of "loyalty oath" to a new Bosnian Serb Republic, or be recognized as a paramilitary terrorist organization. They've given one week to do this."

"Terrorists? Us? Are they crazy?" she replied.

"I believe we now see what's going on in Kozarac. They continue to stir up local Serbs to justify whatever plans they have for us."

Hajra's face grew pale. She looked toward the bedrooms where the children were supposed to be doing their school work.

"What are we going to do?"

"I honestly don't know. The committee is still trying, though time seems to be running out. Meanwhile, I'll do work from home, if I can focus, and the kids will stay close."

Just then the phone rang. It was Tarik.

"Did you hear what was just announced on Radio Prijedor?"

"No. We weren't tuned in. It's tough to listen to these days."

"Well, the Bosnian Serb Army issued an ultimatum that the way to guarantee peace in Kozarac was for the people to turn in their five thousand weapons."

"We don't have all of those weapons. Maybe there are a thousand hunting rifles, some pistols, a few automatic weapons purchased on the black market, even a couple of World War II machine guns. Nothing that will do much against their army, and not the numbers of weapons they claim we have."

"A few days ago, we got a similar ultimatum, which you know about. Lots of us are handing over our weapons in the hope that this will lead to our being safe from harm. I don't trust the SDS. And with the military setting up positions throughout the municipality, how can we feel safe? One more thing, there have been sightings of soldiers setting up posts on rooftops in the city—snipers."

They had said more on the phone than they'd intended to. But the situation was getting grave, and as mid-May approached a feeling of desperation cloaked Prijedor municipality.

***

Elvir informed Hajra that he was joining the local resistance "just to keep an eye on things." She understood why, but she bristled at the news. She tried to convince him that he needed to be home for the children, but he insisted on being part of the patrols to at least monitor what the Bosnian Serb Army was doing. He told her he couldn't be idle while their city was being threatened.

He was part of the midnight shift that met up at the Café Amsterdam, had a cup or two of coffee, and exchanged guns with the previous shift, or brought one that they borrowed from a friend or relative. His good friend, Bosko, a Serb, gave him his hunting rifle.

Each group also had the responsibility of digging trenches around the perimeter of the city should they need to defend themselves, and to slow any attack by the army.

Kozarac's hastily created crisis committee was finally granted meetings with the SDS, but the same ultimatum about turning in guns was the gist of their demands despite protestations that there were nowhere near five thousand weapons in Kozarac. But the SDS told the committee there was no negotiating this, and they punctuated the point that not turning in the weapons, and by not agreeing to the loyalty oath they were, in essence, signing their own death warrants.

It was May 14th and Elvir was getting ready to call his brother, and then his father. He picked up the phone and began to dial, but stopped abruptly. He heard nothing. He tried calling again. Nothing. He put his ear closer to the phone. Dead.

"Hajra. I think they cut the phone lines."

He handed her the phone. There was no dial tone. She tried pushing some of the buttons to elicit a sound, but heard nothing.

"Dead. You're right."

She hung up the phone and hugged Elvir.

"Can you hear my heart pounding? We're sitting ducks. What are we going to do?"

He held her tightly, but had no words to say.

At dinner that night, which was just some jarred vegetables

and fruit, some day-old bread, and water, they informed the children that the phone lines had been cut.

The discussion that evening was about staying calm and staying indoors. A feeling of desperation had begun to take up permanent residence in the household.

The spiral downward was marching at a lightning pace.

The lives of all in the municipality who were non-Serb had been altered irreparably. Even some of the local Serbs, who were sympathetic to their neighbors, were acutely aware that their lives were in a very precarious predicament.

Two days after the phone service stopped, Elvir came home after his patrol shift unable to hide his angst. He found Hajra sitting at the kitchen table watching the news on the small TV, which was now only possible when the electricity was available for the few hours a day it was working. Her face had drained of its usual bronzed complexion from sleep deprivation and worry.

"On patrol last night, Adis told us that his father had been on a bus to Prijedor, but it was stopped at a checkpoint. All of the Muslim and Catholic passengers were ordered to get off and walk back to Kozarac. Serb passengers were allowed to remain."

As if reading Elvir's mind, she said that they should gather the children to talk about what was happening.

No one was able to actually sit around the table. The nervous energy would not allow for that. Danis held onto his mother.

Elvir spoke, and tried to remain as even-keeled as possible. But this was not going to be easy.

"I want to be truthful with you kids. I don't want to scare you, but we need to be prepared. I heard that the committee you've heard about, the one trying to negotiate with Serb authorities, has run into the same roadblock. Since we can't comply with what they want, to turn in all those guns that we supposedly have, they've made it harder to be in Kozarac."

"What do you mean harder, Dad?" asked Amir. "It's already tough. What else are they going to do?"

"Well, we now know that they've mobilized their military units in Prijedor. I have no way of speaking with Tarik, and I'm scared as hell for what's going on there. But we may be next."

Everyone stiffened. Hajra tried to hold back her tears for the sake of the children, but moisture still formed around her eyes.

"I'll be on patrol again as long as I can, and I'll let you know what I learn. In the meantime, we have to hunker down. Remember, we have a basement that, if need be, we can stay in to keep safe. I'm very tired, so let me lay down for a little while, but we just have to keep vigilant for now."

On May 22nd, with food market shelves having been emptied some time ago, they gathered for carrot soup for dinner.

It was then Elvir told the family that the patrols were disbanded; that there were not enough of them or weapons to repel the military.

"Dad, do you know where those explosions we've been hearing are coming from?" asked a clearly shaken Amir.

"They're coming from Hambarine, probably even Prijedor," said Elvir. "From the patrols, we can see the shelling. What is important right now is that we need to make sure that we're safe here in our home."

"For one, we should leave the curtains drawn. No need to call attention to ourselves," said Hajra.

"I'm scared, Mom," said Danis. Halima echoed his feelings. Amir remained tight-lipped.

"We'll do everything we can to take care of you children. You know that. Just listen to us if we need to do something more. For now, just stay calm, and we'll be alright."

"Remember, if we have to, we'll go to the basement for safety. It's underground, and should provide us with needed shelter," Elvir told them.

"We can get through this if we stay together," Hajra said, hoping that her emotions did not betray the hollowness she felt in uttering those words.

"In any event," Elvir quickly responded, "we can't panic."

The family remained on high alert. At meal times over the following couple of days, there was little talk. Halima moved the food around her plate, and excused herself from dinner. She went over to the sofa, and tried to read. The boys played cards, but Danis kept getting distracted, asking Amir if he'd "heard that noise outside?"

They continued to hear the sounds of artillery in the not-so-distant direction of villages around Kozarac.

Halima and Danis moved into their parents' bedroom and were too frightened to get much sleep. Truth be told, the whole family was in a visible state of alarm.

They were on an island in their own home. No communication with anyone other than among themselves. This point was not lost on anyone, and was at the core of their distress. Only Elvir ventured out to check on his elderly neighbors and to bring them what little food they had to share.

It was just shy of four weeks after the fall of Prijedor that the Kovacevic family's fate was sealed, as was that of the entirety of the non-Serb population of the municipality.

Chapter 5
The Fall of Kozarac

Two days after the phone lines were cut, a Serb tank parked in the main square, which was actually situated on the road from Kozarac to Trnopolje, not far from Elvir's company storage facility. It loomed like a large and dangerous animal scouting for its prey. The gray-green of the tank's façade eerily settled into its position as if on its haunches awaiting the right moment to unleash its wrath upon the defenseless people of Kozarac.

Elvir's neighbor told him that he had been near the highway, and with binoculars could see a large contingent of army convoys heading up and down the road. Unfolding events in Prijedor, and particularly in the surrounding villages of the municipality, were unmercifully leaching into Kozarac.

Other military vehicles were moving into place on the road surrounding their city. But no one could know the extent of this mobilization because they stayed in their homes.

Elvir and Hajra were frozen in place. The family ate in silence mostly, except for the TV that was periodically on for any news that affected their lives directly. But Serbian TV had taken over the air waves some time ago, so when the propaganda spewed, they shut it off. Radio was no different.

It was early Sunday morning, May 24th. The sun rose as it always does, and the spring birds were chattering away from their perches on branches hidden by the multiple green shades of the deciduous trees.

Radio Prijedor began playing a Serb nationalist song over

loudspeakers. The family was awoken from their usual restless sleep as the music shattered whatever minimal peace dawn might bring.

By mid-morning the song stopped, and all was eerily quiet.

At 2:00 that afternoon, vicious shelling put an end to the pregnant silence.

"Quick," yelled Elvir, "get down to the basement!"

They raced around the outside of the house to the basement with the sounds of the blasts rattling the ground beneath them. Elvir fumbled with the key, but managed to get it in and twist it to unlock the door. An explosion not four blocks away rocked them as they lunged down the stairs to what they hoped would provide some modicum of protection and a chance to think about what to do next. More shelling and houses getting leveled nearby.

The small room was something Elvir used for his business. With its concrete floor and walls, it contained some spools of fabric, cleaning supplies, and brushes. There was a single light bulb with a pull-string to illuminate it. A tiny transistor radio was tuned into Radio Prijedor. They hunkered down wondering if the shelling would stop. They were all disoriented, and in disbelief that this was really happening. Danis was crying, and Hajra wrapped him up in her arms.

They could smell the smoke from the burning structures as the fumes made their way through the cracks in the door.

"What do we do, Dad?" Amir asked in a tinny voice.

"We need to sit tight. I know that this is a big request, but this is the safest place we can be for now," replied Elvir.

"Staying in the basement will only be temporary," said Hajra. "Maybe if this stops, we can go to the woods as we've talked about. That may be how we avoid the shells hitting us here."

Hajra held the two youngest close to her, feeling their shivering frames against her own trembling body.

With each explosion, screams came from Halima and

Danis.

"They're going to hit us, Dad. I know it!" yelled Danis.

"We're safe here, Danis," said Elvir, though he had little confidence that this was true.

After almost two hours of non-stop bombing, the thunderous noise stopped.

Radio Prijedor was announcing that there would be a cease fire for thirty minutes, so that the residents of Kozarac could turn in their weapons. The family remained in the shelter taking stock of what had just occurred. But, as people began to venture out of their houses, the shelling resumed. It had only been fifteen minutes since the announcement. It was a trick to lure them outside. Those in the path of the new rounds of artillery were slaughtered.

With the almost continual assault, the next day found thousands of residents fleeing. Many tried to leave in their cars and tractors, but they were either gunned down or flattened by the tank-launched grenades. Many others raced toward the woods with the destination atop Mount Kozara for perceived safe haven, twelve kilometers away.

With a brief pause in the shelling, the two parents made an instantaneous decision to head for the woods.

"We need to leave now!" Elvir shouted.

As they exited the basement, they joined the hundreds of others doing the same.

The forest was just a few blocks from their house. Hajra and Elvir grabbed some of the jarred food, and a few blankets they had managed to bring to the basement the day before, and they ran the short distance to a small entry road into the forest.

"Just stay with us, Elvir shouted. "Keep your eyes facing forward and look straight to the trees over there. It's best not to focus on anything else: just the trees and our protection in the woods."

As they hurried to what they hoped was better shelter than

their home, burning houses loomed nearby. Embers could be seen jumping from roof to roof. Smoke darkened the sky and made it difficult to breathe. And there was now a smell of death, and dismembered and bloodied bodies scattered about the streets.

Crossing the threshold from street to forest, they moved further and further into the dense woodland with what now appeared to be several thousand other residents. They found the dirt fire road that veered off to the left within a kilometer of entering the forest, separating themselves from others that went deeper inland.

They sat amidst the nervous chatter of those who fled, shocked by what they were witnessing. Though they were somewhat hidden, no one felt any measure of safety whatsoever.

"Mom, I tried not to look at the...the bodies, but I couldn't help it. I didn't want to step on..."

Hajra pulled her children closer and hugged them tightly. Elvir had his arm around Amir's shoulders wishing he could have prevented them all from seeing what they just saw in the streets.

Taking a deep breath, and trying to distract her children, Hajra spoke.

"Maybe they won't come in after us?"

"Maybe." replied Elvir as his gaze turned upward at the blue sky above the treetops.

There was little solace Elvir and Hajra could bring to the children; only the physicality of their presence, holding each one close.

They had been there for an hour when Hajra broke the silence.

"I brought some bread for you guys. Would anyone like some?"

"Not hungry, Mom," said Halima. Amir and Danis agreed.

She put the bread back into a sack she'd used to carry the

food. She felt the same way. Hunger was secondary to the fear that could not be extinguished by a small piece of stale bread.

The restlessness of those in the woods was mounting. All around them mothers and fathers tried to salve the crying children's fears with cooing and gentle songs.

"We can't sleep out here. This is too much," said Halima.

"We have no choice, sweetheart," responded Hajra. "The soldiers don't seem to be coming in. Maybe they won't. Lie down and at least rest, even if just for a short time."

They laid down on the dead leaves and twigs that had fallen from the previous winter now mulching in the dirt. The sun had set, and voices of the many settled into low whispers. As the night wore on, the grenades and gunfire continued to pour into the city just a few kilometers away.

The next morning, loudspeakers perched astride tanks by the edge of the woods repeatedly blared: "Muslims come out. Muslims come out. Surrender and everyone will be safe! You must go to the soccer field."

They all stood up as if being called to attention by a greater authority. Those with radios said aloud that they were hearing reports that they'd then be accommodated in Prijedor, presumably to then return to their homes.

Amir was the first to speak.

"What do we do?"

"We have to surrender," an exhausted and trembling Hajra quietly acknowledged. "It's our only hope."

"I agree," said Elvir, kicking at the dirt below him.

"We have no choice," Hajra reiterated. "It's clear what we have to do. I don't know if I believe them about going to Prijedor, but they are presenting that possibility."

They were operating in uncharted territory, but had to do what they could to save themselves, especially to save the children.

"You must listen to what Dad and I say once we leave the woods," Hajra said sternly.

"It's important that we stay together," instructed Elvir. "Their soldiers are saying it will be safe for us if we go now, and go to the soccer field. I don't know what to expect, but we'll have to follow their orders. We can only hope they keep their word."

Everyone nodded their heads in understanding as to what they were about to do. Elvir suddenly gathered and hugged his family.

They emerged from the false shelter of the trees, and were met with smoke and flames rising from houses that had been struck and the sounds of explosions nearby. Soldiers were pointing their AK-47s at them. Some were being beaten if there was even the hint of resistance.

Hajra gasped, "Oh my God, look at this. What have they done?"

The rest of the family was speechless. The burning cars strewn along the road had belonged to those who tried to flee out of the city, but were destroyed by Serb shelling.

Body parts and blood littered their path to the field.

"Just look straight ahead," yelled Elvir. "Be careful not to slip, but don't look at anything below us. Just walk. Stay close."

To their left, one of the city's mosques lay in ruins where a large group of people had been killed. The chaotic and apocalyptic scene was too much for some as they flung themselves to the ground. Those who didn't get up were forcefully yanked by the soldiers. Those who still couldn't rise were shot.

There was no time to process what was going on.

Amir and his father led the way with his siblings clinging to their mother close behind. It was like a scene that had been replayed over the vast millennium of prisoners being marched to their fate. There was little talk, only numerous outbursts of crying and screaming. This was their Kozarac, but it had slipped away.

Their world was suspended in a surreal scene of smoke,

fire, soldiers fading in and out of view, and tanks off in the distance. A preternatural silence now visited, as the shelling had halted.

They did as they were told, walking to the field. Danis and Halima were quietly whimpering, and Amir seemed to be in a state of disbelief muttering quietly the same thing over and over again—"Why?"

Elvir defied his own advice to just look straight ahead. He looked over at three soldiers who had just infiltrated the column of marchers.

He saw two men being pulled with whom he presumed were their wives pleading for them to stay. The men did not resist as they entered into a house across from where they had just been. As the soldiers entered, he could make out large knives being withdrawn from their military knapsacks. Within seconds they reemerged without the men. Elvir had to suppress a wave of nausea. He hoped his family was too caught up in the moment to have seen what had just occurred. None of them had noticed it, and for that he was thankful. Still, he witnessed another unspeakable act during what was the most sinister day of his lifetime.

The family was being shepherded to the field with the promise of going to Prijedor. Elvir recognized neighbors, friends, acquaintances, shop owners, and others from his city, all with the same dazed look.

As they continued forward, they passed the Catholic Church. Three men who had been policemen in Kozarac were removed from the line. They were pushed to the front entrance of the building and shot in the head. This act was so sudden, swift, and without remorse, that no one had time to react.

The children were in shock, blankly staring into the abyss ahead of them. Halima tripped over a rock and almost fell. Amir instinctively reached out for her, and he almost fell, too. Danis buried his head into his father's chest.

As they closed in on the soccer field, Elvir spotted Jovan, a man in his twenties from one of the minority Serbian families in the community, shouting to the soldiers below from a balcony that he and another soldier stood upon. Jovan was known to be a nationalist who had gotten into scuffles with non-Serbs. Muslim and Croat men were being identified and pulled aside. A group of those men, including a doctor, two lawyers, a judge, a store owner, and a police captain, had been separated from the rest. These were some of the elite people in town; the ones who wanted to see Kozarac grow into prominence. Some of them were on the committee to meet with the SDS. *Why were they pulled from the line?*

In a moment he learned why. Jovan was pointing out those citizens for that very reason—the town leaders were the targets. *Why target them?* he wondered. He then had a gnawing feeling that the Serbs wanted to rid Kozarac of those who could rebuild what had been destroyed.

Elvir quickly processed what was about to happen.

"Look down at the ground, Amir, Hajra, kids. Watch each step so you don't fall. Just keep moving. Listen only to me. Please!"

While he was imploring them to follow his words, two of the men—the lawyers—were shot in the backs of their heads on the spot. The judge was taken into a house nearby. Only the soldiers emerged moments later. The store owner, an entrepreneur like Elvir, and the police captain, had their throats slit and lay face down in the dirt, leaving an oozy, red-brown mud.

Elvir realized that Jovan knew that he was a prominent business owner, too. As he and Amir approached the balcony, Jovan shouted out for the soldiers to detain the two of them. Elvir froze. Amir couldn't speak, but his contorted facial expression seemed to indicate his confusion as to why them? And Hajra screamed.

A soldier pulled out his long knife and jabbed it into Elvir's neck ever so-slightly. A trickle of blood dripped down to his collarbone. Elvir swallowed hard, his body stiffening. Amir looked on in horror with unblinking eyes. The soldier had a smirk on his face.

"No, the two of you deserve better. Get back in line with the others. I have a lovely place for you to take a nice relaxing holiday."

As the soldier withdrew his knife from Elvir's neck, he and Amir released the breath they'd unconsciously drawn in and held, and walked the remaining distance unsteadily toward the field. The ominous message of the soldier clearly indicated that they were not going to Prijedor.

When they arrived, there must have been 4,000 people on the field being guarded by several hundred armed soldiers and police. No sooner had they entered when families were being forcibly separated and ordered into awaiting buses with large Serbian flags draped over the side view mirrors.

"Men over the age of fifteen, move to this side of the field. Women, children, and old men over sixty-five to the other side.

A soldier's rifle butt shoved the now separated family toward the newly forming lines. Danis and Halima shouted for their dad and brother, but it was useless. They clung to their mother who was caught up in the pushing and shoving.

"What's happening?" Halima yelled to her mother.

"Just stay with me," shouted Hajra as she practically dragged Danis further and further from his father and brother.

"Where are they taking Dad and Amir?" screamed Danis.

A soldier showed up next to Hajra.

"Shut your children up, or else I will," he ordered.

Hajra tensed her body as she implored her children to keep still.

Halima's question about her father and brother's fate, as well as their own, would soon be answered as they were now teetering on a precipice that was about to find them all in a hell no one could have imagined.

Chapter 6
Omarska

As they entered what had once been a thriving iron ore mining company, Elvir couldn't help but recognize that the place hadn't changed much since his maternal grandfather had worked there several years prior.

What stood out for him as a young boy visiting the plant as a guest during an employees' family event with his Babo remained. The big hangar, as it was called, had a rust-colored brick exterior that spanned the length of a large runway or tarmac. The still oil-stained surface was where the trucks drove for their payload of iron ore to be then taken to whatever predetermined destination the metal was to be delivered. Of course, during the visit no trucks were operating, but his imagination pictured the large hulking vehicles coming in and out with roaring engines and the smell of diesel fuel.

There were a few other much smaller buildings near the hangar that were used for offices and storage. The restaurant, where he recalled that it was Greek Gyro Day at the plant, looked the same, too. His Babo's office was in a hallway upstairs from the hangar's huge open-space, and Elvir was excited to sit in the room's chair and look down below through a window to where the trucks entered and exited. He had pulled a blue post-it note from a small middle drawer and scribbled, 'Thank you for the best day of my life,' and placed it on the calendar desk blotter.

Now, there was nothing resembling business operations. True, grease and skid marks from truck tires remained on the runway. And the outer offices were still there. But now, there was a machine gun nest on the roof of the restaurant with guards peering down at the new arrivals. His memories were abruptly interrupted. The thrill he felt as a boy was replaced by the repulsion of what had transpired in recent days, and by being imprisoned.

"Sit on the tarmac," commanded a man named Zivko Miljkovic, who appeared to be in charge. The men sat obediently staring attentively ahead of them.

As he peered slightly to his left and right, Elvir recognized a former police officer from Prijedor, Marko Ristic, who was ensuring that the men did as they were told, though none did otherwise. He recalled that Ristic was fairly unremarkable, and hadn't made much of an impression on him. Until now. *Why is Ristic here? What has he to do with this?*

"You will remain out here for the next couple of nights so that we can identify our enemies: those extremists who want to do harm to the great Serbian people," said Miljkovic.

He spoke calmly, but his tone frightened Elvir.

He then instructed Ristic and his men to stand "at ease" and not direct their Serbian-made automatic rifles at the prisoners. The guards did as they were ordered.

"We don't want to hurt you. We just want to arrest those who want to hurt us," the commandant reasserted.

Elvir noticed some others he knew among the guards. There was a waiter at a local restaurant he occasionally went to, though he couldn't recall his name; a taxi driver named Milan, who Elvir never liked, and who seemed to be smirking at them as they sat helplessly on the hardened dirt under the blazing sun; and finally, there was an older man named Krstic, if he remembered correctly, who had retired from the police force and who looked meaner than Elvir remembered. All of them had an evil light cast upon their faces. He didn't quite trust what was being told to them after eyeing these people. But the commander spoke with reassurances, so it was best to focus on him.

Evening arrived with the "inmates," as Elvir now thought of themselves, cooling off from having been baked by the heat of the day. They were all feeling dehydrated and hungry. But no help on that front was forthcoming. They were mostly silent, staring blankly in front of them.

Elvir kept close watch on Amir, who had not stirred since their arrival. He noted that the sweat and smudges of dirt from the day's events were etched into his son's forehead. He wanted to speak with him, to reassure him, but he was wary of attracting the guards' attention. He looked over at him several times, and only once did Amir look back: eyes wide, pupils dilated.

Two of the guards sauntered over to the men lying on the hard runway. Behind them, another five guards had their AK-47s trained on the prisoners.

They named three men who were pulled from the large group. The rest were told to lie on their stomachs with their heads on top of their folded arms in front of them. They were not informed as to why these three were chosen, but Elvir supposed they were selected because of suspicion that they were extremists.

Elvir knew one of the men taken, and he couldn't believe that this man had anything to do with anti-Serbian activities, if that's what the commandant was worried about. He couldn't discern whether his stomach ached from hunger or fear.

The men didn't return. Perhaps they would arrive later? Perhaps they were even sent home? The prisoners were still being told that if they had nothing to do with extremist activities, they would be able to rejoin their families soon enough.

Amir squeezed his eyes as tightly as he could, tensing his body while telling himself that he and his father had nothing to hide—that they were innocent of anything their captors might accuse them of. This was all a big mistake, he told himself.

As silence reigned over the runway, many of the men fell into a restless sleep. As the late spring sun began to rise, they were awakened to a new set of names who were ordered to join the guards.

At some point later in the morning, the guards told the prisoners that they could put their arms to their sides, but had to continue to lay face down. They laughed as they walked back to their posts.

The morning lapsed into afternoon, but the large hangar's shadow was not ready to relent to the brutal sun.

Elvir turned his head only slightly so as not to arouse the guards' attention. Amir had his head buried into the hard runway, not seeming to care that he was likely hurting his face.

After two days living in the open under the watchful eyes of the guards, the inmates were shown to their new sleeping quarters. Hundreds entered the hangar, replacing the trucks that used to fill up with iron ore when the mining company was in operation. The large floor of the hangar was concrete. The men were told to sit. They were then separated into groups of a few hundred and sent upstairs with guards steadily prodding them to move quickly. They were being directed into large rooms that had been where equipment and furniture were stored.

Elvir and Amir crammed into their tight quarters with the others, and they all sat down. There was little space between them. Dazed from lack of food and water, some of the men whispered to one another their fears for what was occurring, though they peppered their concerns with hope that the innocent would soon be freed.

In the hangar itself a desk was set up in the front with armed guards to watch over the rooms upstairs. Each of the three twelve-hour shifts, the prisoners would soon learn, had its own personality. The inmates' own survival would depend upon knowing which guards to avoid any contact with.

Some men had been told to remain downstairs. The men were taken outside the hangar to another place nearby. *Are they just being relocated, or worse, or are they being set free*? Elvir's thoughts were quite unsettling. Something else was just beginning to gnaw at him: *What is really happening to those separated from the rest?*

Elvir noticed that his son was sitting almost motionlessly as he continued staring into oblivion.

He put his arm around Amir and told him that everything would be alright. This action seemed to jolt Amir into the present. Amir turned toward his father.

"What are they doing to those men? Why take them? What did they do?"

Elvir was relieved that his son spoke coherently, and with a concerned cognizance for their situation.

"There are no extremists among them, I am sure. In fact, no extremists that I've heard of in all of Prijedor municipality. We are all decent, hardworking Bosnians, and most of us have little to do with politics at all. But Amir, we can't call attention to ourselves in any way. That is the best way to avoid being targeted by the guards."

For the most part, early in their imprisonment, there was little understanding of what the Bosnian Serbs wanted from them other than to identify those perceived as their enemies.

But as the calendar flipped to June, there was no further mention of the inmates going home. It was becoming quite clear to the men that there was no escaping the hate that was beginning to show itself full force.

Amir had been pondering what his father had said to him only days before. But he couldn't understand why they continued to be in Omarska. And how they would make themselves invisible in such a place?

The previous day, one of the guards came up to their room and spoke with a man just inside the entryway. The man, the guard told him, would act as a messenger for the others. For Elvir and Amir, that was Bilal. So, their room became known as Bilal's Room. The guard would go no further than the doorway, as if he was afraid that there would be some violent uprising against him and his fellow captors because there were so many more prisoners than guards. However, the prisoners were in no position for a rebellion. Part of the Serbs' plan, they surmised, was to limit their food to a watery broth and stale bread one time a day, referred to by the inmates as breakfast or lunch depending on the time of day they were told to go. Their water intake was restricted severely. If they were able to get to the bathroom to hurriedly sip from the sink's faucet, the warm, metallic tasting water did little to satisfy them. Hunger and thirst were to be a prominent feature of their time in Omarska.

It was during meal time, as they scampered to the canteen, that they were exposed to the sounds of tortured men both inside and outside a building referred to as the White House.

As June progressed, men who had been removed from the hangar a couple of hours before had their bloodied bodies dragged to their rooms, or they did not return at all.

The first time a man was taken from their room, and returned perilously close to death, the stark reality of the concentration camp came into full light. Bilal received him at the door's threshold being assisted by others as they carried him to a small, available space on the floor. When the torturers went back downstairs, a few men went over to tend to the moaning man. A few of the men went into the bathroom downstairs to wet whatever rags they could find in their room to wash off the tortured man's bloodied body. To avoid being seen by the guards they put the rags around their necks pretending that they were hot and needed to cool off.

Elvir was not a man to do nothing. He joined the others to attend to the man, whose name was Ahmed. At first, Amir protested against his father going to the bathroom to get a wet rag to help. But Elvir told him that they needed to take care of each other if they were going to survive.

Lesson one, thought Elvir.

"Then I'm going with you," Amir said. "I'm going to help."

"You stay here. But if you want to help comfort this poor man, I know he would appreciate it," said Elvir as he gave his son one of the rags to wipe down the wounds of the semi-conscious prisoner.

Ahmed was a man in his mid-thirties who lived in Rizvanovici, a village near Prijedor city, with his wife and two young children. He owned a small hardware store that many people around the area shopped at because of the unique items he carried. He always had a hearty wave for Elvir on the streets of Kozarac when he came to town to eat lunch at his favorite restaurant.

"My poor man, what did they do to you?" asked Elvir.

Ahmed slowly responded with a wince of pain as he tried to sit up.

"Don't sit up. I can lean down to hear you."

"They kept asking me where my weapons were hidden. When I told them that I had a hunting rifle only, and that it was in the storage room in my house, they called me a liar. Milan, the taxi driver was there. He was the one who took the most pleasure in beating us. There were others in the room with me. He made us get on all fours while beating us with an iron tool of some kind. We all kept telling him that we have no weapons, that we are friends with our Serbian neighbors, that we would never do anything to harm them. But Milan didn't seem to be listening. 'We have no brotherhood,' is all he said. He and the others just kept beating us. It didn't seem real, but the pain and pooling blood below me told me it was. At some point, I could almost not feel the pain anymore. It was as if my body just wasn't there. I could no longer hear any screams from the others around me. I don't even know how long I was in there."

"You were there for two hours," said Elvir.

"Oh my. They then dragged us out of the building, and they threw me into Bilal's Room, I guess. Do you know what happened to the others?" Ahmed asked.

"No one is sure. Bilal looked through the small window in the door, but saw no one else enter the hangar. But he said he heard shots and believes that they were killed," Elvir replied.

There was a new hush in the room. Others thought as Bilal had. The haze of their dire situation was becoming clearer.

"I was barely conscious and awaited my turn to be killed, to be honest. I would have welcomed it actually. But then I found myself back here with some of you cleaning me up."

All Elvir could do was sigh and shake his head. He looked up and saw Amir next to him. His son had a look of deep sadness, eyes facing downward, mouth frowning at the corners. He still asked his father if he could do something to help. As terrible as it was to see what they had done to Ahmed, and to know what they did to the others, it warmed his heart to know that Amir was willing to help despite his own fears.

"No Amir, but it's good of you to want to help."

Amir managed a very slight smile, Elvir's words were recognition enough for the boy to know that his father loved him. Not that he ever questioned it, but it was not the Bosnian way to be so expressive.

The notion, that the men the guards had just tortured who did not return were surely killed, caved the shoulders of those inside their rooms as they sat unsteadily on the floor, with some muttering prayers. Who would be selected next?

At that moment the door to their room opened and Bilal told the others that they had three minutes to run to the canteen to eat. It was meal time. Those who could, did just that. As they ran to get the tasteless broth, they were beaten with clubs along the way. Anyone who fell was kicked to the side by heavy-booted guards— some shot on the spot. Their hunger for blood equaled the prisoners' hunger for food.

The routine never varied. Each day they were given tasteless broth that contained no more than three beans and a piece of stale bread. The routine was that a guard would tell the inmates to gather in groups to run across the outside yard into the canteen where, like school children in a cafeteria, they would line up to get their meager meal. Given three minutes to eat, they would scarf down the liquid. If it was scalding hot that day, then it would cause blisters inside their mouths. They were rushed to eat so that the next group could come in. There was no talk—no chatter. Only the purposeful attempt to fill their empty stomachs, which remained profoundly vacuous after they finished.

When Elvir returned with some hardened bread hidden in his pants pocket, he gently placed it into Ahmed's mouth. Ahmed slowly chewed the hard chunk as best he could now that he was missing some teeth.

"I heard shots outside," he said to Elvir. "Do you know what's going on?"

All Elvir could do was swallow the lump that had formed in his throat and tamp down the anxiety that was rapidly becoming a familiar weight on his psyche.

Chapter 7
Trnopolje

Her bus slowly moved through the village she and Elvir grew up in—Trnopolje. She knew these farm houses, these roads, and recognized the newly abandoned houses. At any other time, especially when she and her husband visited their parents, it was always a nostalgically warm welcome. She loved the place with all of its sweet memories. After all, this is where she met her husband to begin a life with their beautiful children. She held Halima and Danis as close as possible. As their bus slowed and made a deliberate, wide turn, she noticed the familiar circular driveway they were pulling into.

It was the primary school that she went to as a child for her final two years after recovering from tuberculosis. This is also where Elvir and Tarik went and played soccer games as teens in the pitch just behind a fence in the rear of the building. Except she could see that there was some barbed wire around certain parts of the perimeter now, and the ominous presence of police with semi-automatic weapons greeting them with orders to move from the several buses into the entryway of the main building. As they exited the bus, she noticed Miroslav, the mailman in Kozarac, with a weapon draped over his chest. He looked down at his boots as Hajra and the children passed by, raised his head and gave a quick glance, and resumed ordering the people to move quickly.

The school was all-too-familiar to Hajra. She could picture her mother taking her inside when she was in fourth grade. She remembered clinging to her mom's dress the first day of school, not wanting her to leave. She could see her mother in her mind's eye giving her the biggest hug and kisses, telling her that she would be in the same spot when the school day ended, and she'd bring her a treat. Though she couldn't recall what the treat was, her mother always found a way to make her feel safe. If only she knew where her mother and father were now. If only it could be as simple as her mother giving her a hug and kisses, and a treat at the end of the day. Her thoughts dissolved as she, her children, and others were being herded into an empty classroom that they were told they'd be living in from now on. She noted that others were being directed to the outer field in the back of the building.

There were at least forty other people in their room. There were two older men, while the rest were women and children. Most of them were crying. A large, barrel-chested guard named Vlado Babic, who was a reserve police officer in Prijedor, entered the room and moved an older man in his way with his steel-toed boots. Two older women nearby seemed to instinctively rise to help the man, who was rubbing his rib cage, but they quickly sat back down

"No need to worry. He's fine. I hope I was not too rough. I just needed to get through. So, I must tell you the rules so that everyone is clear about how to make things work smoothly around here. This will allow us to go about our business of identifying extremists, so that you can then return to your homes. You listen when we talk. When you leave here for your meals, once a day, you will not talk, so we can have an orderly exit and return. Mothers must make sure your children remain quiet. There should be no questions," he finished abruptly.

There was a stunned silence as Babic left the room. What was happening? Was this some sort of cruel nightmare?

Halima and Danis buried their tear-streaked faces into Hajra's shoulders with no words except for "why?"

As the evening wore on that first day, the wailing inside

the room settled into occasional whimpers. Hajra recognized some of the women from Prijedor. One was Amir's former sixth grade teacher. Her name was Dzana Paratusic, but the kids called her Mrs. P. She was a woman in her late forties who was married, but never had children of her own. She liked to say that her students were her children, and she rented them during the school year. This always brought a smile to the parents. Amir loved her and she loved him. In fact, she loved all of her students and had a way of making them feel that she cared for each one individually. She was special.

Mrs. P. approached Hajra and the children. Though she had not been Halima's teacher, she knew her and greeted the family with a broad smile.

"This school holds such a special place for me in my life," she said to Hajra. "This is where I started my teaching career. My husband and I could not have children. We never went to figure out why. But as you know, all my students were like my own children—borrowed from their parents, of course."

Halima smiled at that, knowing Mrs. P.'s wonderful reputation through Amir and friends of hers who had her for their teacher.

"I don't know where they took my husband. I don't know where my sister, her husband and two children are. I don't know where my mother is. The only certainty is that my father died two months ago of a heart attack. I was so sad, but now maybe it was for the best. He would not have believed what is happening here," she said.

"For us too," Hajra replied. "My husband and Amir were taken somewhere else. We were separated after being forced to march to the soccer field in Kozarac. I don't know where the rest of my family is either."

Others nearby weighed in with agreement that they, too, had no idea where their families were. But as the moonless sky hovered over the school, a restless quietude settled for the prisoners in room 16.

***

A few days later, as daylight peered through the classroom windows, Babic was back. One middle-aged woman, who Hajra didn't know, began to cry and asked Babic if he knew where her husband was.

"Ahhh," Babic snarled through a sinister smile, "I can take you to him."

The woman was so distraught that she didn't sense the danger that was lurking.

She stood up and straightened out her long dress. As others moved away to clear a path for her, she followed him out of the room. When the door was closed the others whispered their worries for the woman to each other. It was an hour later when she returned.

Babic thrust her into the room, and then he slammed the door shut.

The woman had bruises already rising from her cheekbones. Blood trickled from her nose. Tears were dried along her neckline. Her dress was torn near her lower back. With an unsteady gait and vacant stare, she hobbled to the back of the room. She collapsed on the floor and was immediately surrounded by other women, one of whom cradled her like she was an infant.

Hajra wrapped her arms tightly around her children and pulled them closer. She hoped that they didn't understand what Babic had done. She was in disbelief herself, but the reality of his barbaric act was self-evident.

***

The daily routine of one meal of broth with bits of carrot or celery was hardly enough to sustain them. Halima and Danis were always hungry, and Hajra snuck bread from the cafeteria for them when she could. At night, the guards regularly visited all of the rooms and took women away to be tormented by drunken, vile men. She just prayed that Halima was not to be one of the taken.

***

The school-turned-camp provided the prisoners with views northward. Most of the next several days they could see smoke rising from Kozarac. The flumes of ash and ember found different locations daily, thus indicating where the Bosnian Serb military had struck.

Hajra imagined their beautiful home was burned to the ground as well. It broke her heart. All of the memories of hers and Elvir's lives together likely had vanished. She thought of the family photographs framed on her wall—and in boxes that she had meant to put into albums but could never find the time. She thought of the laughter and joy that being in Kozarac, in their home, had brought them. Erased. Senseless.

Hajra came upon a friend from Prijedor also at the camp. She told her that at the end of May, the old town in Prijedor was destroyed along with mosques, restaurants, and houses. She told her that people were being killed in their homes in all of the municipality. She mentioned names that Hajra and Elvir knew who didn't make it. Their lives vanishing like everything else.

Another, but certainly not final, bit of news was how men were being taken to camps in Prijedor set up in Omarska and Keraterm. Awful places, they were told. Places of great torture and killings.

It was then that Hajra's fears about what happened to the men and boys in her family, mostly Elvir and Amir, entered her consciousness. It was too difficult to ponder what cruelties they might have encountered, so she buried it as best she could. But it rested not too far beneath the surface.

Every day that passed; every day they couldn't wash their

clothing or themselves particularly well; every day that more prisoners entered Trnopolje, some of whom were violated or worse in one way or another; every day, she wondered if they would ever be free again, or even survive.

***

Summer was just around the corner. In normal times, students had ended the school year, and the joys of being young blossomed. Sports competitions in soccer, swimming, and basketball abounded. The sweet weather would bring families together for any reason to celebrate, or no reason in particular other than enjoying each other's company.

This summer saw none of that, of course.

Danis was gazing down at the other prisoners below their room. It was getting hot, so many men took their shirts off and were even fanning themselves with them. He could see the bruises and cuts that they had sustained from beatings they'd endured in the camp, meted out by the crueler guards. Sadly, he didn't react much anymore. This was the norm.

As he peered down his thoughts wandered to his father and brother. He missed them terribly, and having no idea where they were was maddening for him, though he kept it inside. He didn't want to worry his mother with his distressing thoughts.

The mosque in Trnopolje was merely five hundred meters from the school. In fact, he could see one of the two white columned minarets with its balconies and black pointed top from his room. It gave him some consolation that the structure was still intact. His mother had told him that many mosques in the municipality had been destroyed by the Bosnian Serb tanks. At that moment his eye caught someone perched on the lower balcony of the minaret in his sight-line.

What's that guard doing up there?

"Halima, come here. Quick."

As she came to the window, Danis pointed out the guard who was now training his rifle at the men below.

"My God, what's he doing?" she shouted.

Others joined them at the window.

As the guard lowered his gun, the two siblings looked back down at the men by the fence who were now both looking in the direction of the mosque and down at the ground.

They were scurrying around frantically. Just then, two guards came over and gestured to a few of the men to carry the bloody body of the man who had been struck in the head by their comrade's bullet.

Danis and Halima were speechless. When their mother came back from the bathroom, she found them with tears streaming down their cheeks.

"What's going on? What happened?"

Halima pointed to where the murder had just taken place. She could hardly speak, but managed to say just enough to where Hajra grabbed both her children, pulled them close, and led them away from the window.

It was later learned that as those guards left the scene, they were heard lamenting about how much beer they owed their friend for his marksmanship.

***

On the last day of June, as they headed down for their meal, they noticed a new group of men milling around outside. They were gaunt and hollow-eyed. Clearly, they were malnourished. There was some talking among them, but in hushed tones. Hajra was in despair now for her children, and the sight of these hollowed-out men added to her grief.

In Trnopolje, it had gotten easier for those who slept inside to mingle with those who slept outside. Still, they had to be cautious not to draw the guards' attention with any behavior that might seem out of the ordinary. Out of all the guards,

Miroslav the mailman seemed the least concerned about any socialization going on among the prisoners. On that particular day, Miroslav, in charge of the afternoon shift, allowed his charges to wander freely among themselves.

Halima pulled her mom close and beckoned her to lean down so she could say something.

"Mom, that looks like Uncle Tarik."

Hajra looked in the direction of the fifty or so men near the fencing. She focused her eyes on a thin wisp of a man who clearly resembled Tarik. It was hard to tell because her brother-in-law had been a stocky, muscular man only a couple of months before when she last saw him. She moved closer, leaving the children just behind her, but within her line of sight.

The man saw her approaching and at first had a questioning look as if he hadn't a clue who this woman was. But then he greeted her with a warm smile.

He looks so much like Elvir, she thought.

They moved closer, but knew they couldn't hug or greet in any visible way so as not to draw attention to themselves.

"Thank God. It is you, Tarik!" she said quietly..

"Hajra, I can't believe it's you. I can't believe it's really you."

The guards seemed to be unaware of the interaction that was taking place as they smoked their cigarettes, berets pushed back on their heads. But still, Hajra and Tarik needed to be cautious.

"Seeing you is a miracle. Once the phone lines were cut off, we were so worried about you, Merjem and the girls, and everyone else. I'm sure you felt the same."

"Definitely. We were failing at trying to make sense of what was happening. There were killings in the city, and people disappearing; taken away and, at the time we didn't know, likely imprisoned, or killed."

"That's awful. They were closing in on us, too. Please tell

me what happened to you, Merjem, and the children?"

"I don't know that we can be seen together for too long, but I can tell you a bit before resuming another time."

He seemed to be contemplating how to answer. He was also well aware that he and Hajra could be beaten if the guards thought there was anything untoward taking place. Along with a long sigh and in hushed tones, Tarik began to speak.

"I'll do my best to tell you, but it's important that we don't look directly at each other."

Hajra complied and tried to appear as nonchalant as possible. She loved her brother-in-law, and her heart ached to see him in such poor condition. She imagined he might be thinking the same of her.

"Like all of us in the municipality, we were under siege. The soldiers took over the city. We stayed out of sight as best we could. There wasn't a lot of food, and gunfire and shelling was constant all around us. No one slept. We all stayed in our bedroom. Then, at the end of May, there was a knock at the door. There were two police officers, neither of whom I recognized, telling me that they wanted to take me in for what they called an 'informative conversation.' Before I stepped outside, I looked back at Merjem and the girls, who were unable to speak. That was the last time I saw them."

"I'm so sorry. Where did they take you?"

"First to the police station where they asked questions I had no answers for. The so-called conversation was clearly not their purpose anyway. Then, they took me to Keraterm. They turned the old ceramics factory into what I can only describe as a concentration camp. It was awful. Beatings, killings, starvation...well, I don't want to think about that now. They are evil, you know? Of course, you do. I know there has been that here, as well, from what I hear. But it is much less than anything I witnessed at Keraterm."

"I can't fathom what is going on in our country right now. All of this is awful, and makes no sense," she replied.

"I need to tell you something important before you go back inside. There is a man I know from the police force I saw here yesterday, the one at the other end of the yard whose name is Samed, who was in Omarska before being transferred here. I told him about Keraterm, but also asked if he had seen my brother. He said he did: that he saw him and Amir there. I couldn't believe it. Omarska is a very bad place. But at least we know that they are there. We have to hope they can survive and maybe come to Trnopolje, too."

Hajra stiffened at that news, but she had to stop herself from crying so as not to catch the attention of the guards. *I hope Elvir and Amir are alive.* At least she knew where they were taken. Halima and Danis were nearby, but didn't hear what their uncle had told their mom.

Hajra noticed a guard pointing to her and waving her away from Tarik. It seemed that their time together was to be interrupted.

"Elvir and Amir. My God. I hope they are alright. But still, I've heard what happens in Omarska. I need to go now," she said. "One of the guards is coming over here. When we're back outside, I'll find you. Please take care of yourself."

Hajra and the children were ushered toward the entrance of the building. When they entered their room, she told them what Uncle Tarik had been able to share with her. She told them what she had heard about their dad and brother, but downplayed what she knew happened to those at Omarska for fear that the children would be too upset. After seeing their uncle, and learning from their mother about their father and brother, Halima and Danis began to softly cry, and Hajra hugged them even tighter as her own eyes moistened.

The next day after their meal, Hajra lost sight of Danis.

She and Halima returned to their room, but the boy had lingered behind. Hajra panicked.

She asked the others in her room, but no one seemed to have noticed. Hunger made it difficult to pay attention to much else.

Hajra paced around the room. She was at a loss and couldn't come up with a way to find him. Wandering around the camp was not wise even though there were many who slept outside, so it wouldn't be unusual for her to go there. It was leaving the room and not attracting attention that was the challenge.

"Halima, I'm going to go outside to find him. I'll pretend to have an awful stomach ache and tell whichever guard is out there that I have to go to the infirmary. I'll be back. I promise."

Halima was just as anxious as her mom over the whereabouts of her brother. Though she didn't want her mother to risk being seen in a panicked state, she knew something had to be done.

As she exited the room and went down the stairs, she made sure to place her hands on her "aching stomach."

"Where are you going?" one of the guards asked her.

"My stomach. I need to go to the infirmary. Maybe they have something for me?"

"Isn't that too bad. Your stomach. I'll escort you there," he said in a rather disquieting tone.

He told her to walk in front of him. She could feel his gaze looking her up and down. It made her skin crawl.

When they got to their destination, he told the lone doctor, who was a Muslim man, and had a practice in Prijedor, about her stomach. He sneered at her as he left.

The infirmary was stark. There was not much in the way of medical supplies other than a few cotton balls in a jar, some iodine, and a beaten up stethoscope around the doctor's neck.

Hajra sat on the torn up gurney.

"So, your stomach hurts. Must have been the high-quality food they serve here."

Hajra attempted a weak smile, but concern for her son superseded any banter.

"All I know is that right here in the upper part of my

stomach it burns."

"Sounds like an antacid will help. They only gave us those bottles that have expired, but I think this should be OK. Take a few. Do you want to lie down before you go back?" the man said with a genuine note of concern.

"No, thank you. I'll just chew and swallow these, and go. My children will be wondering if I'm gone for too long."

Hajra's mission was to find Danis. Any delay would be a waste of time.

She left the infirmary and stealthily made her way to the back of the school where many were relegated to sleep, and where she had spoken with Tarik.

Since there were other women outside, it was easier to blend in. Still, this was unfamiliar to her. She recognized no one, and even though these were Muslim and Croat prisoners, she trusted no one.

She looked for Tarik and saw him at the far end of the fence.

"Hajra," he whispered, "what are you doing here? If you get caught, you could be punished."

"I know. But Danis is missing. He didn't come back inside after our meal. Have you seen him?"

"No. My God, where could he be?"

After a pause, he continued.

"Let's split up. Don't call attention to yourself. Walk slowly nodding your head to others as if you belong here. We'll meet back in a short while."

Hajra's head was spinning. Danis was missing. It should not be hard to find him if he was still in the camp. But was he still in the camp? Children had been known to disappear under disturbing circumstances.

When they met back up having seen no sign of him, their panic peaked.

"What am I going to do?" she whispered, albeit almost in a shrill way.

"Let's take one more tour of the grounds. But you have to get back to your room very soon. Dammit, he can't have left the camp. He's got to be here somewhere."

Hajra, of course, knew she had to get back to her room. Every minute outside risked being caught if a guard decided to make a show of it. The good news was that she was reasonably anonymous with Miroslav off-duty. But she couldn't be sure that no other guards might recognize her.

They both walked in opposite directions, veering in and out of the dirt encampment, hoping that they may have missed him.

Tarik saw some movement behind a storage shed in the far corner of the soccer field. There were no men there, so it was dangerous for him to go over to the shed to investigate. He hovered as close to the small, wooden structure as possible.

Crawling out from behind the shed was a boy: it was Danis!

As he lifted his head to see into the crowd of prisoners, Danis spotted his uncle. He raced over to him, arms outstretched, hugging him like he'd never let go.

"Danis. What's going on? Are you OK?" he said while trying to gently loosen his clinging nephew from him to avoid any unwanted attention.

Holding back his tears, the boy blurted out, "I couldn't go back into the room. I am tired of it. Tired of this place. Tired of being hungry. Tired of not being in my home with my family!"

"Poor boy. I know what you're saying. I am missing everything normal, too. I wish we could turn back the clock."

"I'm so scared every day. I worry about my dad and Amir, and my mom and sister. Seeing you and what they did to you makes me so mad. I just want to go home," he said as the tears, now unleashed, streamed down his face.

"This morning, I saw something that I can't stop thinking about. I saw...I saw a baby get shot while in his mother's arms.

I was right next to them when it happened. She was just holding her child right over there. A guard shot him. He shot a baby. The mom and everyone around her screamed. My mother came running over to see what had happened. She knew that I was talking to a friend from school who is here. I screamed, too. Uncle Tarik, he shot a baby in its mother's arms!" he blurted out as Tarik wrapped his nephew up in a protective hug.

"I'm so sorry you saw that. I am so sorry. I heard about this, too, but I didn't know you were right next to her. My God. It was horrible in Keraterm, but I thought they'd be less cruel here. Let me tell you something," Tarik said as he kneeled down to look at his nephew.

"I've seen some awful things, too. Especially at the other place I was in. None of it made sense to me. I'm still trying to figure out why this is all happening."

He looked directly into Danis' moistened eyes.

"When your father and I were younger, we saw a man get hit by a truck right in front of us. He was old, and didn't see the truck coming, I guess. We ran over to help him, but it was too late. I won't describe the scene for you, but Elvir and I were pretty shaken. It's not like what you saw, of course, but it stayed with me for a long time. The guy didn't deserve to die like that. I even had some bad dreams for a while. I would scream in my sleep and your dad would wake me up. I'd tell him about the dream, and he listened. He didn't shut me up, or tell me it's going to be alright. He just listened to me. After some time, I stopped having those dreams. So, maybe telling your mom about your fears will help a little. We have seen too much. And you, being so young, should never be seeing any of this. I am so sorry, my boy. So sorry."

"OK. I'll try to talk to her. I'm sure I'm going to have bad dreams, though, I know it."

"You might. Let me take you to your mom now. She was so worried about you that she risked coming down to the yard to find you. Come with me."

Tarik wiped Danis' tears with the cleanest part he could find on his ragged shirt. When they found Hajra, her face released its deep creases, and she put her arm around her son. She told him that they would talk when they returned to the room.

Giving Tarik a squeeze on the shoulder, and a broad smile, then briefly gazing into the heavens, mother and child returned to Room 16.

Chapter 8
The Camp Visitor

The camp visitors, as those outside of the military or police were euphemistically referred to by the commanders and guards, included Dusan Pavlovic.

Pavlovic was a restaurant owner in Kozarac. He seemed well-mannered and even tempered from what Hajra knew of him. His parents were said to be good, decent people who taught their children to be the same. When Hajra crossed paths with him in town, he was always polite, asking how she was, and how Elvir and the children were doing. But power had a way of corrupting even the good ones if they were not mindful of their transition to evil.

It was only a couple of evenings after she'd first spoken with Tarik that Dusan Pavlovic summoned Hajra for "interrogation." As she slowly arose, the children screamed their protests and grabbed at their mother's shirt sleeve to hold her back, but the guard who forcibly yanked Hajra upward for Pavlovic swatted Danis away, landing the back of his hand on the young boy's jaw. Halima grabbed hold of Danis and tended to her crying brother while their mother assured them she would be alright. The other women and children in the room went silent.

Entering the room where the guard had led her to, Hajra stood trembling as if her body temperature had plummeted. Pavlovic's breath smelled of alcohol and his militia uniform was disheveled. He didn't address her by name and acted as if he did not know who she was. There was a florescent light that cast a doomful shadow onto the floor with its sparse furnishings that included a desk, small table, and a file cabinet. There was the stench of alcohol mixed with cigarette smoke that permeated the small space.

He moved in and slapped her hard across the face. She was stunned for a moment and put her hands on her right cheek to see if it was bleeding. It was not, but she felt woozy. He spun her around and threw her onto a table bending her forward. He pulled down her skirt as he unfastened his belt from his pants. She struggled at first, so he punched her hard in the kidney. The blow knocked the wind out of her and a sharp pain seared through her, but she remained upright. She then felt him as he began violating her roughly.

Hajra let out a brief, stunted scream, but gathered herself despite the incredible fear she was now feeling. She had thought about this moment some days before, knowing that this was now a common practice of those vile Serbs who would perpetrate such acts. She decided then that when her turn came, she would show no emotion, make no sound, have no reaction.

She no longer uttered a sound. He was hurting her, but still, she would not react. He screamed profanities at her calling her a Muslim whore, but she let her mind wander as if she wasn't even there.

I will not succumb. He will not feel anything from me. He will not derive any power from his cowardice. That will be my small victory over his evil.

When he finished he said nothing. There was another guard outside his office who was told to take her back to the room. She straightened out her ruffled skirt and lifted her head as high as she could, not showing the humiliation and physical pain she felt.

When she was returned to the room, she was met with the cessation of conversation by the others. She briefly scanned the room, and noted that the women's heads were turned away. She sat down next to her children. One of the women moved next to her and began to gently stroke Hajra's hair and place an arm around her shoulders. The warmth of touch was an adequate antidote to what had just happened, but the dirtiness she felt inside could not be salved.

Halima, being the older, seemed to have an understanding of what had just happened. She hugged her mom and told her she loved her. Upon hearing this, Hajra's eyes welled up with tears, but she forced them back, trying to maintain a sense of dignity that Pavlovic had tried to exorcise.

It was the same routine over the next five nights. Pavlovic would summon, and Hajra would follow a guard to the same room. Each time he seemed more bellicose. And each night Hajra swore she would show him no sign that he had won.

On the last night before she left for the classroom, he finally said something to her other than the profane rantings of a drunk rapist.

"You are nothing. You can't even satisfy me. I'm sure your husband felt the same way."

Hajra found a small victory in what was a horrific act against her. In her mind, she hoped he suffered great pain someday. And when this madness was over, if she survived, the world would know what a cruel and awful monster he was. Somehow, she would make sure that people would never forget what he had done.

***

For the next several nights Hajra waited for the door to open to be summoned again by Pavlovic. Others were taken from their room, however. And others returned in the same state of shock and shame. They were now all sisters of the depraved plan to impregnate Muslim women with Orthodox Christian Serb seed.

She confided in her friend, Ida, who had also been violated

by Pavlovic, that she would rather die than be pregnant with his child. Ida felt likewise.

Two weeks after the last time Pavlovic had raped her, she felt moisture trickling into her tattered underpants.

"I need to go to the bathroom," she told her children.

She strode down the hallway with a vague sensation of cramps. Was she menstruating? Did she avoid a fate that she believed was almost worse than death?

There was no one in the bathroom when she entered. She looked at herself in the grimy, cracked mirror and she noted that she looked like hell. But this was certainly not the time to assess her looks, and she quickly walked the few steps into the doorless stall.

Here goes. She slowly lifted her skirt above her waist, and placed her fingers on the outer edge of her underwear. Pulling back at the elastic band, she peered downward. A red streak was smeared below. She grabbed a few sheets of toilet tissue and stuffed them inside. She pulled her skirt back up and exited the stall.

Exhaling the breath she had been holding in, she paused before exiting. *Thank you, God. Thank you for sparing me the painful decision I would have had to consider was I to carry his baby."*

Chapter 9
Just Before Summer

Many new prisoners entered Omarska in the coming days and weeks. They spoke of the war that was raging all around Bosnia. They were hearing reports of cities and villages being marauded by Bosnian Serb army units and police reservists, and even criminal gangs that were exacting vicious attacks against all non-Serbs.

One man who entered Bilal's room had a story of how he was saved and then caught. The others listened intently.

"I live in an apartment building in Prijedor with my wife. A neighbor of ours, a Serb man named Dragan, was our dear friend. It was late afternoon just a few days ago when we heard rapid knocks on our door. "They're coming," he told us as he stepped inside our apartment. He had a look of panic. We didn't need to ask any other questions."

"Those are courageous neighbors," said Elvir.

"Yes, yes. Wonderful people. We hurried into their apartment and hid in a closet. The soldiers went into our place. Later, we saw that they stole our TV and some jewelry. We heard them take some of our other Muslim neighbors away. It was awful. I heard them punch an older woman who refused to go with them. She screamed, and they dragged her through the hallway as she swore at them. Poor woman. When they left, we went back in and grabbed our documents and some clothes, and stayed the night at our friends'. The next day, very early in the morning, we managed to take the car to my cousin's house in Puharska. There were no signs of Serb soldiers in his village, so we thought we were safe."

Staring silently at the man, their sallow faces remained fixed on him.

"My cousin took us in, but we were always in danger with what was going on in Prijedor. Of course, our hiding came to an abrupt end as the soldiers entered Puharska and told everyone to surrender. We had no choice. Some of the people ran and were gunned down. The image of this haunts me. They took us back to Prijedor and I was taken here. I don't know where my wife is, and I am beyond worried for her safety."

With a woeful look, Elvir simply said, "I am sorry, my friend."

As the month of June plodded forward, not only was there an increase in the inmate population, but an escalation in killings. There was no longer even the slightest pretense on the part of the commandant that only the extremists would be rooted out. If that was the case, all prisoners must have been considered extremists because they were subjected to dismal living conditions and beatings that often lead to death.

One of the bright spots, if you could call it that, was cigarettes. This became a highly regarded commodity and was exchanged only as a result of a quasi-black market.

When pipes burst or bulbs needed replacing, the maintenance supervisor, a Serbian man who had been at Omarska when it was an operational mine, still came on-site a few days a week. His name was Milos, and he was well-liked by his colleagues; all of them, no matter what ethnicity or religion had only nice things to say about him when they all worked together. He was always eager to help anyone who needed his or his team's assistance.

One of the inmates in Bilal's Room, Edin, had been an engineer at Omarska who worked with Milos. In fact, they had periodically drank a beer or two together in Prijedor with other employees before the war.

While repairing a broken window in the camp one day, Edin stealthily approached Milos. He told his story to the inmates sitting near him.

"I asked him if he could visit my wife, who I believed was still at our home, to tell her that I was OK. He said he would, and would be back in a few days. It took him a week to come back, and of course, this had me worried. But he found me and gave me money she'd sent with him. He even gave me his honey sandwich seeing how starved I was. And that money got me these cigarettes you've seen me smoking that I bought from one of the guards."

"At least," said Elvir, "there still is some humanity left in our neighbors and friends."

Edin pulled out a pack and traded one cigarette for an extra piece of bread that someone had, one for a few coins from another, and one for a bandana that Elvir had stuffed away that might help to wipe away the sweat in the stifling room. Now, the four who bore the fruit of Edin's labors lit up and gently tugged at the filters as they inhaled the smoke. It was a moment of ecstasy that was to be short-lived in the coming days. As they dreamily continued to puff, a few others circled around them. Edin, Elvir and the two others smoked theirs down close to the filter as their "audience" looked on. Elvir handed the remainder of the cigarette to a man standing just behind him. The other men did the same. It was a ritual that was repeated whenever the black market was selling.

***

It was a couple of days before the beginning of summer, so the heat and humidity began to surge in Prijedor. The men and teenage boys, and the few women who were present as well, were locked in the cavernous compound of Omarska teetering between life and death. There was no escaping the fact that Bosnian Muslims and Catholic Croats were the targets of this mass incarceration. The police presence in the camp was composed of the local Serbs who assumed the role of persecutors. They wore uniforms of short-sleeved light blue button-down shirts, dark pants, berets, and Ak-47s poised for use at the slightest infraction. Torture was their primary source of inflicting their will upon the prisoners. And they relished the opportunity to unleash whatever cruelties they could devise. Since many knew one another before the war, it was clear that they were settling old scores; perhaps some as far back as grade school.

On weekends, soldiers from the Bosnian Serb Army came by to test out their own skills at torture. This madness, and the absurdity of it, was beyond measure. It was as if there was a contest to see whose creativity could inflict the most pain. This was their revenge for comrades lost on the front lines far from Prijedor.

The prisoners were in a concentration camp with people who considered them to be subhuman—expendable. They were stuffed like sardines into rooms with little space to move. Some prisoners died from asphyxiation in the extremely tight quarters. Many continued to lay on a hard storage room floor and just stare into the empty space above them. There were other rooms upstairs, former offices really, that were currently used as sleeping quarters for the overflow in the hangar. In the administration building there was a room above the restaurant where "interrogations" took place. Interrogations, administered mostly by professional police inspectors from Prijedor and Banja Luka, were a euphemism for torture, of course, as the prisoners were heard pleading and crying for mercy.

The building referred to as the White House had become the place where those who entered its rooms were subjected to the worst of the torture, and who often did not survive.

Casualties in the camp were beginning to pile up.

As more prisoners were brought in, and with the heat of

the day lingering inside their rooms, they were sleeping so closely together it was as if they were connected.

They had to lie so close to one another that the only way to give themselves even a millimeter of space was to lay on one side all facing the same way. The prisoners couldn't move, as it was impossible to influence the others to change position. No one could manage such a feat.

"Dad," whispered Amir, "I can hardly breathe in here."

"I know," Elvir quietly responded, "my hip aches, but we can't do anything about it. You can hold me even though I can't see you. I'll know you're there."

The prisoners had lost a lot of weight. Their hair was long and matted, though some had completely shaved heads, with scraggly beards that were etched into their gaunt faces.

There was groaning from a man not too far away from Elvir and Amir. Amir recognized him: he sold and repaired equipment for his soccer team. Amir whispered as much to his father.

"I think he has a fever," said another man nearby. "I'd guess that the beating they gave led to an infected wound."

Just then, the massive guard, Dokic, opened the door to their room. No one had noticed that he had opened it ever-so-slightly. He spoke to Bilal loudly enough for those nearby to hear.

"I heard that," Dokic said. He told Bilal to tell the man to join him outside. The message was given.

"Let me inspect your wound," Dokic snarled as they both stood outside the doorway to the room. The man stood unsteadily as the guard seemed to be contemplating how to approach the problem.

The inmates inside heard a pounding sound as if a weight was repeatedly being heaved into the man's cracking rib cage. Dokic was unleashing blows with cruel fury. Each time he hit the man, a weakening scream emanated from him until there was silence. Then a single shot rang out ending the man's life.

Dokic returned to tell Bilal to inform the other prisoners that the infirmary was closed, but if anyone needed further care for their fevers, he would be happy to reopen it.

Amir grabbed his father's sweat-drenched shirt and pulled his dad closer, if that was even possible.

Elvir could hear his son's muffled sobs. Amir, wanting to show his dad that he was a man, too, released him while pulling back his tears, as he silently peered into the darkness. Elvir recognized that Amir was struggling between the two worlds of being a child and a young adult. What he could see was that his son was unmercifully losing his childhood in this barbarous environment.

***

Back in their room after returning from their meal, Elvir's good friend, Hasan, was sitting next to Amir. Hasan was a light-hearted man who could sometimes banter with others in a way that would make them forget about the hell they were in.

"Amir, when I get out of here, I am going to greet my wife with a huge hug. And, with a bag of groceries in-hand, I'll get down on my knees and beg her to make us a sumptuous meal. We'll start with dolma, and yogurt with garlic sauce. This is always a good way to begin, you know. She'll then make her famous Begova Corba soup with chicken so soft it melts in your mouth. I love it when she puts in lots of carrots and potatoes. I could smell the aromas of the pepper-spiced broth even now. We like to put a nice, cool sour cream on top."

Others listening in were mesmerized by Hasan's fantasy.

"You've got to try her Bosanski Lonac. The way she layers the meat and vegetables is like art. Michelangelo has nothing on her. We'll end with Ustipci. I like them with honey, but she'll fry some of that dough with jam because that's her favorite. Finally, she serves the coffee. How I miss that coffee."

Elvir smiled as the conversation about food continued with others adding their own wishes. It was a welcome relief. But he looked around at the gaunt, unclean and unshaven men in filthy clothing with body odor that reminded him of livestock, and felt a pang of sadness. He wondered if any of them would get to eat like they used to in a warm, casual home surrounded by family and friends, ever again.

***

It became clear which guard shift was a bit easier on the prisoners and which was not. There were so many prisoners called out by Ristic's shift that never returned. Contrasting that, on rare occasions, Markovic, who ran the easier shift, gave the prisoners a brief moment of freedom. During his shift, the prisoners were allowed to go to the bathroom without time restrictions. This was a moment when inmates would meet those they knew staying in other parts of the hangar and exchange information about their relatives, or simply smoke a cigarette together. Sometimes it was even possible to 'visit' another room with permission of the guards.

On one particular day at the end of the second week of June, shift leader Markovic allowed the men in Elvir's room to sit outside to get some air.

This is the only time they saw the thirty or so women inmates not in the canteen. There, it was their job to cook the food, and clean up afterwards. If they were not being too closely observed, they would give the men some extra food. One time, Amir was so hungry that one of the women slipped him an entire onion. He took it back to Bilal's room and ate it like an apple.

Sometimes they were called upon to clean the blood spilled in Omarska. For the women, their hell included night time visits from guards.

But on this day, the guards seemed to be in a better mood

for some unknown reason. It was one of very few times that the inmates were allowed to go outside and sit in the shadow of the building without being harassed by their overseers. Except while being served their paltry meal, women and men did not see each other.

To his surprise, however, Elvir was sitting next to his cousin, Dzejla, who had worked as a lawyer at the courthouse in Prijedor. She looked quite thin, displaying deep circles around her dark eyes and sunken cheeks, with bruises on her arms. In hushed tones, she said she needed to talk to someone she trusted like him. Elvir nodded affirmatively, encouraging her to go on.

Dzejla moved a bit closer to Elvir, and whispered to him in a way that was barely audible to anyone but her intended listener.

"I want to tell you something, so that if I don't get out alive and you do, you will know the truth. Of course, who knows if any one of us will survive this hell hole," Dzejla said.

"Go on," said Elvir, "they can't see us for the moment."

"Especially that ape, Stevanovic, but the others, too, come into our room every night and drag us to some other part of the camp, and they...they..."

Elvir interjected that he had heard what was happening to women in the camp, in essence signaling her that she didn't need to finish the sentence.

As Dzejla proceeded, Elvir tried to take it all in as best as possible, but it was not easy to digest the cruelty that the women were subjected to. He thought of Hajra and hoped with all his strength that this was not her fate. He had to suppress the lump that was forming in his throat.

"It is awful here, Elvir, as you well know. I don't know what else to say. I just wanted to speak with someone I trust to tell what is happening to the women here. None of us talk about it. We are all walking around in a daze. I wish they would just kill us."

Elvir sat silently, eyes focused on the dirt below him. He then looked over at his cousin who was staring out into the distance. He could see moisture forming around her reddened eyes. There was nothing he could say or do that could take away the pain Dzejla and the other women were feeling. In an instant, shouts from the guards erupted. A new shift had just arrived.

They had had enough of this "generosity," so they rounded up all of the prisoners intending to send them to the hangar. As they stood up Elvir gently touched Dzejla's shoulder, and whispered, "Be strong. Don't let them win."

Before the guards released them back to their rooms, they told the prisoners that in exchange for the time the previous shift had given, they now had to provide something. The prisoners tensed up as they braced themselves for what was to come.

They were made to stand up with their hands over their heads. Then, five prisoners were "chosen" to sing Serbian nationalist songs. The rest were told to then lie on their stomachs with their heads on their folded arms. As the guards laughed and prodded the singing prisoners to do so louder, they began to slam their rifle butts into each one's ribs, doubling them over in pain, and stunting the song coming from each. They kicked them several times with the screams of pain piercing the ears of those lying on the piping hot asphalt, and stabbing at their hearts.

"Now those are beautiful songs that you're singing. But you sound like shit," they taunted.

The injured men had collapsed, broken, in the hot sun on the tarmac that had only moments before provided a brief respite for the drained inmates.

Elvir could see Amir trying to cover his ears with his hands as he was leaning into his folded arms as ordered. He moved his elbow over slightly to touch Amir's, just to let him know that he was there. He could hear the faint breathing of those around him. Like him, this is what was left of any sense of control they had; breathing. Breathing and dreaming of family, friends, food, and normalcy that once was their lives.

Of the five, Elvir could see that two of them died and were carried away by inmates called to do the guards' bidding. Those men, the ones who moved the dead, it was known, didn't always return to their rooms.

Every day bodies were piled on the opposite side of the hangar for disposal. The yellow van that delivered the food was the same van that left with the bodies. It was another in a long series of evil acts set upon the prisoners by their captors.

On June 20th, one day before the official start of summer and while all the prisoners were in their rooms vying for whatever oxygen they could find in the crushing heat, a horrifying act of violence took place.

Several names of prisoners were called out including Elvir's neighbor, Emir, who was in their room. Emir slowly exited with eyes pointed downward. One could almost hear him swallow hard to keep from vomiting.

Immediately screams of excruciating pain were being heard throughout the building. Some of the men in Elvir's room were staring out of the door's small window in horror, including Elvir.

"They're beating these men with metal clubs and those heavy rubber hoses with the steel weights on each end. My God!" shouted Elvir.

He immediately turned away from the window understanding that his acute nausea could serve no purpose.

Amir wanted to see, but his father would not allow him to be witness to such madness. All of a sudden, he heard Dusan Pavlovic's voice order another man to "bite" Emir's testicles.

This is not possible. What is Pavlovic doing?

Elvir grabbed Amir and hugged him hoping to cushion the awful noise coming from outside their room.

When the carnage was over, there were eight disfigured

and dead men. Pavlovic ordered others from some of the rooms to "take the filth outside to be disposed of."

As Elvir stood, stomach churning from what had just occurred, he nor the others had any words to comfort one another. There was no way to comprehend what had just taken place. No way at all.

***

It was quite clear that the inmates were living by a thread. For those who survived there was a hollowness of body and soul that made them unrecognizable from their former selves. Their remaining human form consisted of sunken, dulled eyes, with cheeks to match and ribs that flared outward.

It was a Saturday afternoon when a message was sent to summon a man in Bilal's Room, Dino, a Croat man, and several others in adjacent rooms were taken. Those called somberly left the hangar knowing that they would be beaten or worse. Dino was a teacher from the village of Trnopolje, and was well-liked by students and parents alike. Sometimes on weekends, Dino and Elvir would meet up at a local café to catch up on their lives. Now, Dino's life was in clear danger.

He and the others entered the White House and its four rooms where they were greeted by the regular army soldiers looking to prove their might. Screams echoed throughout the torture rooms. The beatings were of their usual vicious nature.

Neither Dino nor any of the other men returned.

Those who remained in the rooms were sent off balance by a strange ritual of every three or four days; the taking of attendance.

"Elvir," said Hasan, "do we know if Dino and the others were exchanged?"

"Hard to know. That's what they tell us, right? But are they just giving us false hope? Every time they 'take attendance' they tell us that some of those who were taken were exchanged. Are they just saying this, so that we think we may be traded for their buddies imprisoned by our army? What about the bodies lined up across the way? But I'm not so sure of anything anymore. Perhaps some of us do get to leave alive."

This became an all-too-familiar pattern. Many left, and most did not return. The despair and gloom made it impossible for the still hundreds inside to communicate for the most part in any meaningful way. There was mostly silence during the long days. Silence and waiting.

Amir was almost unreachable. Elvir would hold him close when he had the energy to do so, as the hunger, thirst, and heat sapped him of the strength to do much more than to stare into the abyss. His son's hollow countenance frightened Elvir, but he hoped that this was what Amir's brain needed to do to insulate itself from this madness. At least they hadn't been tortured. Yet.

Chapter 10
The White House

Lists. This was the way an inmate learned of his fate. A guard would go to Bilal's room, as was done in all the rooms, and announce who was to be taken for "interrogation" and who was to be exchanged for Serb soldiers captured by the Bosnian Army during battle. The exchange was always the preferred selection, of course. This meant getting out of the camp. It was an odd acknowledgement that your life was at least worth the life of a Serb soldier. Yet, there were always questions as to whether this, too, was a ruse. Could "exchange" actually mean you were to be executed instead?

The most feared place to be taken to was the "White House." It had been both a storage facility and an office for supervisors of the iron ore company to coordinate the trucks coming in and out of the complex. Currently, it was a place of torture.

Late one hot evening on the first of July, the inmates were doing their best to conserve what little energy they had. Milan who seemed to relish in the pain he inflicted, opened the door for Bilal to pass along the following: He gave six names of those on his list who were to come outside. The list included Elvir.

Father and son glanced at each other knowing what this meant. Sweat began pouring off of Elvir as he dragged himself upward from where they were sitting.

"Daddy, don't go. Don't let them take you. Stay here with me!" Amir whispered, knowing that if he betrayed his true feelings by yelling, he too might be taken.

"I'll be OK, my son. I'll come back to you soon." Elvir said with an uncertainty in his voice that he'd hoped Amir didn't detect.

As he turned away, he could hear that Amir was trying to mute his sobs, and he himself could feel his knees begin to wobble. Elvir's friend, Hasan, went to Amir's side to console him as best he could.

Elvir felt dizzy and numb and terrified all at once. Images of his family flashed before him. His heart was pounding as were his temples. A despondency he had never felt before overtook him. It was an odd resignation to the very real possibility that they may never see them again.

He slowly exited the building and walked the short distance across the tarmac to the White House. There was no breeze to brush away the perspiration beginning to emanate from every pore. He and the others selected were greeted by the chilling gaze of Milan as they crossed through the entrance of the room that would be their torture chamber. It was one of four rather cavernous spaces that was devoid of furniture and dimly lit. The walls were made of plaster with a sickening, pasty white texture. Looking around all Elvir could see were instruments of pain, and smirking guards ready to inflict their will upon the helpless.

Elvir recalled that Milan was even known to be somewhat sadistic in Prijedor. It was rumored that he ran over cats in his taxi for sport. In all three of the Prijedor camps his reputation preceded him.

Without hesitation, they were met by two guards who slammed them in their heads with metal rods. The men dropped to their knees in pain, scattered about the room like flattened bowling pins.

One of Milan's more terrorizing tactics was his silence. He said little as he went about the business of his craft. In very few words he told the guards to select two men so he could set the stage for what they all would face.

Mirza and Mehmed were chosen. Elvir knew them both from Prijedor. Mirza was a barber, and everyone loved him. He was a jokester, but never offensive to anyone. In fact, he could be somewhat self-deprecating. Elvir always thought that going into his shop one could find more than just a good haircut. It was entertainment. Mehmed was a more serious man. He was an assistant bank manager in Prijedor: friendly, but one who took his job at the bank quite seriously. Both had a wife and children from what Elvir knew of them. Both were honest, decent people. And right now, both were about to be in deep trouble.

Milan took out his favorite implement. It was a thick, rubber hose with heavy iron knobs on either end. Making them get up on "all fours like a dog," he began whipping both men with ferocity on their backs, shoulders, and heads. When one of the men collapsed a guard would pull him up again to receive a new round of pounding. The thwacks made a dull sound as the hose met flesh and bone. The men screamed in agony with each lashing.

Milan and the other guards burst out with sadistic laughter as they beat the men. At one point, Milan lowered his face near Mehmed's.

"I am tired and can't beat both of you."

At that, the beefy guard Dokic, the police reservist from Prijedor who made the rounds at the three notorious camps in the area, turned Mehmed onto his back. While Milan returned to beating Mirza, the other guard, with brass knuckles, began to punch Mehmed in the chest. He was aiming for his heart! The man yelled out in a scream that pierced through the taunts of the tormentors. The other men watched all this in horror, eyes trying to avert what was happening, but alternatively looking at the scene before them. As the blows met their target in his chest, the others could hear the air rushing out of Mehmed's lungs. And then the beatings of both men ceased.

Mirza was laid out on the floor with blood oozing from wounds beneath his shirt, but also from the exposed areas like his head and neck. His moans were barely audible now. Mehmed was not moving.

Dokic dragged them out of the White House to be "taken care of."

Before he left the room he nodded to the shift leader Marko Ristic and a comrade, a guard called Zoki, who had been casually leaning against a wall awaiting their turn.

Ristic then displayed a thick wooden pole the size of a fence post. He told the four remaining men to sit and face the wall. He rotated around the room pummeling them from behind. One of the men, Nihad, was screaming and crying, yelling for him to stop.

While the others were writhing in pain, Ristic dropped the wooden post near the door. He flipped Nihad onto his back and with brass knuckles pummeled him on his face. Blood spewed from his nose and mouth as the cracking bones sounded like wood being split for a pot-belly stove. His eyes closed up and already began to shine a blackish blue hue. His comrade had brass knuckles, too, and he was beating the others.

Ristic seemed to tire of this. He turned to Elvir and kicked him several times in the stomach with his steel-toed boots. He then motioned for Zoki to take over. Zoki unleashed a flurry of blows with his brass-knuckled fists into Elvir's face. Blood spurted out of his nose, as he faded in and out of consciousness.

Ristic then went to the door and opened it, breathing heavily from the exertion of his deeds. Zoki kicked Elvir in the face as he joined the other near the door.

"You two," Ristic said, pointing to inmates who were assigned to move the dead. "Take these bloody Turks back to their room unless they die first. This other goes for disposal," he said, pointing to Mehmed.

When Elvir was tossed back into the room, four men including Hasan and Amir, ran over to tend to him. Amir was distraught beyond tears. He wanted to burst out crying, to fix his father if such a thing was possible. He swallowed his pain knowing that he had to help his father. The scent of death hovered nearby.

Elvir was unconscious and bloody. Amir knew he could not focus on this, or he would collapse in anguish. He needed to help him. He didn't want him to die.

They brought some water from the bathroom in soaked rags. One of them, a young man from Hambarine named Jusuf, brushed Elvir's face to clean him and cool him off. The men had to gently move him into a position that was the least uncomfortable using his undulating moans as a guide. They laid him down against a wall with old clothing on the other side to keep him as still as possible

Amir was silently praying that his father wouldn't die. Hasan told him to just hold his dad, that the others would clean out his wounds, and a shaken Amir complied. The others continued to bring old water-logged shirts that they'd found, and gently wiped the shredded skin to remove the oozing from his wounds.

"Dad, can you hear me?" Amir said.

There was no answer.

"We're going to help you," whispered Amir, trying to hold back his tears once again.

Amir wondered if he had to say goodbye to his father. The thought terrified him. He repeated the small prayer to himself that he had learned from his grandmother, his majka.

Elvir was alive; his breathing was shallow, but it was steady. Although those in the room were now called to get their daily meal, Amir and Hasan stayed with him.

For the rest of the evening, Amir wiped his father's forehead. He and Jusuf took turns throughout the night. Early in the morning, with his strength sapped, he fell asleep next to his father. When he woke up, Jusuf was still there aiding Elvir.

It was mid-morning, and Elvir opened his black and blue eyes. He was very sore and it was difficult for him to move, but he was conscious though unable to talk.

With great relief, Amir welcomed his father back to the living. Elvir managed a half-smile as his son looked him in the eyes. *Amir is now a man*, thought Elvir. This was not the way Elvir wanted his son to grow up, but this was the harsh reality of Omarska.

In the evening, Elvir struggled to tell his son that he was going to get better. Amir stroked his father's hair, and smiled broadly. Though he was in pain, Elvir was on the mend.

Over the next few days, several of the men in Bilal's Room brought back any extra bread they could scrounge from the canteen for Elvir. One of the women in the canteen gave Hasan a soup ladle that he and the others could use to gather water from the bathroom sink for Elvir to drink. The clandestine operation saved him.

After two weeks Elvir's healing was making progress. Still, it was difficult for him to move easily, and the wounds and deep bruises were tender. Elvir noticed that the sleeping arrangements had changed. The inmates in Bilal's Room were not sleeping one next to the other.

Where did they go? What happened to the others? thought Elvir. He didn't want to ponder this any further.

Upon awakening one morning, Elvir looked over at Amir, who was staring at his father at that moment.

"We must stay strong. For mom, Halima, and Danis, and for Bosnia." said Elvir.

In his private prayers to a God that he believed he lost faith in long ago, Elvir asked to ensure that his family was safe, and that his desires to stay strong for the sake of them would be answered.

Chapter 11
Dysentery

Two days after his father showed signs that he was able to care for himself, Amir came down with dysentery. Hygiene was practically impossible to maintain in the camp. The inmates wore the same clothing day-in and day-out, and the battle with lice were just some of the issues they were confronted with in the dismal living conditions that plagued them.

On a typical hot and humid afternoon, the prisoners returned from their meal of watery and tasteless broth per usual. Amir was suddenly hit with sharp pains in his abdomen, and he doubled over holding onto his father.

"What is it, son?"

"Shooting pains in my stomach. I feel like I'm going to explode," he said as he winced.

"Lie down here. I'll see if Bilal can get a guard to call the doctor."

Dr. Mesonovic, a non-practicing Muslim also captive at Omarska, who stayed in a place with many other prisoners called "Mujo's Room," was the only doctor allowed to help the inmates around the camp. Other doctors who were captives might do what they could in the rooms they were held in, but many had already been killed. Dr. Mesonovic did the best he could with the limited medical supplies he was given for the tortured and sick prisoners. But he also often treated the Serb guards themselves, who, when drunk, which was often enough, misfired their weapons and either clipped a foot or leg with a bullet, or shot their comrades. He was a good man and well-respected in Prijedor by Muslims, Serbs, and Croats. Yet, he had Muslim blood, so that disqualified him as a full-fledged human being, according to the dominant Serb doctrine of the day. He often felt helpless to do much to save the abused prisoners, his own people, who were the targets of brutal and sadistic treatment.

"He has dysentery. Treating dysentery with antibiotics and keeping hydrated is the best way to help the patient," the doctor told Elvir, but he had no means of providing either to his son.

"Get as much fluid into Amir as possible. In these conditions, it is so difficult to treat something that should be easily remedied. I wish I could do more for him. I am so sorry," the doctor told Elvir.

Elvir knew that dysentery could kill if not mitigated. So, as Amir continued to anguish in pain from the parasitic invasion, a tremendous anxiety filled him. *He must get fluids. Clean fluids. I will not let him die.*

Jusuf, the young man who had helped Amir tend to his father, offered to help once again. *What a special young man, this Jusuf*, thought Elvir. Hasan, his loyal, long-time friend, offered the same.

The three acted as nurses to ensure that Amir stayed hydrated. They alternated sneaking into the bathroom with the soup ladle that was hidden in their room. They filled it with water from the sink, hydrating him when the lead shift guard was not Ristic. There were times at night when guards got drunk somewhere in the complex after the commander had gone home, which would do one of two things: dull their awareness of the prisoners' movements, or enhance their belligerence and cruelty. When Amir soiled himself, Elvir, Hasan, and Jusuf alternated bringing his clothing to the sink to rinse it off.

However, going downstairs was much more difficult. Recently, hundreds of men were placed inside the hangar within a wire-cordoned area. They were sleeping on the cement floor replete with its dirt and motor oil-stains. There were also men sleeping on narrow stairs that went down from the rooms to the bathroom. There were even men sleeping near the toilets.

So, when Elvir or the others went downstairs in the middle of the night to the bathroom to provide whatever help they could for Amir, they had to walk over, and sometimes on the men on the stairs, depending on how urgent Amir's needs were at that moment. Elvir tried not to hurt the men, but he desperately wanted to help his son. For some of the sleeping men whose conditions were so compromised, they didn't react to being stepped on. It all broke his heart. The enormity of the indignation piled on without any means of reconciling what was happening.

Elvir rocked his son, holding him as he had done when he was an infant. He looked upon his innocent face and thought back to the days when he and Hajra acknowledged that their love for this recently born boy was more than they could have ever imagined before having their own child.

For Amir, undulating waves of pain included vivid hallucinations. He saw his mother floating above him, reaching out but unable to touch him. She tried to speak to him, to tell him that she was there to help. But her voice was a faded, raspy version of the sweet maternal sounds he was familiar with. Suddenly, as she hovered just feet from him, her face disappeared, leaving only her hands outstretched toward him. He could hear himself screaming for his mother to become whole again, to look at him, but it was to no avail. *Am I dying? Is my mother dead and calling for me?*

Responding to Amir's moans, in a soothing voice Elvir said, "I'm here, my boy. I'm going to do whatever I can to help you get better. I'm here. I'm not going anywhere"

Elvir felt he was losing his son. He rocked him gently and poured what little strength he had into the love he felt for him.

It was all that he could do anymore. The sadness he was feeling was almost suffocating. He had to have his son back. He closed his eyes and prayed once again. At that moment, Hasan tapped him on the shoulder.

"Look, my friend," Hasan said.

Amir's eyes were open and they had a look of recognition aimed at his dad.

He felt miserable, and seeing his dad look at him in a piteous way was actually worrisome to him.

Amir whispered, "I can't leave you. Who will take care of you when you trip and hurt yourself?"

Elvir smiled. Had Amir returned from the almost-dead? It seemed he had. The worst was over. *Praised be God*, thought Elvir.

It was nearing their once-a-day meal, so Elvir stayed with his son while Hasan and Jusuf brought back whatever bread they managed to confiscate.

It had taken four days, but Amir miraculously pulled through.

"I'm typically not a praying man. That is more your grandmother's department, but I prayed for your recovery this time. I didn't know what else to do."

"Though you will never be an Imam, thank you Dad."

He stared at his father through glistening eyes.

Looking away for the briefest of moments, Elvir peered off into the most distant part of the room and dared himself to have a fleeting image of his family back together again in their home in Kozarac.

Chapter 12
The White House Redux

If a prisoner had to go to the bathroom, he might be taking a grave risk. Depending on the shift leader, relieving oneself was almost solely determined by this fact. Shift leader Krstic was notorious for not granting permission to go to the bathroom. If you asked, the inmates quickly learned, you could be taken outside, beaten and taken who knows where, never to return.

Every week, Krstic and his fellow guards entered the front door of the hangar and selected the first inmates they saw.

"You all have made the bathrooms disgusting. You are disgusting. Here is the cleaning solution and rags. You five," he'd order, "clean it now!"

The men scrambled to their feet and headed to the bathrooms. Urine, feces, and vomit were stuck to the toilets, on the floors, and in the sinks.

The chemical they had to use was a chlorine derivative. It was quite powerful at cleaning, but also at stinging eyes and nasal passages. The men who had to clean with it gasped and choked. They tried to cover their mouths with one hand and clean with the other, but this acrobatic act did little to lessen the fumes' impact. When finished, they emerged gagging and coughing, tears racing down their cheeks. And when the prisoners were given permission to use the bathroom soon after the cleaning, they too came out finding it difficult to breathe.

It was the middle of July, and desperation had long ago taken hold. Elvir had healed as well as he could under the circumstances. But all of the remaining prisoners, with numbers dwindling because of the mass murders, and at times increasing with new captives being brought in, were gaunt with a permanent gray pallor. Most now just blankly stared into the unforgiving space of their prison.

Routinely, men were taken out of the rooms, and sent to the White House for torture. With windows open, albeit it minimally, it was easy to hear the screaming that echoed throughout, often punctuated with the sounds of gunshots.

The selection of who was next for the White House was so anxiety-producing that Amir was regularly awoken from his nightmares. The same scene appeared to him in which his father and he were being dragged to the White House by several guards who spat and cursed at them. When they got to the torture chamber his mother and siblings were waiting, bloodied and looking away, unable to communicate. He awoke drenched in sweat. Not wanting to upset his father, he would only say that he had a nightmare, but couldn't remember its contents.

One evening, Elvir was selected, once again, along with two others.

"Don't go, Daddy, please don't leave me, please! Not again." whispered Amir.

"I have to, my son. You know that if I refuse, I will surely be killed," replied a trembling Elvir.

Amir knew his father was right. At least he had a chance of returning alive, although in what shape was difficult to fathom.

But Elvir was unsure of whether he'd return this time. His head ached, and his heart raced uncontrollably. Taken with him were two brothers who were only in their twenties, Adin and Imran. Both of them were excellent soccer players who Amir admired greatly, but who now looked like old, withered men.

They entered the White House where the last beating that

Elvir endured flooded back to him. And it was Milan again. "Milan the Terrible" as some referred to him. His deeply set, dark eyes looked even more menacing.

He said nothing. He just took out a metal rod and began beating Elvir first on the back of his legs, knocking him to the ground. He then turned to the two others and beat them across their faces. Both men screamed in agony.

Milan whipped back around hitting Elvir on his back and shoulders.

"You don't deserve to live, you filthy Turks. You don't deserve my mercy." And he returned to his cruel dance.

Milan continued to beat the two brothers.

He turned to Elvir and dropped the bat he had used. Instead, he picked up brass knuckles and punched Elvir repeatedly across the face. The pain Elvir felt was almost unbearable as it seared through him like a hot poker from a wood stove.

But the vicious beatings suddenly stopped. They were all dragged outside. Elvir was floating above his body. He was losing his battle to stay alive—to return to Amir as he had promised.

He recalled one image before he passed out. Just outside the White House there was a barrel that filled with water from the typical rainy days of July. Milan shoved Elvir's face into the filthy water as it reddened with his blood. As he faded into darkness, he heard the mocking laughter of his tormentors as Milan said how it was good practice to wash your face before going to bed.

Elvir had been unconscious for the better part of five hours, but when he opened his battered eyes Amir was tending to him with wet rags, rocking him in his arms on his lap.

Was he dreaming? Hadn't he died like Milan had promised he would? How had he avoided that fate?

"Dad, can you hear me? Dad..."

"Yes, Amir, I hear you. What happened?" he replied in barely a whisper.

"You were taken back here after they beat you. You're in bad shape."

"Where are the two who went with me?"

"They didn't come back," Amir said in a hushed and sullen voice.

His tone had changed in the two plus months they'd been there. It was clear that Amir adopted the survival mantra that the captives needed to have in order not to go insane, or to find a way to kill themselves.

Elvir was lost in pain and jumbled, gauzy thoughts. *Am I dying? Am I dead? Is this really Amir? Poor Amir. He is witnessing the worst of humankind.*

He and Hajra had tried to instill in their children that people were inherently good. Sure, there were those who were not, but they weren't born that way. It had to be learned. The treatment the prisoners were subjected to ran completely counter to what he wanted to believe.

So, where did these people learn to be so monstrous? Minds are pliable. The messages that we Muslims are somehow to blame for their problems has led to this. And now Amir, Jusuf, and so many of us are the recipients of their brutality.

He faded back into a tortured oblivion.

Amir didn't want to leave his father, but Jusuf said he would forgo the meal to watch Elvir. Amir accepted his offer and brought back some bread for Jusuf and Elvir.

It took several days before Elvir could move with only minimal pain. Still, he now walked with a limp as Milan had battered his right leg quite severely with a bat.

The first day of August was insufferably hot. The windows of the hangar were barely opened, making it hard to breathe. This further cruelty, in combination with little water allowed to be drunk by the inmates, resulted in many deaths inside. The stench from the recently dead mixed in with the infected wounds of their battered bodies—and the poor hygiene—made it even more unbearable for the prisoners.

"The Turks want to take a shower," Ristic said. "The poor lads are hot and sticky from all of their hard work. Let's give them a shower."

The hundreds inside the hangar were ordered to come outside and stand in the hot sun. The air was still. Some of the men collapsed. The guards chose some others to drag them away.

A young guard named Bogdan, probably not more than twenty years old, was given the task to prove his manhood by his comrades.

"Bogdan," one of the older guards yelled, "cool off the boys, they're hot."

Bogdan had the fire hose in hand and it was now flowing full force. He was spraying the men, many of whom were falling like dominoes from the heavy stream of water, their gaunt bodies unable to stand against such a torrent.

Some tried to turn in such a way that they could capture some of the water in their mouths, but this was near impossible. While the guards laughed and mocked the prisoners, Bogdan gave a three-finger salute, the Serbian greeting among soldiers.

The cruelty stopped and some of the fallen were taken inside by those who were strong enough to do so.

When the prisoners returned to their rooms they just slumped downward onto the floor. The silence that filled their quarters was overwhelming. No one spoke. No one could do anything more than lay down and close their eyes in a vain attempt to shield themselves from the terror that had invaded their lives since coming to Omarska.

Amir laid down next to his father and rested his head in the crook of his right shoulder. He exhaled slowly and wept quietly. Elvir moved his chin over to where his son's head rested. He set it upon his flattened and greasy hair. Most of those in Bilal's Room fell into a fitful sleep and awoke early the next day to find that the nightmare hadn't disappeared.

Chapter 13
Keraterm

For a number of years Prijedor was known for its ceramics works. Just outside the city center was a large factory that produced well-known tiles, plates, pots, and anything ceramic for home and commercial use. The textiles company, called Keraterm, closed down not long before the Serbs began their genocide of Muslims and Croats living in Bosnia and Herzegovina.

Now, it was used to rape, torture, and murder.

Prijedor had three concentration camps: Omarska, Keratem, and Trnopolje. Of the atrocities committed there, the severity of the cruelty imposed upon non-Serbs in the Prijedor municipality was the least inflicted in Trnopolje, which was often described as a "detention or deportation center," though either was only a relative term.

There were plenty of rumors about Keraterm. Actually, verifiable rumors were transmitted from those prisoners who had been there and transferred to Trnopolje, telling of its horrors.

Keraterm had four corridors used for storage of ceramics when it was in operation. Each corridor's large room was used to house its prisoners. Each of the four rooms was given a number by the Serb guards starting at number one. The point was for the guards to know where they were putting people from the same village and nearby villages. From there, it was not uncommon for ten to twenty inmates to be dragged out of the rooms, never to return.

It was well known that the prisoners in Room 3 were the recipients of particularly severe savagery. Certain guards: Boskovic, Lazic, and Knezevic, had reputations for their brutality. They and their families had been the good neighbors who Muslims thought they knew, and might even call their friends. At Keraterm, they had no sympathy for their non-Serb neighbors.

And, of course, there was the big guard, Dokic, who visited all of the camps in Prijedor, and Milan, who was rumored to have murdered over one hundred prisoners by his own hands, who took pride in meting out punishment.

Many times, the result of their handy-work was to drag out the dead, or to finish the job with the nearly dead with a bullet outside on the grounds of the camp.

***

The day after Tarik had found a hiding Danis, Hajra was outside with her children looking to speak with him long enough to follow up on what he'd first told her.

While Miroslav smoked cigarettes at his post a short distance from where the prisoners were milling around, Hajra and her children wandered over to where the men near the fence lingered. Tarik spotted them, and he slipped quietly to the back of the group. His eyes lit up as he saw Hajra and the children standing next to him.

"My God, look at you kids, such a short time in this camp, and how you've grown," he said wryly.

He managed to get a chuckle out of all three of them.

"It's the nutritious food they feed us, Uncle Tarik," Halima teased.

"Danis, how are you doing?"

"OK. I took your advice and talked with my mom about stuff."

"It's going to take a long time for him, or any of us to forget what we've seen. Thank you, again, Tarik, for being there for Danis."

"Of course. Halima, you look grown up already. How are you?"

"Not great, Uncle. But as my mom always says, we have to survive to show them that they didn't win."

"I like that. I'll remember that one."

Knowing that their time together would be limited, Hajra addressed Tarik directly.

"My dear Tarik, we don't know how long Miroslav and his comrades' generosity will last. Sometimes, as you've seen, they get a little testy with us and order us around if they feel like it, so can you please tell us what happened to you and your family? It's good for the kids to hear this. In fact, they requested that I allow them to," she said.

She yearned for Elvir, especially so that he could know his brother was alive.

The thought of Elvir brought a momentary pause of sadness, but Hajra quickly went back to her original query when they first saw Tarik in the camp.

"You told me that they took you to the police station to interrogate you, and then to Keraterm. I didn't really talk to the kids about this part."

He hesitated for a brief moment before speaking. He was not sure he wanted to tell the children of the horrors he survived or had witnessed. He cleared his throat and spoke in a slow, deliberate manner.

"Oh, yes. Well, the station was filled with Muslim and Croat men, and my heart was racing. I was telling myself that this was all a big mistake—that we would be back with our families after they spoke with us."

"So, where did they take you again, Uncle?" Danis asked.

Tarik continued, "Do you remember the old ceramics factory in town, Keraterm? That became my new home. Well, not exactly a home. It was the worst place I could ever imagine. I was consumed with not knowing what was happening with your Aunt Merjem and the kids. The times I wasn't thinking about them, I was thinking about my parents and everyone else, like you guys. I was starving and thirsty a lot. And they would beat me. But I didn't give in to them. They learned too well from the Chetniks, I'm afraid."

"You're so skinny like us, and the wounds that you have on your chest look painful," said Halima, her eyes drawn to her shirtless, gaunt uncle.

"They beat me regularly, sweetheart. After a while, and I know this sounds odd, I would be thankful when they only beat me for a few minutes instead of an hour. The one who was the cruelest was the big guard, Dokic, who I saw come through here yesterday. I tried to avoid him, hiding among the others here at the fence. He is a very bad man. But my wounds will heal."

The three of them cringed at hearing this. Tarik sensed this, especially recalling what Danis had recently witnessed, and stopped being quite so graphic. He thought about the time Dokic beat him so severely that he sincerely believed he would die right there. That was Dokic's specialty—beat you to within an inch of your life, and then throw you back to your room to suffer, only to come back another day. If his victims died later, so be it. And he mentored his colleagues well. But there was no need to tell his family any more, if for nothing else than to not worry them that Elvir and Amir may have met up with Dokic or another of his ilk in Omarska. He shuddered at the thought.

"Do you have any idea what happened to your parents or mine? Or my brothers for that matter?"

"No, I'm afraid not. I've heard there's another camp at Mount Manjaca near Banja Luka that some are being transferred to. Actually, I've heard they've set up camps, big and small, all over Bosnia"

"Why did they send you here from Keraterm?" asked

Hajra.

"I don't really know why. But, to be honest, Trnopolje seems like a breath of fresh air compared to that hell-hole I was in. I'm sure you don't feel this way, but I'm just glad to be out of there."

Miroslav was ending his cigarette break after smoking at least half a pack. Gripping the gun across his chest, he ordered that the "party" was over.

Everyone returned to where they were supposed to be.

Before Hajra and the children went back inside, they told Tarik to be careful, and that they would find him the next day. Tarik, who rarely was seen crying even at funerals, trained his moistened eyes on them and didn't look away until one of the guards, who surprised him by standing centimeters from him, dug a rifle butt into his back. He let out a muffled yelp. He was sick of their bullying, and he would not give in to it by uttering any indication that the guard had hurt him. The pain that he truly wanted to get rid of was the mental anguish; the one that his tormented dreams revisited on a nightly basis during his restless and stunted sleep—the one where Merjem and the children were laughing and enjoying being together in their house in Prijedor, with his brother, parents, and all those whom he ached to hug. But then suddenly, they are all gunned down by Serb semi-automatic weapons, and his nightmare goes black.

***

The next day Tarik was gone. He had been in the camp for four days, and it was as if he was never really there. Hajra had the children fan out to see if they could find him. But he had simply disappeared.

When they gathered back together Hajra beckoned them to head back to their room.

"He's not here," said Halima. "What did they do with

him?"

"I don't know. I asked some of the men near the fence, and they saw some guards take him away this morning, and he never returned. They said that others were taken, too."

"Oh no," said Danis as he dropped to the floor, clutching his head in his hands.

"Danis," Hajra called as she sat down next to him with arms around him.

"No, Mom, no. What did they do to him?"

An equally distraught Halima sat down on the floor, too, her own arms wrapped around her body.

It would be another day before any of them left the room to eat the watery broth with its bits of carrot and occasional onion, and days-old bread at meal time. In fact, for a week afterwards they didn't go into the yard at all.

***

On August 5th, from their room, Hajra and others peered out of the window into the yard. Their angle was not very good and they could only see a few men at the edge of the group. However, more were moving into an area that allowed those at the window above to get a better view.

Halima wandered over to her mother as Danis, exhausted from lack of nourishment, slept in the hot room.

"What's going on over there, Mom?" she asked.

"I'm not sure. But there is a TV camera near the fence and what looks like reporters speaking to the men," she replied.

"Who are those men? I haven't seen them before. They look like...like...Uncle Tarik did when he arrived. And why is that barbed wire there now?"

"They do look like him in a way. I'm guessing they're from one of the other camps? And I don't know why they're separated from the rest and caged behind the barbed wire?"

"Why are those people with a camera talking with them,"

Halima asked.

"I don't know, my darling, but I believe they are British or American from what I can tell by the writing on the camera. If they are English-speaking reporters, maybe there is finally someone here to tell the outside world what's happening in Prijedor," she said.

"Oh, mom, if that's true," she stuttered, "if that's true, then maybe we can get out and find Dad and Amir if..." she stopped, not wanting to jinx any hope that something good might be on the horizon.

Hajra silently peered down to the yard. She squinted as if to bring a greater focus on what was developing below. *The reporters are hearing from the prisoners. The cameras will bear witness to this horror. Do I dare hope?*

Chapter 14
The List

It was the last day of July, and for the previous few days rumors had been circulating around the camp that reporters were getting wind of the situation in Prijedor. One prisoner, who had actually worked at Omarska when it was a functional iron ore mining company, was allowed to periodically sit in what had been his office to listen to the radio, a privilege that one of the guards, who was his colleague back then, gave to him. It was this man who heard news reports about the "discovery" of the camps. It was not long after that those rumors gained momentum.

The first few days of August brought about another strange event. The guards were taking inventory in all of the rooms. They were checking off names of the living and the dead. Included in their survey were the names of those who had been exchanged for Serb soldiers captured by the Bosnian Army.

On August 3rd, most of the women were transferred to Trnopolje, though the other inmates in the camp didn't know of this movement at the time. The remaining several hundred prisoners continued to endure the crimes being committed against them.

Hasan was the one who noticed that women had left the camp. He and Elvir agreed that this was worrisome. There had been many killings as evidenced by those taken, never to return.

One ray of hope had emerged. Elvir had heard from one of

the later arrivals to Omarska that there were negotiations in London to stop the war. The man told him he had heard that the participants had wanted accountability from Karadzic for the concentration camps that had been reported about. Karadzic, of course, denied the allegations and welcomed reporters to visit the camps to see for themselves.

The news had spread in their room. There were hushed discussions of what it would be like if they were let out of this hell. They even fantasized about going to their villages and cities to get back to some semblance of normalcy even if they knew the reality that their homes had likely been destroyed by the Serbs. They'd rebuild, is what they said.

The lists of prisoners were amassed by the guards as a way for the captors to organize distribution out of Omarska to Trnopolje and Manjaca. Of course, the prisoners had no way of knowing that this was why inventory had been taken. They also had no clue that the exodus was to take place on August 5th with the expectation by Bosnian Serb leaders that the reporters were to come on the 6th, so there would be no prisoner on the premises. But plans don't always go as devised.

***

By late July, there were reports finding their way around the world that non-Serbs who lived in Prijedor, as well as other cities and towns in Bosnia and Herzegovina, were being targeted by the Bosnian Serbs for extermination in concentration camps. This was confirmed in an article in the now defunct *Newsday* newspaper out of Long Island, New York, by Pulitzer Prize winning journalist, Roy Gutman. His reporting on the death camps in Prijedor was the first witness-generated and verifiable story linking the Serbs to these atrocities. That was very quickly followed up by a team of reporters led by Ed Vulliamy of Independent Television News (ITN) in the UK.

"This was the stuff that made up the Holocaust," noted the senior investigative reporter, Vulliamy to his colleagues at ITN. "Is this actually happening again in Europe?" he asked his team.

His team was determined to find the truth following Gutman's revelations. They contacted Bosnian Serb leader Radovan Karadzic, who then challenged ITN to see what the "detention centers" were actually doing. He claimed that the prisoners were, in fact, captured soldiers from the Bosnian Muslim extremist paramilitaries who had initiated the fighting against the Serbs, prompting his Bosnian Serbs to retaliate.

The ITN team took up Karadzic's challenge. After days of wrangling with the Bosnian Serb leader, the reporters were given permission to visit the camps in Prijedor.

As the lead reporter would later tell, Serbian leaders in Prijedor Municipality were expecting them on August 6th, but they arrived a day early. This caught them off-guard. It resulted in a couple of hours of heated discussion where the officials insisted they go to Manjaca near Banja Luka, which was brutal, the reporters had heard, but nowhere near meting out the cruelty to the degree that was reported to occur in any of the three big camps in Prijedor, especially Omarska and Keraterm. But Keraterm was emptying out, sending its prisoners to Trnopolje and Manjaca. So, that left Omarska and Trnopolje as places of interest for the news team. The lengthy negotiations allowed Prijedor's city leaders to call ahead to the commandant in Omarska to warn him that the reporters were soon heading their way.

The call prompted the order that the guards quickly empty out the White House, and all other rooms that prisoners were in, and to stuff them into the hangar, while those already in other quarters such as Bilal's Room, were to remain in them. There was to be no evidence of their captives for the reporters to see.

***

Toting a camera that was ready to roll, the reporters arrived at Omarska later that morning to be greeted by the commandant, a guard shift leader, and a translator.

While this encounter was being filmed, for several minutes they were outside of the main building arguing with Commandant Miljkovic about what they would be allowed to see. Miljkovic clearly was not going to capitulate, and told them in no uncertain terms that they would be allowed in the canteen, and that would be it.

The ITN reporters continued to try to persuade him that Karadzic said they could have brief access to the other buildings, but the commandant wouldn't budge.

"That's not what we were told," the commandant said through a translator. "And we have protocols to follow in this camp. Besides," he said, "there are no women or children here and the men are treated quite well for being our enemies. There is no need to see anything else."

With no persuasive argument working, the reporters, along with their cameraman, moved into the canteen.

On this day, a list of thirty names were chosen by the guards to go to the canteen for the meal. This was unusual, of course, because the routine was that each room would just be randomly emptied for their daily feeding.

Amir, who looked much older than his fifteen years, was selected, along with Jusuf, and those that seemed to be the stronger of the lot, although "stronger" was a relative term for those in Omarska. They were told to run out of the hangar in a single file, and not to look at, or to speak with the reporters, who they would see once they entered the room.

There was no time to process what he had just heard. *Reporters? God, are they here to see what's going on in this place? I hope they're not Serbian,* thought Amir, understanding that Serbian media was quite slanted toward only reporting what the government wanted them to say.

They were given their usual three minutes to slurp down the day's scalding gruel and, when ordered, to run back to their rooms.

This charade was clearly designed to fool the reporters into thinking that they were being treated well. All of them were the "pick of the litter" as one of those in Bilal's Room would later say.

The reporters, whose English gave away their UK origin, tried to ask questions as they filmed the spectacle before them. Answers were not forthcoming except from Jusuf, who happened to be sitting next to Amir.

Ed Vulliamy asked the men at the table near him how they were being treated.

"I cannot tell lies," said Jusuf, "but I cannot speak the truth either."

As they ran back to the hangar and upstairs to Bilal's Room, Amir glanced over at Jusuf with incredulity. Curiosity piqued when the group returned.

One man spoke up.

"I am not sure I can honestly say what just happened. I know that there were reporters who spoke English. And Jusuf, well..."

Amir turned to face his friend, as did the others.

"That was something," uttered Amir, "and you are incredibly brave."

Jusuf replied to Amir and the others nearby, "I either just signed our death sentence, or if the reporters show important people what they found here, maybe they have just gotten us released in the nick of time."

For the rest of the day, the aura of what had occurred seemed to linger and provide a ray of hope. However, allowing oneself to hope always came with the risk of disaster.

Unbeknown to any of the prisoners, that evening and the

next, one hundred and twenty-four inmates from the camp would be executed and buried in a mass grave in a place called Hrastova Glavica.

Chapter 15
Trnopolje

The ITN team was loaded into military vehicles and taken from Omarska to Trnopolje, which they were told was a detention and relocation center. They had gotten footage of the canteen in Omarska, which was damning enough. The gaunt bodies, and fear-laden expressions, revealed so much about the treatment at the camp. And it was clear to all of them that these men were window-dressing: the creme de la crème being offered up as evidence to support how well the Serbs were caring for their internees.

Yet, even with clothing on, reeking in their unwashed state, one could see the bones protruding that were clear indications of malnutrition. "Lantern jaw" is how Vulliamy described the prisoners' hollowed out faces, as they discussed their findings with each other.

The road to Trnopolje was normally seen as a beautiful drive to a bucolic Bosnian village if it was not for the purpose of seeing the concentration camp just over an hour from Omarska. When they arrived, the camera started filming.

The video began capturing the run-down old primary school with a fence, behind which were about two hundred men. There were women and children, many of whom they later learned slept outside as well. However, they could also see onlookers, women mostly, peering down at them from what were presumed to be classrooms. As the reporters came close to the fence, they could see the emaciated bodies of men who had clearly been mistreated, or worse.

The twenty-minute footage was later relayed to their station in London. It was included with what they had witnessed in Omarska, which on its own was almost enough to condemn the perpetrators.

The men, many without shirts and clearly with infected cuts and gashes, and bruises apparent on their bodies, huddled together, some standing, some sitting. The reporting team found a few of them who spoke English and asked questions about treatment.

The first group of men they approached had arrived just this day from Keraterm. They joined others in the camp who had been there longer, to mill about and sleep outside. They didn't know why they were transferred, but the few who spoke, obviously desperate to tell someone, tried to convey what they had experienced without being so overt that they would later be killed for speaking their truths.

"How are you being treated?" asked reporter Ian Williams to a man who spoke English quite well.

"OK. We just got here today from another camp at the city limits of Prijedor," said the young man.

"But are they treating you well here?" the reporter continued.

"It is only our first day, but this seems to be better than the other place."

"Do you mean Keraterm? What did they do to you in the other camp?"

The man appeared unsure as to how to answer this question. Averting his eyes from the camera he replied, "Yes, that is the camp. We were not treated that well, but we're here now."

The man then went mute.

There were a few more men who spoke English that followed suit with scabs and wounds belying the brutal treatment they received in Keraterm.

Hajra could see this from the window in her room, though

she couldn't hear what was being said. This was, in fact, a new group of men from Keraterm she had been told, which is where Tarik had come from weeks before. She could see a man who she knew was a colleague of her brother-in-law in Prijedor speaking to the reporter. She recalled how Tarik told her of the brutality that occurred in that camp, and she hoped this was being exposed to the news team.

She saw the reporters leave. Without uttering any words, a slight shift in posture by those in the room told of the ray of hope that the news team had brought.

The next day the sun was unrelenting.

There was a strange air in the camp. Stranger than normal. It was hard for Hajra to put her finger on it. The reporters had interviewed and filmed the men by the fence most assuredly to show to someone. That was an encouraging sign. Yet, several of the Keraterm prisoners who she'd seen the day before were gone.

A few days later, the International Red Cross arrived and began to make conditions at the camp better. There was even talk of being deported to Croatia—that negotiations by the United Nations and Red Cross with the Serbs were targeting such a move. It seems the news report had hastened that determination.

But still, worry turned her thoughts back to her husband and son, and Tarik.

Later that night while holding her very thin children against her exposed ribs, she dreamed that it was up to her to find them. She tried looking in Prijedor and Kozarac. She recognized the cafes and shops of those two cities, even running into smiling citizens, though none could speak, and all shook their heads that they had not seen any of the three. She went walking on the road nearby and ended up in her birth village. She searched Trnopolje, but it was void of anyone. And finally, she wandered the grounds of the school-turned-concentration camp. But they were nowhere to be found. They had simply vanished from existence.

Upon being jolted from her sleep by the dark dreams, Hajra stayed awake the rest of the night praying that those images were not an ominous foreshadowing, and that the momentous events of the previous days would bring their living nightmare to an end.

Chapter 16
New Lists Revealed

With the charade at the canteen of the day before behind them, the prisoners were greeted with a new surprise. As they awoke Elvir, Amir and the others were informed of the following by an announcement from the shift leader.

1,200 prisoners were to leave for Manjaca, the military POW camp. This list included Elvir and Amir, while 780 were headed to Trnopolje.

The lists' purpose was unclear to the inmates, but not to the Serb perpetrators. In order to find the number of buses needed to take the prisoners away and continue to hide the truth, this task required planning and organization.

As each group returned from the canteen after their meal, provided that morning, the guards allowed the prisoners to sit on the dirt outside the hangar to await transportation out.

As Elvir moved over to sit with his son, he had tears in his eyes, almost not believing that they were to leave, but feeling relief and joy that this was to soon be a reality.

Noticing Elvir's tears, one of the guards mocked him as he said to a colleague, "Look at this one, he is sad to leave us, maybe he had such a good time that he should stick around?"

At this point, however, Elvir didn't care what they said. He was leaving. That's all that mattered. He'd deal with Manjaca when he got there, but he was leaving Omarska.

As the masses of prisoners sat awaiting the buses, the guards got nervous. Their concern was that the men could overtake them due to their sheer numbers. So, they made them all get up and go to whatever room they found in the hangar, just to clear them away to avoid any hint of rebellion that could have been brewing.

Elvir lost sight of Amir, who had been standing next to Jusuf as they scrambled into the hangar. But with so many people, it was impossible to keep track. He kept peering left and right, up and down, to see if he could find Amir, but to no avail.

There were only two lists: one for those going to Manjaca, and the other for those to Trnopolje. At least that is what had been learned through the camp's rumor mill. However, a friend of Elvir's standing next to him informed him of another list that took Elvir's breath away.

"I just heard that you and I are on a third list. Ristic is outside and he called our names," said Kemal.

"I don't get it, aren't we going to Manjaca? a dumbfounded Elvir replied.

"Not anymore. We are to stay here," Kemal said as his voice dropped off into a whisper.

Elvir didn't know how to respond. As the others began to vacate their rooms to get on their respective buses, he and one-hundred-seventy-three others were told to go to the garage nearby. The garage was a small, windowless space used to repair trucks and other vehicles for the mining company. It was not a place for one-hundred-seventy-four people to be. In fact, they were so tightly packed that they had to stand on one foot, alternating with the other to maintain an upright position.

It was early afternoon, and Elvir was one of the last to enter the garage. For that he was grateful because he could be near the door, and one tiny window above it allowed some air inside.

"Dad. I can't leave without my father," Amir said to Hasan as the group headed for Manjaca was being herded into the buses.

Hasan did his best to calm Amir. "We all need to hold on. I don't know what their plans are for us once we get to Manjaca, but with all that we've been through, we need to have some faith that we'll reunite with your father. You must be strong. I must be strong, too."

As the bus drove away, Amir looked back knowing that he may never see his father again. Beleaguered, he just stared out of the window as the bus passed through the heavily guarded gate at the camp known as Omarska.

***

Being in the garage, and not being with his son on a bus to Manjaca, was the hardest thing Elvir had experienced. Harder than getting beaten. Harder than nursing his son back from dysentery. Harder than the torture of life in the camp.

Elvir just kept saying to himself, *we will meet up again, Amir. Be brave. Be strong. You must take care of yourself. I know you can.*

Elvir felt such despair as he had not felt before. At least his son had been with him in the camp, as horrible as their lives were. They could look after each other, sleep and eat with each other, and were mostly within arm's reach. In an instant that was over, and the uncertainty of what would happen to them, especially now that they were separated, was overwhelming. The depression Elvir felt was so deep that he didn't know if he could pull himself out of it.

And now, as he struggled to maintain some semblance of composure so as not to lose hope completely, a guard entered the garage and chose five of the men, including Elvir.

"You will go into the White House, and clean up the mess that is left on the floors and walls. No trace of any of your dead Turk friends can be seen by anyone."

Elvir and the others grabbed cleaning supplies left at the White House door and silently went about the business of clearing the place of any remnants of the torture and death that filled the rooms.

It was mid-afternoon when he returned to the garage. As the day wore on, there was less and less noise outside as the buses drifted away. No one spoke inside their new holding cell. One man toward the back of the space died. And all were aware that the night before, another group of one hundred and twenty-four selected prisoners, spent their last moments of life in the garage before being taken out of the camp.

Elvir wondered why it was his turn? As he looked around, he saw some politicians from villages around Prijedor municipality, two policemen he knew from Kozarac, and a resistance fighter. He understood that this was to be revenge for the Serbs. But why him? He had been in the JNA, but not for long. Did they think because he had military training, he was a threat?

Afternoon turned into evening, and then the night arrived. It was eerily silent now. The buses had come and gone, and it was only those men in the garage who remained.

It was now just us and them, Elvir thought.

At 11:00 that night, the door to the garage opened. One of the guards just gestured for the men to exit. He pointed toward Mujo's Room and said for the men to go inside—that this was to be their new living quarters.

Confused, they all entered the room.

As they sat in Mujo's Room, with some relief, no longer having to endure the confines of the garage, they just waited. Most just stared out into the darkness.

At 1:00 in the morning the sound of a truck engine could be heard from their room. Elvir's mind, once again, returned to the men who had been taken away and killed the night before. A guard ordered them out of the room.

This is it, he thought. *My life ends now.*

Heads bowed, they slowly exited.

A truck was waiting on the tarmac.

Trucks await us, Elvir thought, *trucks to take us to our deaths.*

But in the next moment, a few of the prisoners were told to lift the rear door of the vehicle. Inside, there were one hundred and eighty metal-framed bunk beds with mattresses and pillows.

"You will unload these beds, and set them up in Mujo's Room, where you will now be staying. You will then put pillows on top of each bed."

For extra measure, however, some of the men who were too exhausted and weak to help were pulled aside and beaten.

Elvir was part of the group willing themselves to haul the beds into the room. While doing this, he was piecing together what had taken place the past few days in order to understand why these beds were brought in.

He thought about the reporters exposing the truth. He understood now that this is why the camp was emptied. The beds were military-style and Mujo's Room could almost pass for army barracks. But were these for their soldiers to make it look like barracks, so that if other reporters visited this is what they'd think? If this was the case, what was going to happen to the remaining prisoners?

It took four hours to get all the beds out of the truck and set up in the room. Elvir was exhausted. He had no energy whatsoever. He still believed that he very well might be killed, but his brain was too fatigued to contemplate anything, let alone his execution. The guards had bullied them, beaten some of them, called them names, and reveled in the entire early morning's activities.

A bed, Elvir thought to himself. *At least we'll have a bed to lie on.*

Elvir couldn't wait to crawl into one—to feel its warmth even if it was hot and muggy in Mujo's Room. He couldn't remember what it felt like to sleep on a mattress.

Then the fantasy was interrupted by one of the guards.

"At no time should you consider the beds for your use. You are to lie on the floor if you need sleep."

Elvir felt hopeless.

After the guards left, he just shook his head in disbelief at the depths of their inhumanity. The beds were for "show" only. They were the most inviting things any of them had seen in months, and now they were being denied access to them.

He and the others laid down on the floor. It was nearly dawn, and they had not had any sleep in almost twenty-four hours.

There was no energy to speak with one another. They all knew that any of a number of things could happen to them in the coming minutes. They were almost beyond exhaustion as the sounds of snoring perforated the dense air in Mujo's Room.

Two hours later, when the 7:00 a.m. shift of guards arrived, a marked change occurred.

One of the guards, a good guy actually, announced to them, "Good morning, people."

He called them people. Elvir had not heard them ever referred to as humans. But now, no demeaning names. No threats.

The guard then followed with, "You can stay in Mujo's Room, and you can use these beds. The International Red Cross will come to register you in the coming days, and journalists will come, too. We expect you to say how it is here now. Is that clear? You will tell them that you have been here for between five and fifteen days. And let them know of the beds you get to sleep in."

They all crawled into the army-issued twin bunk beds with thin, cheap mattresses, but that didn't matter to the men. To them, it felt like they had just laid down on imported Swedish thick-foamed, king-sized beds with four mahogany posts. Their exhaustion had found a resting spot—a place to ease the pain of the past twenty-four hours— actually, of the past several months.

There was a strange sense of calm, of peace. Daylight had arrived. A new day had indeed begun.

Chapter 17
The Ride to Manjaca

Amir anxiously wrung his hands speculating about where they had taken Jusuf. After he and the many others boarded the buses for Manjaca, he lost track of his friend who had been called out with about fifty others. It made him queasy thinking of one potential outcome, and he tried to push the thought out of his mind. Hasan sat next to him and noticed the boy with his face buried in his hands. He put his arm around Amir and comforted him as best as he could.

The buses passed through the countryside toward the mountains. Mount Manjaca, which is what the camp was named for, was not more than a couple of hours away. Amir had been at that mountain with his family when he was younger to camp and hike, which included his Uncle Tarik, Aunt Merjem, and his two little cousins.

He remembered that, even in the summer nights, it could get cold up there. They all snuggled in their sleeping bags and tents after sitting by a blazing fire pit singing songs and telling stories.

His uncle would point out different constellations in the crystal-clear sky, and in his imagination, Amir was part of the international astronaut crew as the first Bosnian ever to be launched on a mission to outer space.

He could dream of the future back then—of accomplishing anything he set his mind to. His parents supported his imagination, and encouraged him to excel at whatever he pursued. In the past months, however, his only dreams were to stay alive.

Just then the bus stopped. A soldier with an AK-47 climbed up the steps and began walking over the men seated on the floor of the overcrowded bus. He slammed his rifle butt into anyone within reach as he made it to the back of the bus and then returned the same way stepping on those on the floor. Yelps and groans echoed throughout the bus. Amir cursed under his breath as a gash formed on his forehead. Hasan was punched in the nose, which caused a rush of blood to spurt downward across his mouth and chin, and onto his lap. He took an old, ratty tee shirt he had stuffed into his pocket and attempted to impede the flow. He tore the unaffected side of the shirt and gave it to Amir to tend to his wound.

The soldier made it back to the steps of the bus, but turned around to speak to the driver. Before the driver stepped outside for a smoke, he turned on the heat to its maximum setting and closed the door. The bus remained idle for another twenty minutes while the prisoners could hardly breathe, and sweat poured profusely drenching their ragged clothes that stuck to their overheated bodies.

Hadn't they been destined for Manjaca? Was their hope of arriving there and then being deported to Croatia a ploy on the part of the Serbs? Why did the madness never cease?

When the driver returned, he lowered the heat, opened his window, and put the bus into gear presumably to the camp in Manjaca.

The men said very little from that point. Amir was contemplating what had just happened. His forehead stung, and Hasan was still trying to control the nose bleed. Some of the men sprawled out on the floor had little energy to avoid lying on one another.

They arrived in the city of Banja Luka as the sun was setting. Surprised by the numbers of people occupying the streets, Amir could see dozens of Serb soldiers and ordinary citizens turning toward them with threatening looks as they peered into the passing bus. No doubt that this was a purposeful display of victory over the vanquished as the bus paraded the prisoners, slowly snaking its way through the city. The onlookers were banging on the bus swearing at its riders; pointing fingers and calling them Turks, Mujahedeen, Ustasha whores, and pieces of shit.

Amir thought of his aunts and uncles, and cousins who had lived there. He thought of his grandparents visiting them earlier in the spring. *Were they still alive? Had they been separated from one another as his family had? Did they suffer the same fate that he and his dad had?*

These thoughts found the melancholy that he had been trying to ward off. He leaned his head against the window as the bus moved beyond the city center. The coolness of the glass provided only slight relief to his flushed face.

As they exited the once beautiful city and returned to the road there was a sign stating that the city of Sanski Most was thirty-five kilometers away. Just past the sign the driver veered off onto the grass. An imperceptible heightened vigilance from the exhausted men reappeared.

The door opened as if expanding its jaws, and a sergeant in the Serb army entered brandishing a club. He strode over those on the floor and viciously swung at them. He did not spare those seated who also received his wrath. Amir waited for his beating. He had no energy to do anything more than accept that he was about to be battered. However, the soldier stopped abruptly midway down the aisle, and stared menacingly at one of the prisoners.

"Ah, my old friend, Arif. You know that I owe you some money for repairs you did on my car. I have a much better way to repay you."

He grabbed Arif by the hair and dragged him over the others and down the steps. He then threw him on the ground and began to pound him with the club. As the man writhed in pain yelling out for mercy, the soldier pulled out his long-blade army knife and stabbed Arif through his heart. He then threw two men off the bus, and told them to bring the lifeless body back onto the bus. Eyes bulging, and mouths agape, the men did as they were told. They dragged him up the steps and placed him a few seats behind the driver in a now-vacated seat while his blood left a long streak on any surface the body had touched, including some of the other men.

The soldier got back on the bus and pronounced that his work was done here. They could now freely travel to Manjaca, he said, where other "treats" awaited them.

When he finally had some energy to do so, Amir turned his gaze toward Hasan and spoke quietly.

"I don't know if I believe we're going to Manjaca. Look at what they're doing to us?"

"I'm not so sure either. I was so hopeful when we left Omarska. I feel like this has become a smaller version of that place, but on wheels."

"I mean, I think we're headed in the right direction. I went to the mountain with my family when I was younger."

"Yeah. Your dad told me. If we get there, this won't be a holiday though. Too bad, too, I brought some lamb sausages to grill."

Amir gave Hasan a slight smile.

Thankfully, within an hour they were at the prison called Manjaca. The sign said "No Entry" but not for them, of course. Yet the Serbs were not quite finished with the transfer, serving up one more reminder of their domination.

They were told to sleep in the bus—that no one could process them at night as was protocol. The bus driver turned on the engine and the heat. With windows closed, and the stench of death and sweat on top of clothing that had not been changed in months, sleep was impossible. The men were leaning on anything and anyone in the overcrowded bus. They had not been given food or water since leaving Omarska where they had last eaten tasteless broth.

Amir was feeling nauseous and held back the vomit he felt lurching upward. His mind was playing tricks on him, as well. He imagined he was hearing the engine of the bus speak to him saying that he was to get off at the next stop: Kozarac. He was seeing blood-red flashes of light undulating before him. At that moment, the driver came back on and turned off the engine, and the heat stopped. This jolted Amir back into a foggy sense of reality. The driver told them to open the windows, that they smelled like shit, and that in the morning he would make sure that after they dragged their dead friends off the bus, they would clean it so that no trace of filthy Turks could be detected.

Chapter 18
Last Days in Omarska

They were given a heartier version of the slop they had been forced to eat for the past two-plus months, and they were told meals were to be twice a day from now on.

"The Serbs act as if they were sending you to a fine restaurant in Prijedor," one of the men said to Elvir, out of earshot of the guards, of course.

At least it had a piece of potato, bits of meat and carrot in it, and even a pinch of salt. The bread was fresher, too.

They were allowed to go out and sit in the sunshine, and the increased food helped the prisoners feel stronger. The guards left them alone, and the men and few women left were feeling a new sense of calm.

Two days after the camp was cleared out minus Elvir's group, a reporter from Sweden arrived. Elvir was told by Ristic that he would be the one to speak to them because he could speak some English.

"How long have you been here?" asked the reporter.

"I have only been here for fifteen days," said Elvir. I have a bed to sleep in and food to eat. They treat me well."

The reporter pressed him further.

"Can you describe what you mean by treating you well?"

"I have only been here for fifteen days," repeated Elvir. I have a bed to sleep in and food to eat. They treat me well."

"Have you sustained any injuries? Have they harmed you in any way?"

"I have only been here for fifteen days," said Elvir once

more. I have a bed to sleep in and food to eat. They treat me well."

Clearly frustrated, the reporter left.

"Well done," said Ristic, who understood very little English, but knew that Elvir said what he was instructed to say.

Elvir smiled politely at Ristic, and with a sense of calm he casually walked twenty meters to join the others milling about the tarmac.

On August 12th, the International Red Cross entered the camp. They were there to register the living. Elvir and the others were ecstatic, though they couldn't quite show it. Their whereabouts were now being logged.

There were five women who remained in the camp. They served the food. Whenever reporters or the Red Cross came to the camp, the women were hidden from their view. Therefore, they were not registered.

It went this way for two weeks. Reporters, better meals, taking in the bright sunshine, minimal harsh interaction from the guards, and wondering when it was their turn to leave.

It was August 21st, and the announcement was made that the prisoners were going to Manjaca.

Later that morning, trucks were awaiting their transport out of the camp.

Amir, God willing, I will be with my son again.

Before they loaded the trucks, two male prisoners were removed from the group. One had been a politician who had loudly resisted when the Serb nationalists first took over the municipality's government in Prijedor, and the other had led an ill-equipped armed resistance as the soldiers entered his village. This man had managed to survive by not going to the daily meal, while his brother brought bread back to him, and cared for him when he was sick. However, he was now revealed to the guards. Revenge murders, Elvir sullenly surmised. They were never seen again. It was later reported that of the five remaining women prisoners at Omarska, two were taken to Trnopolje, while the other three disappeared on the day that the notorious camp closed its gates forever.

Chapter 19
Open Reception Center

The Red Cross workers came to the camp within a week after the ITN reporters did their investigative reporting. Hajra and the children were already seeing some changes that the Serbs were forced to make, including better food and serving it twice a day, and allowing for more hygienic practices, including bringing in portable showers for at least a once-a-week rinse-off, or so they were promised. Also, donations from a Muslim relief organization in Croatia were beginning to ship clothing in via Red Cross trucks.

Despite these changes, the prisoners longed to be free.

However, as it was told to them by one of the Red Cross administrators, "Of course, the Serbian authorities say you are free to go, but there is a 100 percent chance that you'll be shot."

It was early September and life at the camp had improved dramatically. There were no more beatings and abuse. The barbed wire was taken down and the camp was kept much cleaner. In fact, the camp was now used by the Serbs as a place for foreign visitors to inspect if they wished.

"Mom," said Halima, "look at the new sign they put up."

Standing in the yard chatting with friends she'd made in the camp, Hajra turned toward the entrance that her daughter was pointing to.

"Open Reception Center," it read in English, German, and Serbo-Croatian.

Hajra was dumbfounded.

"I wonder what they're doing?" she replied.

At that moment Danis pointed to some visitors coming their way.

A man and a woman with UN credentials were walking toward the family with clip boards in their hands.

For some reason, they wanted to speak with Hajra.

"Hello," they said in perfect Bosnian. "We'd like to ask you a few questions if that's alright?"

Hajra did not trust them despite their friendly demeanor, and the fact that the UN was a recognized organization to aid those caught up in a humanitarian crisis didn't initially put her at ease. She was wary that anything she said might go to the Serb authorities.

"I can answer a few questions, but I have some for you, as well," she replied.

"Sure," said the man named David who was from the U.S.

"Are these your children?" David asked.

"Yes. This is Halima and my son is Danis. I'm Hajra," she said, but wondered if even this was too much information for the American from the UN.

"Where are you from?" he asked.

She hesitantly answered. "Kozarac, not too far from here."

"I know Kozarac," he said, "my partner Anita, who is from Germany by the way, and I just passed through there. Sadly, there is nothing left."

Hajra's heart stopped. She had a clear recollection of the devastation that rained down upon them when they tried to escape. She remembered how strong Elvir was as he did his best to get them to safety, even believing that the soccer field was their one glimmer of hope. She paused for a second, thinking of Elvir and Amir.

"I'm not surprised that our town is destroyed. The last few days there were maddening. We were scared for our lives. My husband and fifteen-year-old son were separated from us, and we are not sure where they are. Or if they are alive..."

Hajra began to tear up thinking about Kozarac, but especially about Elvir and Amir. *Where are they?* She had heard that the two most notorious camps, Omarska and Keraterm, were completely cleared out now. *I have to hang on to the hope that they are alive.*

“We don’t mean to upset you,” Anita said. “We’re trying to establish what is going on here. There were British reporters here and at another center last month, and their stories and accompanying video seems to have woken up a world that is still mostly asleep about what’s taking place in Bosnia.”

Her mistrust was beginning to fade as they seemed to be very earnest about their mission to discern the truth. She wanted to tell them what she had seen. And she desperately wanted people to know the truth. But she had to be careful not to disclose too much, or even to be seen with these people for very long.

“First, I have to know that if I tell you the truth, we’ll be safe from reprisal by the Serbs?

“Absolutely,” said Anita, “they know that our reports are for the UN. They have no illusions about this.”

Hajra took a deep breath and spoke.

“We saw the reporters here in early August. We are not extremists trying to rid Bosnia of Serbs. It is quite the opposite,” Hajra said.

“Can you tell us what it’s been like in Trnopolje?” Anita asked.

“Things have gotten a lot better over the past month. But we want to leave so badly. And the kids need their father and brother, and I need my husband and other son. I guess we need to know if they’re alive, and where they are,” Hajra said.

“I don’t know if we can help you with that at this point. Perhaps the International Red Cross can help. They are registering survivors of the camps here in Prijedor to ensure that they are accounted for, and to match the names against those that are missing,” said David.

Hajra continued. "Yes, we have registered with them. Maybe someday when we are truly feeling safe, I will be able to speak about it fully. I can tell you that there were very sinister things happening here. I heard about beatings, murders, and rapes. Up until recently, there were a lot of starving people here. But, as I said before, it's gotten better."

Hajra was careful not to disclose the information in a personal way, particularly what happened to her.

"I will leave you with one more thing. It has taken all I have to not go mad here. Keeping my children safe has been my sole priority, and although I never actually felt like I had control over that, I vowed that the guards would have to kill me first before they'd touch my children. It never came to that. I don't want to say any more."

"I understand," said Anita.

"I will share this with you," David said "It may be that the goal is to clear your country of all non-Serbs. That is why you can't go anywhere just yet. It is dangerous out there. We are here to gather information, so that they will stop what they are doing. I hope you and your family reunite soon."

As the UN representatives exited the camp, Hajra wondered if she had said just enough to indict the Serbs, but not too much to put her and the children at risk. No matter, she thought, any information will help to shed some light on what was happening in her Bosnia.

Chapter 20
Manjaca

It was August 7th when Amir arrived at the summit of Mount Manjaca. The POW camp contained a couple of large buildings for the hundreds of head of cattle to sleep during the winter. Now was grazing season, so they stayed in the fields nearby. Each of the total of roughly three thousand prisoners, most of whom were civilians, were crammed into two buildings with three large stalls in each. There was enough space to sit two long lines of prisoners facing each other with a narrow passage separating them.

The buildings were separated by barbed wire. Stalls one, two, and three were part of Wire One, as it was known. Stalls four, five, and six were part of Wire Two. The floors were concrete and covered with ferns for the men to sleep on top of in the cramped quarters just as the livestock had done.

The facility was part of a JNA military complex with offices, and living quarters for the commanders and soldiers, as well as munitions storage.

Before the men were allowed to go to the stalls they were cursorily examined by doctors and their injuries were catalogued. They were then given a small cup of water, but still no food.

Amir noticed that the prisoners here were from many different parts of Northwestern Bosnia by the nuanced dialects that he heard being spoken. He could barely focus because of the harrowing bus ride, and his hunger and thirst. His entire body ached from the cramped conditions and a faint hint of nausea remained from the wretched scent on the long ride. Fortunately, Hasan was assigned to his stall, number three. He missed his father beyond words, but at least he had this kind man to lean on.

The camp commander announced the new set of rules, promising the prisoners, who joined those already there, that they would not be hurt if they followed them:

"When walking anywhere here at Manjaca you will keep your heads bowed down and your hands behind your backs. There is a mess tent for your meals that you will find right over there." He pointed to the large, enclosed tented area, which was to be where they were fed. "Most of you will be given jobs while you are here."

"One more thing," the commandant said, "that barbed wire separating the two buildings and all those armed soldiers speak to the fact that you are POWs now. And the space in between the two fences out there, you'll find, is loaded with mines that will certainly alert us that someone has either tried to escape or made a misstep—likely his last misstep."

At least, thought Amir, the place didn't seem like Omarska. The commandant was more military, and seemed to want order more than anything. Not that the prisoners wouldn't be punished for not following the rules, but the initial sense was that torture and murder were not to be the primary mission here. But of course, he and everyone else were skeptical and they would have to be careful. Yet even their skepticism was muted because they were too exhausted to do much thinking at all. They went to their stalls and quietly lay among one another.

"Hasan, do you think this will be our last stop until we can leave?" Amir asked.

"I don't know. My hope is flimsy, but at least it's still hope. Still, we'll try to keep one another strong so that we don't lose the little optimism we have. OK?"

"It's strange, but I can't remember the faces of my mother

and my sister and brother. My fear for their lives was even snuffed out at Omarska. I am so tired. And my dad, what could they be doing to him back there?"

Hasan could hear the resignation in the boy's voice, and he put his arm around Amir's shoulders. He had no words. He had no strength. He needed to stay alive if for nothing else then to help Amir. Hasan's wife and ten-year-old son were in the house in Prijedor when he was taken by the Serbs. He prayed every night that they were safe. He looked at Amir like he was family, too.

They both laid down on the ferns that covered the cement floors, and fell into their usual restless sleep.

When they awoke in the afternoon, they were being called to order for their 3:00 dinner. They lined up near their stall with heads down and hands behind their backs as they slowly made their way to the mess tent where the food was just as tasteless as at Omarska.

It was August, but the sweltering days and cool nights were quite different for Amir, who was used to the heat certainly, but not the chill of Mount Manjaca.

He was malnourished, but the hunger was long ago numbed by the pitiful circumstances of the past three-month internment in the camps.

Upon returning to the stall, he laid down and closed his eyes. But he couldn't sleep. His thoughts took him to a dark place.

Am I losing my mind? My ability to think? To figure things out? I can't lose it. For my dad's sake when I see him again, I can't lose it. I have to stay strong.

But it's hard to think clearly. I remember when I was in school, I was a pretty good student. I made my parents proud. But now, simple things that I should know, like what types of clouds are above my head. Are they cumulus, or cirrus? I knew that stuff in school. I liked science and especially studying Earth Science was fun. I think that was what the class was called? Now, when I look up at them, I have no clue. The only information I've put into my brain in the past months is how to avoid being beaten up or how to take care of those who have been. I need you, Dad, please get here soon. I need you.

He had come to love Hasan like an uncle, and knew that he was watching out for him in his father's absence. But he wanted his father so badly that whenever he had dreams, they were about him and his dad hanging out in Kozarac. He worried so deeply about his entire family, but the grim thoughts he had he still managed to submerge. Yet, because he had spent so much intense time with his father, he couldn't shake the feelings of dread now that they were not together.

A hopeful sign emerged five days after their arrival. The International Red Cross began coming to the camp. The prisoners were informed by the aid workers that they would be visiting every Wednesday to ensure that the men were not mistreated, to bring some limited supplies, and to register them so that they could account for where the imprisoned non-Serbs were located. Equally critical was that the cruelties at the POW camp subsided, so that the newer prisoners would be less impacted by the previously experienced torture, torment, and murder.

It had been two weeks since they entered the stalls at Manjaca. Standing outside their building with others from Wire Two, Hasan spoke to Amir.

"New buses are arriving," Hasan pointed out. "I wonder which camp they're from?"

As was protocol, the beleaguered prisoners on the buses had to get the perfunctory medical exams first, and then listen to the commandant's speech before finding out which stall they were assigned to. Within that time, the existing prisoners were ordered back to their stalls.

The new arrivals were marched by the armed guards while doing exactly what the rules demanded: heads bowed, hands behind their backs.

This was a smaller group. There seemed to be less than two hundred. *Where are they going to fit?* Amir thought, which he reckoned was a strange notion because why would their captors care whether they were comfortable?

The seated men in the stall stared at the incoming to see if they knew any of them. Hasan could sense these were people from Omarska. Their tattered clothes, gray-green skin color, and hollowed, deep-set eyes spoke of the horrors they endured. Yet he took note of a strange vitality that emanated from them as they walked to open space at the far end of the stall.

Amir's gaze was leveled at the new arrivals, too. He had to rub his eyes to make sure that he was not hallucinating like he'd done on the bus ride to Manjaca. He assured himself that he was not.

Indeed, it was his father! Since the guards would allow no talking or movement from the others, Amir could not leap to his feet and yell for Elvir. He poked Hasan with his elbow and nodded his head toward his dad. Hasan's eyes lit up. He gestured to Amir not to say a word. Elvir didn't see them with his head bowed down. He moved past them and was prodded to the back.

When they were all seated and the guards left, Amir pulled his tired body upward and slowly moved to where his father was.

As he waded between the two rows of prisoners, his smile got wider. Almost reaching his father, Elvir looked up to see what the commotion was as the others understood the reunion that was about to take place.

"Oh my God! He exclaimed. "Oh my God! Amir!

"Don't get up, Dad, don't get up."

Amir practically landed on his father just as he squeezed by the last man seated to his dad's left. His father kissed the top of his head repeatedly, and the two stayed embraced for at least a minute.

"My God. Amir! Amir!"

A man sitting next to Elvir moved away to give father and son a little more space. "Praised be God," was quietly uttered by the few prisoners who had the energy to do so.

Chapter 21
Father and Son

It was late September, and as withered as their bodies and spirits were, father and son were well into the routines of Manjaca. Every day the guards woke them up at 5:00 a.m. The prisoners splashed some water on their faces and got ready for breakfast, which began at 6:00. Hasan had to get up at 4:00 to begin to prepare the meal he would serve in the mess tent. Somehow, though the kitchen workers were generally from Sanski Most and had arrived earlier in the summer, Hasan managed to talk his way into the job.

"Must have given someone lots of cigarettes to get that esteemed position," Elvir teased.

After breakfast, they each had assignments to do.

Elvir was a corn shucker. It was monotonous, but it gave him something to do to distract from the painful reality they were living in. Each day, hundreds of ears of corn were brought into the camp, and the prisoners assigned to this task pulled the husks off and tossed them into a large bin. It was so tempting for Elvir to hide an ear or two of corn in his clothing to bring back to the stall for Amir and the others, but he knew if he got caught it could potentially mean a beating or worse.

Amir was assigned to cut wood in the forest nearby. The wood cutting crew sawed downed trees and then cut them further for firewood. Each had to be cut into one-meter-long pieces after which the wood cutters hauled them uphill to be deposited in trucks. The nights were getting cold in the mountains, so wood was needed for the pot belly stoves of the guards in their homes. None of the wood ever saw its way to warm the prisoners at Manjaca. The guards either took the wood for themselves to dry out and "season" for next winter, or they would sell it to augment their military pay. The only warmth the men got was from the clothing on their backs, and huddling close together in the stall.

The food had gotten better over the weeks. Soups now consisted of beans and lentils, and they even got meat once in a while. More than occasionally, they were given a small can of fish. Also provided was a good-sized piece of bread and sometimes an apple. However, the United Nations High Commission for Refugees, known as UNHCR, only delivered new food supplies every three days. Often, it was plundered by the guards, so that when it came to the prisoners' meals they were more meager than they should have been.

The days were long, and the rainy season had begun. This was not a gentle summer shower, but a harsh, wind-swept storm that often included claps of thunder and lightning. The prisoners could see the lit-up skies through slits in the roof of the stall where droplets of rain water slid slowly across the wood beams and down onto the floor.

Often, the men would take the five-liter jerry cans given to them by the Red Cross and capture the dripping water to drink something that was reasonably clean for a change. Otherwise, they were only drinking water that came from the lake they would visit each day to fill their cans—a lake that was used by the cattle nearby for drinking and depositing their waste. More than occasionally, the guards would pee in the water, and then make the prisoners fill their bottles. This was on top of the oil and dirt from the tanks that were stored on-site that oozed sludge when the soldiers were made to wash the large vehicles down.

The trek to the lake served two purposes: it gave the prisoners an opportunity to fill their canisters. But perhaps, more importantly, it allowed them to leave the Wire.

Exiting the gate that read "No Entry," was psychologically freeing. The prisoners could walk through the mountain paths to the lake, done usually in four columns of one hundred each. They were accompanied by machine gun-toting guards who might find it to be the right time to exert their dominance.

If you were in the back of the last column, with one of the guards as your escort, there was a fair chance that you would get hit with the barrel of his weapon. And if the guard was in a particularly cantankerous mood, he might request a Serb nationalist song to honor his "great heritage." This put those unfortunate prisoners in the rear at a distinct disadvantage.

On a crisp afternoon in September, one man, Armin from Kozarac, found himself in the back of the line. He had tried to line up sooner, but the sole of his right shoe had fallen off, and he tried to tuck it under an overhanging piece of leather from the inside. It was clearly a feeble attempt at repair, but Armin had no other solution at the time.

He hobbled as best he could, trying to coax the shoe to remain intact. He mostly dragged it, and made it just before the last of the group saw the gate latch behind them.

The rear escort requested that those prisoners near him sing a Serbian song. There was no response.

Now, with the surly guard getting angrier and angrier at the lack of interest in singing a song that would please him, Armin began to sing of the glories of Serbia. Several others joined in, as did the guard.

With eyes pointed downward, as they had been conditioned to do at Manjaca, the columns of men finally skidded to a halt at the lakeside. The singing stopped. Armin and others took in a deep breath having avoided beatings.

Armin filled his two canisters, and scampered up the hill to find a spot in the middle of the column. He would not be able to find the strength or courage to accommodate another song "request."

When he got back to Wire Two, Armin sat next to Elvir

along the wall on one side of the stall and very quietly told him what had happened. He told no one else. Word got out that the guard was looking for the Turk who sang so beautifully, but no one identified Armin. How could they, was the standard response, their heads were pointed downward per camp rules.

In early October, one of the men in Elvir and Amir's stall washed his nice, leather jacket with water he had retrieved from the lake. This jacket was his pride and joy. He had hoarded several cigarettes and what amounted to a box of cigars to trade with another prisoner whose family had just sent it to him. Surprisingly, it had not been stolen by one of the guards, which was often what happened to items brought in by the Red Cross for prisoners that magically disappeared when the relief organization left. He walked over toward the barbed wire, and hung it up to dry. As he stepped back a mine blew up, and tore off his leg. Elvir happened to be looking over at the explosion as it happened and saw the limb separate.

The man was screaming in agony, blood spurting everywhere. A couple of guards tied a rope around the man's thigh to slow the bleeding, and then they carried him, and the severed limb, to the infirmary.

After witnessing this gruesome scene, Elvir raced over to a nearby tree and vomited.

The man was taken to a hospital in Banja Luka, or so that's what the rumor mill had heard. No one knows for sure because he never returned to the camp.

There was always uncertainty as to whether there were actually mines buried near the fence. The talk was that this was just another way to keep the prisoners in line. There were even bets as to the veracity of the rumors. Any skepticism was quelled after that day.

***

Each stall was said to have about six hundred men, though

likely a bit less. There were also the "camp commanders" as they were referred to by the guards.

These men were still prisoners, but tasked with keeping order in the stalls by reporting to the administration and medical staff if there were any problems. Though they slept on the same fern-covered concrete floors, they were given privileges including extra food, time outside while the others were inside, and access to visiting the offices of officials in the camp to have a smoke.

A few of these men could not be trusted, but mostly they were seen as OK by the others. The prisoners were unsure as to why they were chosen. Perhaps it was because they had served in the Yugoslav Army with the Serb soldiers, some of whom were guards at Manjaca now. After all, they were all part of the same army defending Yugoslavia. But when Slovenia, Croatia, and Bosnia and Herzegovina declared their independence, only Serbs were left to fight. Though Muslims and Croats may have left the army, some of them still wanted a unified Yugoslavia, not independent republics. The suspicion was that they agreed with the Bosnian Serbs, not so much about expulsion or extermination of non-Serbs of course, but that none of this would have happened if their countries hadn't voted to be their own republics.

Hasan referred to a one of them as a "Nazi collaborator" out of sarcastic homage to those in the German concentration camps who would sell their souls for their own safety. If nothing else, it was important to be cautious around them—to not say or do anything that could jeopardize one's safety.

Ajdin, an auto mechanic from the town of Ljubija, was quite trustworthy: a quiet man who was assigned to be a camp commander in Elvir's stall apparently because he did such an exquisite job maintaining the cars of several of the guards that rotated through the camp.

Ajdin was exceedingly careful and went about his role with the fidelity expected by the guards and camp officials. It was he who reported when there were injured prisoners needing medical assistance. It was he who told low-level guards that all was quiet and inconsequential in the area of the stall he was responsible for. And it was he who entrusted Elvir with some highly sensitive information that he learned while performing his duties.

Every day for thirty minutes, the prisoners were let outside in small groups of about fifty. Guards stood at their posts watching the men mill about on each side of the barbed wire that separated the two large buildings.

A few different times, Ajdin had approached Elvir and engaged him in conversation. Unbeknown to Elvir, Ajdin was assessing whether he could trust him. It was three weeks after they had met that Ajdin began a conversation with Elvir outside, acting no different from the other times they spoke.

“There are prison ledgers,” he told Elvir. “I saw one in the supervisor’s office, which I was asked to clean up. It was very odd. There were names of all of us with our disposition at the end of each line. Those in pencil were safe. Those written in pen were not; that meant a permanent solution for those poor souls. It is why Muhamad did not return after being taken yesterday. He was deemed destined for the ‘Military Detention Center,’ which I fear means torture and death.”

Elvir managed a slight smile so he wouldn’t betray his alarm at hearing this, but also not to alert the guards that any unusual conversation was in progress. But, as Ajdin moved away giving a quick wave of his hand, Elvir thought about Omarska—about those hundreds who didn’t return. It made him sick to his stomach. But he also wondered why Ajdin entrusted him with this information, and if he could trust the man.

***

“Dad, said Amir one night, “when will we get out of here?”

"I don't know. There is no sign that they will free us, so I just don't know," said Elvir.

"I am so glad we're together, but I am feeling so...so hopeless," Amir said.

"All we have is hope, as flimsy as it seems."

"I'm so tired. Cutting down trees for wood wouldn't be that hard for me if I was doing it in normal times. But after a couple of hours of doing it I'm drained, and sometimes the guards are cruel. Today, when a man from Glamoc named Hamza couldn't hold an axe any longer, he dropped it and himself to the ground. One of the guards came over to him and kicked him in the ribs to get up. Hamza could hardly move, but he screamed out in pain. The guard ordered him up, but Hamza couldn't do it. The guard then kicked him a few more times, and let him lay there until we were all finished cutting the branches into firewood. He then told me and Ismail from one of the other stalls to drag Hamza up onto the truck. Poor Hamza, he is as thin as a rail and his ribs almost showed their bruises through his shirt. When we got back to the camp, he was sent to the infirmary, so I don't know what's happened to him since then."

"I am so sorry to hear that. That's the type of crap we saw at Omarska. I will ask Hasan when he takes some food to the infirmary to check on Hamza. Now, come close to me so we can both stay warm, and let's lay back in our beautiful, soft cushioned bed with its down pillows, and plush comforter. It's time to rest up for another day of fun-filled activities here at Camp Manjaca."

With a smile, Amir thanked his father, and then moved closer to him as they drifted off into another restless night battling the demons that punctuated their endless time in a concentration camp.

The next day after their 3:00 meal Hasan told Elvir that Hamza had been transferred to a hospital in Banja Luka. Hasan was told by his contact in the infirmary that the official report read "heart attack." When Elvir told his son, Amir bit his lip. He didn't utter a word. When he looked up again at his father, he just shook his head. Though it was certainly better for them at Manjaca, there were still many reminders that they were expendable.

***

Cigarettes were currency at Manjaca. Every two weeks the Red Cross gave one pack per prisoner. For most who smoked, that wasn't enough to get them through. So, they gambled. Poker was a big deal to pass the time. The more cigarettes one had, the more currency one had to trade for other items. Five cigarettes were worth a half a loaf of fresh bread, while bread that was a couple of days old was only worth one cigarette. Other food made its way to this black market, too. Additionally, a few packs could get extra boots if they were new. Used but solid boots would cost about ten or so cigarettes. This was the camp's economic marketplace, and it was lucrative for those who were more entrepreneurial.

Elvir was a pretty decent poker player. Amir watched from the side of the game and admired his father's ability to not give away his hand.

"Where did you learn how to play, Dad?" he asked.

"My brief stay in the army taught me a lot of things. Some of which I am not so proud of, but I'm not going to tell you about those," he said with a smirk.

"I learned that I was pretty damned good at poker. Then, of course, we played for money. Not that soldiers had very much, but it passed the time in the barracks. Back then, we Muslims were seen as no different than Croats or Serbs. We were all just soldiers. My, how times have changed," Elvir said.

Hasan interjected.

"So, did you learn how to cheat then, too?

"Oh, is that how you think I'm winning now, my friend?"

Elvir joked.

"I guess not, Amir would be all over you if he knew you did that. He's the one with the conscience of the two of you." Hasan let go of a hearty laugh.

The chilly night air of the mountain, which made it difficult to get warm, could be cut a bit by the jocularity that the prisoners were able to find. This was not Omarska, and despite the tragedies that still managed to find their way in at times, Manjaca allowed for a more relaxed atmosphere. With the regular visits of the Red Cross and UN, the Serbs were far less likely to pull anything.

Still, there was always an air of melancholy. After all, they were like caged animals who had to live by the rules set forth by others who controlled their lives.

"You know," said Armin, "we Muslims are a doomed people in Bosnia."

"I agree that this may be true, but tell us why you think that?" replied Elvir.

"It almost seems like here at Manjaca I can finally think about what has been going on in our home, our Bosnia. And with Kozarac destroyed, and all the other villages in so many municipalities experiencing the same fate, what will we have to go back to now?"

A man named Ali from Prijedor spoke up.

"I feel the same. I hate it here, but at least we have time to figure out what happened. Not worrying about being beaten and killed like in Keraterm is a bonus. I don't mean to sound like it is a benefit in any way when I say that, but we do have more time to reflect on things. Maybe that's not always a good thing, though."

Elvir pondered what those in the conversation were saying.

It was true that so many non-Serbs had been killed, so many homes and buildings destroyed, so many people that were now homeless and maybe even without a country to return to—at least a familiar and welcoming country. And so much heartache in his beloved Bosnia. Perhaps the sentiment about having time to think about the unthinkable was not always a good thing. Yet, there was a reality that they had all lived through, and that reality might likely mean that they could never return to their homes.

He had been mulling over these thoughts since he acclimated to life in Manjaca. These were the ruminations that continued to bring him down. He also realized that at least he and Amir and the others were alive. He desperately needed to know that Hajra, his children, his brother Tarik and his family, his parents and all the relatives and friends they'd had before the destruction, were alive and safe. This would be his new mission should he get out of Manjaca. In a very real sense, going back to Kozarac was secondary to knowing that those he loved were still with the living.

One early fall morning, Ajdin saw Elvir coming out of the mess tent having finished breakfast.

"I hear the Red Cross and the UNHCR are working on getting us out of here," he quietly said while walking past his confidant. Elvir looked up, but Ajdin was far ahead. *Did he actually say what I think he said? Was it too risky to hope?*

For the first time, as he peered off into the hills surrounding the POW camp, Elvir noticed the crispness of the fall colors as the reds, yellows, and golds of the leaves shone in the reflection of the brilliant sunshine up above.

Chapter 22
Leaving Trnopolje

It was October 1st, and the "Open Reception Center" had been in place for several weeks now. Though the conditions certainly improved dramatically, Hajra and the children, and all the remaining prisoners, were feeling trapped until this morning. Though she had heard about possible deportations out of the camp, she didn't want to get the children's hopes up until she knew for sure.

"Today brings good news," Hajra announced to Halima and Danis. "The Red Cross just helped over 1,500 of us board the many buses outside the camp to go to Karlovac in Croatia. We could be next!"

"Oh mom, if this is true, we could be free," exclaimed Halima.

"Yes, my love, we could be free," Hajra replied, hugging her daughter tightly.

"But what about Dad and Amir?" said Danis.

"That's exactly what I am thinking, my sweet boy. But I am wondering since the Red Cross has registered all of us, maybe Dad and Amir are on a similar list. If that's the case, we can know where they are for sure."

Hajra said this knowing that they could learn a horrible truth, too; that Elvir and Amir were dead. She pushed the thought out of her head, but it was still lingering at the core of her anxiety. And she knew without even asking that her children were thinking the same thoughts.

Three days later, the Red Cross named another 1,000 to go

to Karlovac. This included Hajra and the children.

They were given the previous afternoon and evening to get food, water, and to clean up a bit. The next day, the buses were waiting for them outside where school children used to be dropped off and picked up before the school became a concentration camp.

"Mom, it's actually happening! We're leaving this place," said an excited Danis.

"Don't be so scattered, Danis. You're forgetting your soccer uniform, shoes, and hooded sweatshirt," said Halima teasingly. She was feeling light-hearted, as were all of those leaving. Still, there was a slight fear of the unknown, and a reticence to leave Bosnia.

The stipulation for being able to leave was to sign over their property in the municipality. Apparently, this was occurring in all of the camps and locales where the Bosnian Serb military was in control. It was the ticket out for those who were not otherwise imprisoned, tortured, and killed.

"If you want to leave, you must sign over your property to us," was how it went for non-Serbs throughout Bosnia and Herzegovina.

"Someday we'll come back to Prijedor to live," Hajra said as if she could read her children's minds. But she was not so sure about that.

Hajra certainly felt a weight beginning to lift at leaving the miserable conditions and torment that she and others endured while there. Not forgotten was the indignation that Pavlovic had foisted upon her—the pain and humiliation notwithstanding the small triumph she had in not giving in to him. Still, she was violated, and the emotional scars were there. Her children knew what she had been subjected to, and that alone hurt. But they also saw the strength she displayed throughout their time in the awful camp. She felt deeply saddened for her children, and all children that had been subjected to the terror reigned upon the victims in the atrocities perpetrated by the Serb nationalists Milosevic, Karadzic and Mladic, and their followers. How will they be able to reconcile what happened to them and achieve the bright futures that many of their parents had envisioned for them? And the war had begun not too long ago, so there was likely more pain yet to be suffered by so many, including innocent Bosnian Serbs, if this thing didn't end soon.

Of course, just leaving Bosnia was difficult. This was the only country she knew. This was the place she grew up in, had so many family members and friends in, got married in, and had children in. There was never a thought of leaving before, but that was not to be her new reality. And there was a nagging thought that she may never return—or at least not return for a very long time.

How strange it feels to not have a country to call my own. To not be able to plant my feet in my own soil and know that I can do the same tomorrow, and the day after. Homeless is how I am feeling. But that idea is too narrow. Actually country-less would be a more appropriate term. Hollow is what I feel.

She wondered what the future would bring for her own children, of course. And then there was Elvir and Amir. Her thoughts resembled numerous forks in the road.

Are my husband and son alive? If they are, what kind of indignities or worse did they have to endure? How will we find one another? If they are dead, how will I survive such a tragedy? What about my parents and Elvir's, our siblings and families, and our friends?

So many unanswered questions. So many difficult choices ahead. Strangely, she now had choices: something she'd had very little of in the past number of months.

***

They boarded their bus with a bag given to them by the Red Cross that included a sandwich, fruit, two water bottles each, a small package of baby wipes, and local Croatian currency equivalent to about five US dollars.

The eight-hour ride would be long, but it would be worth it to finally find freedom. The Red Cross workers in Trnopolje said that there were many people from all over Bosnia in Karlovac, and beds for them to sleep in. The goal, they said, was to have the refugees remain for only a short time before finding a third country to take them in.

As the bus pulled out onto the road, the air of tension that had permeated the family before leaving seemed to disappear. They were bound for Croatia: the bus was their first stint of freedom. They peered out of the window lost in their own individual thoughts. Hajra looked at her two children with a mixture of deep love, awe, and worry.

"Mom, they called us refugees. Is that what we are now?" asked a fidgety Danis.

"I'm afraid so. But it's better than being prisoners in a concentration camp," she replied.

"A third country," Halima chimed in. "Do they mean we'll have to stay out of Bosnia? Not live in our own country?"

"Perhaps. But I can't think that far ahead. Right now, we have to focus on Karlovac. Please don't worry about much more than that," Hajra replied while reaching around to give both children a hug simultaneously.

The three resumed staring out at the passing fields and villages, returning to their own thoughts.

Hajra reflected back to their time in the camp, and even before the war began. They had been through so much. It seemed like years had passed, but it was only months. She had her own personal heartache to process, but also the hope that the future could bring. Perhaps now they could take hold of their own destiny?

"Danis, we're going to be free, and that's the best news we've had in so long," said Halima, continuing to gaze out of the window.

"Maybe now we can look for Dad and Amir?" he said.

"I hope so," Hajra responded.

They passed through Prijedor on their way to Croatia. It was a strange sight. Burned-out buildings in some areas, particularly in "Old Town." Danis, whose nose was pressed up against the window, reached his hand up and tapped the window as he pointed to it.

"Mom, look at what they did," he said, pressing his entire right hand against the warm window.

She and Halima just stared, at a loss for words.

All of the passengers muttered about the devastation they were seeing, including as they passed through Kozarac, which had little left resembling its former self. Hajra saw this, and recalled how the UN representatives she spoke with a number of weeks prior told her of its total destruction.

Halima and Danis both buried their faces in their hands. Seeing their city destroyed was too much for them. Hajra touched their shoulders with an outstretched hand and could say nothing. She, too, was distraught at seeing the ruins. She squeezed back the tears that were threatening to make their way down her cheeks. She wanted to remain strong for her children.

Their bus driver stopped for a cup of coffee to-go in the village of Svodna. With the motor running and passengers anxiously waiting to get back on-the-road, some local Serb citizens jeered at them. They pounded on the bus yelling obscenities, cursing. The passengers were being peppered by Bosnian Serbs proclaiming one last moment of disgust for the "Turks."

Danis turned to Halima.

"What is wrong with them? What have we ever done to them? I don't even know these people or this village. I can't wait to get to Karlovac."

"I know, neither can I," she replied.

However, thought Hajra, after what they'd been through, this was nothing. Still, it hurt that they were being derided like this. She paid no more attention to the jeers, asking the children to do the same, and focused on what her next steps would be in Karlovac, a small city in Croatia she knew little about. What she did know was that they were no longer in Trnopolje. She hoped beyond hope that they were, in fact, actually going to Karlovac. She was worried that this was all another ruse, and that the bus would turn around and head back. She just wanted to find her relatives, and especially Elvir and Amir. She wanted the Red Cross in Croatia to provide her with some tangible proof of their whereabouts, even if that truth pierced her through the heart.

***

It was getting dark when they finally pulled into Karlovac. The bus slowed down as it reached the city limits. There were police cars with their lights spinning escorting them. There were people on the streets waving to them, and throwing kisses. Danis and Halima were entranced with what they were seeing. And relief in the form of smiles and utterances of "We're free," punctuated the conversations throughout the bus.

The bus slowed to a stop, and the driver told the passengers that they had reached their destination—that it was time to disembark.

The three newly-minted refugees grabbed their belongings and stepped down onto the street with a mixture of emotions, but primarily exhalations of relief that they felt having arrived in Karlovac.

There were many other refugees milling about; the newly-arrived joined others who had done so right before them, as the flow of buses seemed endless. Those who had no family or friends to greet them were directed to Red Cross and UNHCR representatives who guided them to nearby barracks to get clean clothes, food, and to be given sleeping arrangements—

the barracks set up for hundreds to sleep in very near the UNHCR headquarters. This, thought Hajra, would be the preferred place for her and her family for now. She and the children were overwhelmed with the sights and sounds of this new place. And, they were free. Landing in the security that the barracks provided would be the first step in finding some stability.

The children held on to their mother, tightly gripping her pullover. They were following the other refugees being directed by UNHCR representatives toward a large set of buildings.

As they neared the entrance of what they were told were barracks, Danis turned his gaze in the other direction.

“Look,” he shouted.

The others swiveled around to see Zlata, Merjem, Fatima, and Azra headed their way.

“Oh my God!” Hajra screamed.

Though they were told at the camp that family would be alerted of the arrival of those released from the camps, she hadn’t counted on that happening to them.

“Hajra, kids,” Merjem yelled, “I can’t believe my eyes. It’s incredible to see you. I can’t believe it!”

The cousins jumped at each other hugging and kissing, yelping, and screaming.

“How was the bus ride? Did they feed you? You must be hungry, and so tired.”

Marjem and Zlata could hardly contain themselves.

The two women embraced Hajra and the children with a warmth that had been void in Trnopolje. Their joy spilled over on the walk to Merjem’s cousin, Esma’s house.

“How did you know we were coming? We’d heard that there might be family to greet us, but I guess I didn’t want to believe we’d be so lucky.”

“The Red Cross informed us that you would be on one of the buses coming to Karlovac. We just weren’t sure which one.

We've been anxiously awaiting your arrival. The kids were like little squirrels each time a bus pulled up, spinning around, jumping up and down, yelling that this may be the one. Zlata's arms must be aching from all of the pulling on them that the girls did. All four of them are practically pulling her down over there," she said as she pointed to the cousins' Majka being mobbed by her grandchildren.

"I remember that your cousin Esma and her husband live here. I suppose I didn't want to believe that we would be greeted by anyone unless I saw it with my own eyes. I didn't even tell the kids that there was a possibility. But, seeing Zlata, you and the girls here is a dream come true."

As they walked and talked and chatted about the last time they saw each other, and about how they were doing, Hajra looked upward as if appealing to whatever higher power she now believed in as if to say, *Thank you. Thank you for getting us out of Trnopolje. Thank you for bringing us together.*

They walked past the army barracks with local police stationed outside.

"What happens in that building, Aunt Merjem? Is that like the school we stayed in in Trnopolje?" asked Danis.

"No, nothing like that. They are old army barracks for people coming here like you to sleep and eat in temporarily. Most are either waiting for relatives coming from elsewhere in Croatia, or even Austria to find them, or they will apply for asylum in other countries." she replied. "They'll find safe places to go," she said as she wrapped her arms around her precious nephew.

Hajra was half paying attention to the conversation Danis and Merjem were having. She was so thankful to be where she and the children were at that moment. Yet, it occurred to her that only these family members were here to greet them. Where was her husband and son? Where was her father-in-law? What about Tarik whom she last saw at Trnopolje before he disappeared?

Those and other questions would be answered soon enough. With some trepidation, she continued toward what promised to be a new and difficult chapter.

Chapter 23
The Lost and the Found

They entered the modest-sized house that was a few short blocks from the UNHCR building. There was a small kitchen, living room, one bedroom and a bathroom on the first floor. The white plastic blinds that hung from the two windows in the living room were drawn. The linoleum kitchen floor consisted of small black squares set into slightly dull white larger tiles. There was a sheer patterned curtain above the kitchen sink. The kitchen light consisted of two long fluorescent bulbs underneath an opaque plastic cover. The ceilings looked freshly painted and the lamps in the living room seemed like they were family heirlooms.

Upstairs was a larger bedroom with a bathroom where Merjem's cousin, Esma, and her husband, Ivan, a Catholic Croat from Karlovac, slept as did their newborn, Dalila, in a crib next to their bed. There was also a smaller bedroom with a bathroom in the hallway. Zlata, who had been sleeping in the downstairs bedroom, had moved her things to join Merjem and the girls who slept in that room, which had a double bed and two single mattresses on the floor. Overall, it was a pleasant and well cared for home made even more so compared to where they just came from.

Hajra and the children were ecstatic to be with family, and to feel safe. There was a smell of dolma and fresh baked bread wafting from the kitchen, fresh fruit in a bowl, and juice and water in containers on the table. This was the comfort food they'd been longing for.

The three were shown to their room, which was on the first floor. There was a double bed for Hajra and Halima, and a small rolling cot for Danis. Merjem had gone to a small warehouse set up by the Red Cross that had clothing for them donated by a Muslim relief organization nearby. The clothes were already laid out on the bed.

They were given towels and took showers in the small bathroom next to their bedroom. Each took an extra-long, very hot shower, luxuriating in the feeling of getting clean for the first time in months.

Halima exited the shower and was the last to join the group seated at the kitchen table.

"My skin itches from the months of not showering. It felt so strange to use soap and shampoo. I think it will be many more months until I finally get all of the dirt out of my pores. I didn't want to get out of the shower! Hot water? Soap? Shampoo? I had forgotten what those things were like."

The others laughed, but the truth was not lost on Hajra and Danis, who clearly agreed with Halima.

Zlata had made the dolma. She knew that her grandchildren loved the stuffed grape-vine leaves with ground meat, rice, spices, and chopped vegetables. The children had always believed that their grandmother magically arranged the dolma in the tureen with each piece connecting itself to the next, always prompting Halima to marvel at how much Majka's "Dolma Family" always loved being with each other. As they slowly cooked in their own juices, each ingredient individually excelled at what it did best, but in combination with the others made for a distinct flavor, giving Bosnian dolma its uniqueness—especially Majka's dolma. It tasted like home.

During the sumptuous meal they reminisced about Prijedor, and the beauty and harmony of their homes, and the destruction they saw along the way. They discussed returning someday to rebuild, with the understanding that this may be in the distant future. As they talked about their journey from

Trnopolje the mood mellowed.

Understanding that Hajra and the children were exhausted from their journey, Merjem and Zlata wanted to leave it up to Hajra as to whether she wanted to talk now or another day about what happened to them. Hajra said that she was over-tired, and not ready to go to bed just yet—that she could speak for a little while at least.

"OK Hajra, please let us know when you need to go to bed. We don't want to burden you. You just got here," said Merjem.

"No. I would like to just say a few things, and then, you're right, I am sure I'll be ready for sleep," she said to Merjem.

"If the children wish to leave, they are welcome to go into the bedroom upstairs, and we'll sort out the sleeping arrangements tomorrow," Esma added.

No one moved. They had seen so much in the recent months that nothing that was to be shared would disturb them. And besides, they were too wired to sleep now, as well.

Hajra hesitated a brief moment before speaking. She addressed Merjem and Zlata directly.

"I'll share what the camp was like some other time. For now, though, I must tell you that a few months ago we saw and spoke with Tarik while we were in the Serb camp.

The color from Merjem's face drained.

"You saw Tarik! In Trnopolje?"

"He was there outside near the perimeter for four days, but then he disappeared with several others, and we don't know where he is now. We were hoping he was with you," Hajra said.

"Oh, my God, you saw him. Please tell me more. I am so lost without him. So empty. Azra and Fatima have been so strong for me. And I am trying to be strong for them. But it has been hard for all of us—not knowing. I... we are so scared for him," she stammered.

Zlata shifted nervously in her seat on the sofa at the mention of her other son.

"Oh my God," she whispered.

Hajra continued.

"Well, when we saw him, he was very thin, but his spirits seemed better, compared to what they'd been like in Keraterm where he was first imprisoned," said Hajra.

"He was in Keraterm? We've heard what that place was like," Merjem said.

Hajra proceeded to tell Merjem and the children what she'd learned from him, but she left out the part about the daily torture. She also said nothing about the massacre of those in Room 3 at Keraterm, which she'd learned about later. She did tell them how he helped Danis, though. Merjem smiled at that. Mostly, though, she reported that they didn't feed the prisoners well in the camps, and the conditions were dismal. "So, like all of us," she said, "he didn't get much food."

She added that he seemed hopeful once he was out of Keraterm. He was much happier to be in Trnopolje. But she admitted it greatly worried her that he disappeared, and that she had no clue about where he was taken.

"Could he have escaped?" Merjem asked.

"No, I don't think so. There were many armed guards at the camp in Trnopolje. It was also very dangerous outside of the camp with Bosnian Serb soldiers everywhere.

"We only read about what was going on in the camps in Prijedor in a local Croatian newspaper that Ivan saved. It was big news, he said. The local news station played the British news teams' video here, however, he said he didn't see anyone he recognized, looking for family members he knew. There was a revealing photograph on the cover of the American magazine, Time, of an emaciated man named Fikret Alic with some of the other prisoners at Trnopolje nearby. It was terrifying to see in color what the Serbs had done to them. I worried that Tarik had suffered the same fate. That doesn't matter right now. What matters is that when you saw him, he was alive and in better spirits. Where could they have taken him?" Merjem said as her voice cracked.

Hajra had no answers for her. She, of course, had heard rumors of what the guards did to those they removed from the camps. They were either exchanged for captured Bosnian Serb soldiers, sent to another camp, or killed. But she could not say any more to Merjem and her children because the speculation would only cause them great anguish.

Merjem's eyes misted over as Hajra finished. She was not sure what to make of all that she had just heard. She didn't want to think about the possibilities of what might have happened to her husband any longer. She quietly stood up, kissed Hajra and Zlata and the others goodnight, and with her daughters following closely behind, they all walked upstairs.

Although she had wanted to hear what Merjem and Zlata knew about the rest of the family, Hajra was now ready for bed herself. She hadn't expected the conversation to go this way on the evening of their arrival. It surprised her that she hadn't. *What was I thinking? Poor Merjem. I couldn't hold onto the news about Tarik. I'll try to comfort her tomorrow. I can hardly think straight any more today.*

Esma and Zlata cleaned up the dishes and cups, while Ivan brought out some sheets, pillows, and blankets for the three of them. They hugged good night and went into their bedrooms no longer under the watchful eyes of the guards of the prison they had just left.

***

Zlata awoke early the next morning. She put the coffee on the stove and prepared breakfast. She didn't sleep particularly well, ruminating about Hajra and her grandchildren, but also about her sons and Amir. *Where are they all?* And she wanted to tell Hajra and the kids about her husband, Besim.

Hajra, Halima, and Danis emerged from their room not long after Zlata set the table.

"Good morning, Majka," the kids said as she kissed them on their foreheads.

"The breakfast smells delicious, and I'm starving," an excited Danis exclaimed.

"Eggs and cheese coming right up, kids," Zlata replied.

No one upstairs had stirred yet, so it was the four of them seated at the table.

"Majka," Halima quietly asked, "where's Babo?"

Zlata took a deep breath. She knew she'd have to tell them about Besim some time, though she dreaded the moment. But realities were harsh for Bosnians these days. And this was as good a time as any.

"Let me make breakfast first, and then we can sit down and talk," she responded.

As the aromas of the morning's fare made the kids salivate with anticipation, Zlata brought the frying pan to the table and doled out the breakfast on all of their plates. As she sat down herself, she spoke.

"I'll tell you about Babo, but first I want to share some good news," she said.

"Sure, Zlata, you tell us whatever you want," replied Hajra. "Good news is always welcomed, of course."

"I believe that your parents, brothers and their families are OK," she said to her daughter-in-law.

The children stopped chewing their food mid-bite.

Hajra set her cup of coffee down with such deliberateness that some of the steaming liquid dribbled over the side.

"Oh my God. Oh my God. How do you know?"

Halima and Danis continued to stare at their Majka in disbelief.

"Of course, I don't know for certain, but I've heard there were a number of people who escaped Banja Luka before all this madness began. A friend of your mother's and mine who lived near them—you remember Sajra?" Hajra nodded. "She is here in Karlovac, too. I saw her a few days after I arrived in a market not too far from here, which made me so very happy. Anyway, she told me that your mother asked her to go with them to Germany where they were headed. Sajra, whose husband died a few years ago, said she would, but her two sons who lived near her in Trnopolje, did not want to leave. Like so many of us, they believed that the Serbs could not hurt their fellow Bosnians. And they knew that there were checkpoints beginning to be set up along the roads making it difficult to leave. Sadly, a few weeks later, her sons were murdered by those same Serbs. She was so lost and desperate. Poor woman is still so distraught."

"How awful. I knew her sons from school. They were a few years older than me," said Hajra.

"I knew them, too. I am just so heartbroken for Sajra," replied Zlata.

Zlata took a deep breath.

"Let me continue with how I know that your family is safe. Sajra was offered a way out by going to Karlovac. As you may know, her mother was Serb. She had some hospital documents to prove it. She bought a bus ticket to Karlovac and is staying with a cousin now. Apparently, your mother was able to get through to her by phone somehow to tell her they were headed for Germany from Banja Luka with her sons and their families. Although Sajra has not heard from your mother since, she is hopeful that they are there."

"I can't believe it," Hajra shouted. "I can't believe that they may have all escaped. Until I speak with them, I can't know for sure."

"Do you know how to get in touch with my family,?" asked Hajra.

"Yes. Sajra said that she checks in with UNHCR daily to see if a message came in from your mother. She will let me know as soon as she hears."

Hajra did not know what to say. Her hope was tainted with the realities of what was happening in Bosnia. But she had to hope.

Just then, Esma and the baby came downstairs.

"Good morning everyone. How did you sleep?" she asked.

"Good, good. Thank you so much for letting us stay here," Hajra said.

"Please, you are family to us. We could do nothing less," Esma responded.

Zlata had a faraway look in her eyes.

Halima didn't want to ask her grandmother about Babo again. They were all sensing that the news about him was not good.

Zlata refocused.

"I'll share other news with you about Babo later. Let me clean up. I want to prepare other meals for today. Can we talk more about this after dinner?"

"Of course. As I said, whenever you want to. I'm so grateful to hear about my family. We'll talk later about Besim."

Zlata pulled a tissue from the box nearby, and softly blew her nose. It didn't go unnoticed by the others that she was crying, but it was best not to ask anything more of her just then. It was clear she hadn't the strength just yet.

***

The day went on with some food shopping, the children playing with Dalila, and the adults continuing to ask about people they all knew from Bosnia. It was light talk—reminiscing really. Hajra was anxious to learn more about her parents and brothers, but knew that she'd have to wait for Zlata's friend to get something more concrete to go on.

The evening meal came and went. There was no discussion about Besim. And no one pushed. In her time, Zlata would tell them.

The exhaustion returned not too long after dinner, and Hajra and the children went to bed early.

They all hugged goodnight. In their small bedroom, Hajra and her children spoke about what they had learned from Zlata that morning. They were all cautiously optimistic. But sleep found Danis in the midst of their conversation, and Halima and her mother agreed that perhaps they should join him and try to get some rest themselves.

Sleeping in bed next to each other, Hajra heard her daughter lapse into the rhythmic breathing of a deep sleep. The house became very quiet. Hajra's thoughts were racing. *I can't believe my family may be safe. I need to speak with them. I so badly want to share this news with Elvir and Amir. Where are they? Where is my father-in-law, Besim? I didn't want to ask Zlata tonight. So much to take in right now. Still so much to think about. So much to worry about. I must stay positive. If I managed to save my children up until now, I must continue to stay strong for us all. I must continue to believe in miracles.*

She soon drifted off into a series of disturbing dreams. In them, her family was together in a great city in Germany, but she was lost and couldn't find them. Tarik was calling out to her, but she couldn't see him. Elvir and Amir were drifting among the ruins of Kozarac, and her children were outside looking for something, but that something was not revealed.

When she awoke the next day, she had to shake her head of the cobwebs from the previous couple of days, and of the many months prior. She was taking stock of where she was, and all that had already changed.

Chapter 24
More Truths

That morning, everyone got up except for Merjem. Azra said that her mother told her she needed to rest—that she did not sleep well and would be down later.

Esma got a crying Dalila out of her crib and was sitting downstairs feeding her. Ivan had just left for work where he aided the Red Cross in keeping the barracks stocked with furniture and other supplies, and doing tasks related to the refugees' well-being. Zlata was busily getting a breakfast of coffee, bread, and cakes ready. Halima, sensing Majka's distractedness, helped out in the kitchen.

Although there was some good news, with brothers Elvir and Tarik missing along with Amir, and the whereabouts of Besim not known, there was a deep chasm in all of their lives affecting the somber mood in the house now. They tried their hand at small talk, but the elephant was still in the room.

When they sat down to eat, Hajra asked Zlata if she was ready to talk about Besim.

Zlata looked into the coffee cup in front of her. She lifted her soft, brown eyes, with a more heavily wrinkled countenance than Hajra had remembered, and began to speak.

"This is difficult news to share. Babo, your grandpa, kids, is gone."

"What do you mean gone, Majka?" asked Halima softly.

Zlata turned her troubled gaze toward her granddaughter.

"He refused to leave for Croatia despite the threats that were so apparent to me. And he insisted that I go. He could be such a stubborn man. And he trusted people to a fault. He said that these people were our neighbors, our friends, and that this would be enough to ensure our safety. Your grandfather would do anything for his friends and even strangers. I have learned that he is most likely dead, betrayed by some of the same ones he trusted," she said as everyone sat in silence.

Zlata added. "He wanted me to leave just to be sure that I would be alright. I tried so hard to get him to come with me—that we could always go back to our house when the craziness died down. He was such a sweet man. But when he got something into his head, it was almost impossible to convince him otherwise."

She turned toward Halima and Danis. "Your father and I would tease him about his stubbornness, too. But he would just shrug and say that he knew best."

"I had arranged with my friend, Vesna, her husband Stanko, and their two young children, to get out of Trnopolje and get us to Karlovac. They are such wonderful people. It wasn't easy. We were stopped at a few checkpoints, but being that they're Serbian, we made it to Belgrade. From there I had to take buses to Budapest, Zagreb, and finally got here to Karlovac. All the while I worried about Babo. I spoke with Vesna a few weeks after I arrived, and she told me that he was no longer at home. Vesna heard that he was taken somewhere and killed by soldiers."

Danis went over to his Majka, who was crying, and wrapped his arms around her, burying his head in between her shoulder and neck.

"I'm so sorry, Majka. I'm mad at the Serbs. I want to kill them," said a defiant Danis.

"Please don't say that, Danis. I know you're angry. I am, too. But I know there are Serbs who are good and don't accept what is going on. Remember, it was my Serbian friends who got me to Belgrade before coming here. It was a risk for them to take me."

Zlata dabbed her tears on her shirt sleeve. Halima went to the bathroom to get Majka tissues. She then passed the box around to her mother and the others.

"There's nothing more to the story. I'm so grateful to be here with you—that you have found your way here. We Bosnians have to be strong. Our history is full of times when we were targeted by one or another group, but we survived. Someday, this too will pass. It always does," said Zlata as she found her way to the kitchen to get another cup of coffee.

***

It was early afternoon when Merjem came downstairs. She was still in her pajamas and somewhat disheveled. It was clear that she had been crying. Hajra, Zlata and Esma greeted her with kisses. Hajra got her a cup of coffee.

Zlata informed Merjem that she told Hajra about Besim. Merjem just stared into her cup as the steam from the hot brew rose toward the kitchen light.

Since they had finished lunch an hour earlier, the restless children wanted to go out to the nearby city park. For Halima and Danis, it was the first time in months that they could take advantage of being untethered from the grasp of the concentration camp. Zlata said she needed to go to the market, and that she would watch the children. She told Danis that she remembered how much he loved the comic, Zagor, the superhuman hero in the mountains of Pennsylvania in the early 19th century. This was Danis' reference to early American history. He even fantasized that he might someday go see where his hero lived. Majka said she had seen the comic in the local market, and that she would get it for him when she next went shopping. This news was greeted with a huge smile, thank you, and hug from her grandson.

As they raced out of the door, Azra grabbed Danis by the hand, as Fatima grabbed Halima's. Laughter, the true sound of free-spirited children, brought joy to Hajra like she hadn't had in so long. The TV was on low, and the house was mostly quiet, especially with a napping Dalila.

"I'm sorry that I went to bed so abruptly the last couple of nights. I guess hearing about Tarik has really gotten to me, which is why I was in my own world yesterday," said Merjem.

"There is no need to apologize, it's quite understandable. We're all trying to deal with very harsh realities these days. I figured that's why you were kind of quiet," replied Hajra.

Merjem sighed and shook her head.

"If you want to tell me more about what happened to you in Prijedor, and how you got here, I'd like to know. That is, if you feel up to it?" asked Hajra.

"I'm ready, thank you. I want to tell you. As hard as it is for me to talk right now, I think it's important that you know.

"My darling Hajra, I can't imagine what you and the children have been through. We have heard of what the Serbs did to us in the camps. Though you left it out while telling us about Tarik, I know what he must have gone through. It has been awful to try to get answers about what happened to our family," Merjem said.

Hajra took Merjem's hand.

"I'm guessing Tarik told you that he was taken from our home for interrogation. I still remember how he looked at me as he went out of the door. His eyes conveyed to me not to worry; that he'd be back soon. But he never came back. The days lapsed into weeks, and we were beside ourselves.

"Yes," said Hajra, "Tarik told us this. He said he'd thought that he'd be released and back home"

Merjem nodded and continued.

From the end of May to the end of August, we lived as shadows in our own house. In July, they ordered all Muslims to hang white sheets outside our homes. We even had to wear white armbands if we went out. There was little food, and believe it or not, our neighbors, who are Serbs, would leave fruit and vegetables, sometimes even some meat, at our back door. Still, it was unbearable, but more unbearable was not knowing where Tarik or the rest of the family was.

"The girls were very anxious and lost a lot of sleep, as did I. We were worried because we heard rumors about others being taken out of their homes. We were so panicked that this would happen to us. Every sound made us jump. I did all I could do to tamp down the girls' fears, but it was hard for me, too."

"It sounds awful. It's like you were in your own prison, but in your house. But how did you get to Karlovac?" asked Hajra.

"Oh, yes, let me tell you," Merjem replied.

"We could only take very small suitcases. The girls actually took their backpacks with a few clothes and other items of importance. Both of them took the dolls that their Majka had made for them when they were little."

"I remember when she made a doll for Halima, too."

"They are even more special to the girls now. Anyway, I have an uncle in Chicago. Well, he's not really an uncle, but that's what my mother has always referred to him as. He contacted the Serbian Red Cross and paid them a lot of money to get us out of Prijedor and over here to Karlovac. Of course, I had to sign over our house to the authorities. We then took a few different buses and eventually arrived here. To be honest, I wasn't sure we'd make it even with what my uncle arranged. Being here is temporary until other countries commit to taking us in as we cannot stay with Esma and Ivan forever. And who knows when, if ever, it will be safe for us to return to Prijedor."

"I told you," said Esma who was knitting a blanket for Dalila, "you can stay as long as you like."

"I know, I know. You're very kind. But we have to figure out our next steps. It could be that we stay in Karlovac, but that depends on many things. So, we can't commit to anything. What you and Ivan have provided I can never repay you for."

"That's what families do for one another. Please don't ever speak of repaying us. We're so happy that we can be here for you and your children, and now for Zlata, Hajra and her kids," Esma said.

Merjem thanked her cousin once again and continued her story.

"We got here at the beginning of September. As you saw when you arrived, there were others just like us. Many stayed in the barracks. When we arrived it wasn't as crowded. The Red Cross then registered us like they did for you. They also told us that my cousin was here, and that Esma and Ivan were aware that we were arriving. They were standing outside the UNHCR building waiting for us. We didn't see them because we had entered the building another way to first register with the Red Cross. Esma gave them other names of relatives, including Tarik's, to make sure she would be contacted if they arrived. I also gave them the names of my parents and yours, in addition to Elvir, your kids, my brothers' and their families. They told me that Zlata was here, too, because Esma had put hers and Besim's names as family. Actually, they had lots of names, you know, the ones they registered in the camps and elsewhere."

Esma interjected. "Zlata told us that she arrived and told the Red Cross representatives that she had found her way out of her village of Trnopolje before the real trouble started. She lamented over leaving her dear husband. Leaving him was so, so hard, she said. But she told us that with his words still echoing in her ears, she thought this would end soon, and they'd be back together again. She said she had heard of others from Prijedor municipality who had come here. Sejma had friends here to stay with. She learned that I had listed her and Besim as family."

A momentary silence cloaked the room. Then Merjem said one last thing.

"I'm so sad about Besim," she said as a tear slowly dripped down her cheek. "And I am so afraid for my parents and brothers. I'm worried sick for Elvir and Amir. I have nightmares about them. I'm trying to be positive and strong, hoping that they will find us, but I am scared to death," she said.

Hajra stood up and put her arms around Merjem, who now shifted the topic.

"I have heard that the Netherlands, Sweden, Germany, the UK, Canada, the U.S. and other countries have all said they would take Bosnian refugees. To be honest, being away from Bosnia may be what we choose to do. The war is not over by any means. Karlovac seems quite safe, but I've heard talk that fighting may happen here, too. And what can we do here? This is not our home. How will we live? Although I'd love to return to Prijedor, it is Serbian-controlled now, and so dangerous for us. But we want to be here in case Tarik makes it to Karlovac or to learn of any other place in Croatia he finds his way to. Being in this country was always our plan, even if temporarily, this was at least our first stop on the road to safety." Merjem said.

Dalila's cries from upstairs stopped the conversation. Hajra was glad for that. After changing the baby, Esma came back down to feed her.

While rocking Dalila she spoke.

"Merjem and I take turns checking in with UN authorities who work with the International Red Cross to track those who register in Bosnia, to see if there is any word on family. Today is my turn. Can one of you take Dalila while I get my coat, so I can get over there?"

"I'll go. I'll just run upstairs to get dressed. Besides, it will do me good to get some air," Merjem said.

"OK, " said Esma, "I'll go the next time then."

"But you didn't eat," said Hajra.

"I'll grab this apple before I go," Merjem replied.

It was just a few minutes after Merjem left that Zlata and the children walked in the door from the park, got some dried fruit from the kitchen, and gathered in the living room telling the adults about the fun they had on the swings, and running around playing tag. Danis showed his mother the comic book, and spoke of the candy they ate, courtesy of Majka who had decided that the market was close enough that leaving the children for a few minutes would be fine. The raucous and happy voices made for a good antidote to the conversation just had in the house. They all cooed at the infant as Esma placed Dalila on a blanket on the floor, as the others gathered around her smiling at the beautiful innocence before them, while Halima tickled the baby's stomach.

"Where's mom?" asked Fatima.

"She went over to the UN building. She'll be back soon," said Hajra.

However, Hajra noticed that Merjem had been gone for almost an hour. Going to the UNHCR building is no more than a ten-minute walk. She instinctively stood up and peeked out of the front window, but saw no one heading toward the house. She returned to sit on the couch, but had trouble focusing. Merjem's mood had lingered, and Hajra's concern for her sister-in-law had risen a few more notches.

Chapter 25
Merjem's Walk Backwards

When she left the house, Merjem headed straight to the UNHCR headquarters to see if there was any news about anyone in the family. Of primary concern was Tarik. She stiffened at the thought that neither her husband nor her parents and brothers had appeared on any lists to-date. She often thought about Elvir and Amir, hoping that they were still alive. It was all quite overwhelming for her.

She entered the building and there was only one person ahead of her in line. As she gazed around the room, she thought of Tarik the day they were separated. He seemed to try to reassure her that he'd be back. Of course, she didn't know that this was the last time they'd all be together. She had not ever conceived of where he was going at the time. Who could know that concentration camps were in the offing for non-Serbs?

"Next," the representative said.

Merjem's spell was broken and she approached the desk.

"Hi. I'm here again to see if my family has been accounted for on your registry."

Merjem and the woman knew each other because of the many times she'd come in with the same question.

"Actually, as I cross-check our lists, I have some good news for you. We have located your brother-in-law and nephew, Elvir and Amir Kovacevic."

"You have? That's incredible. My family will be ecstatic. Where are they? Will they be coming to Karlovac?" a breathless Merjem asked.

"Well, I'm sorry to say that they are in the POW camp at Mount Manjaca. Right now, I don't have more than that for you. We can only hope that they are being treated well. We have Red Cross workers going in there regularly to ensure that the prisoners are."

"Thank you, Madame, thank you for this news!" she screamed.

"One more thing," Merjem said. "Do you have any information about my husband, Tarik? Any shred of news?"

"I'm afraid not. I'm sorry."

Merjem's grin quickly receded.

"That's OK. I'll continue to hope. That's all I can do. I'll tell my sister-in-law and her children about Elvir and Amir. This is great news. Thank you, again. Thank you!"

Merjem left the building greeted by a chill wind. *No parents, no brothers, no husband.*

She needed to walk a little more before going back to Esma's house to share the good news. She wanted to be as uplifting as she could be for her family. Uplifted was not how she felt at the moment. *I'll just walk a little more. That will help.*

Her thoughts wandered back to an incident she had when she was a teenager.

Growing up in a Muslim household, but with strong secular leanings, Merjem's father would have a shot or two of the locally-made rakija, a liqueur that tasted like vodka-infused with plum, which was plentifully grown in the area. It was a heavy drink, but Merjem often looked at those drinking it with a rather curious eye. Occasionally, her mother would join her dad for a drink, but that was just when the two of them were alone.

Once, when Merjem was seventeen, she and her brother, Adi, who was a year older, bought a bottle of cheap Serbian red wine called Czar Lazar, and went to the dense grove of

Sessile oak trees about a kilometer from their house. She and Adi were the closest of the three siblings and they often did many things together.

She hadn't drunk very much alcohol before, but it was a beautiful summer evening, and they had been talking about doing this when the time was right. And this evening, the time was right.

Their parents went to visit an aunt in a distant village and they were going to stay the night. The siblings said they were going to have coffee with friends in town, and encouraged their parents to visit their mother's sister.

Adi opened the bottle and politely suggested that his sister begin. He was not much of a drinker either, and was a little hesitant at first.

"OK, Adi, I'll be happy to start the party."

She took the bottle and didn't just sip it, but took several gulps of the wine, and handed it back to her brother.

"Ahhh," she said, "not bad. So, don't hold onto it too long or I may swipe it back from you."

Adi took a more measured sip and scrunched up his mouth asking her how she was able to down so much.

"I guess I like it. And now I'm already feeling a bit wobbly. Give me more!"

Over the next half-hour Merjem proceeded to dominate the drinking party. Not that Adi didn't get drunk, because he did. But Merjem was hammered.

"Remember when that biology teacher, Dordevic, would get on a roll about the most minute details. He would go off on tangents," said Adi.

"Yeah. And he always seemed to be having fun—with himself. He'd tell these strange jokes during his lecture and laugh. We'd all laugh, too, but at him, though he never knew it. I was actually worried about the guy," Merjem replied. "There was something off about him."

"I don't think I learned a lot about biology, actually," said

Adi, "but he was kind of entertaining."

She and Adi continued to ramble on about crushes they had, other teachers they liked and didn't like, and questioned why their older brother, Davud, was so serious all the time.

Merjem went on non-stop about Tarik, who she'd gotten to know in high school. Adi knew Tarik, too, and liked him. In fact, he and Elvir were in the same math class, and Elvir mentioned that his brother liked Merjem. This was exhilarating news for Merjem.

"Tell me more, Adi. Did Elvir say anything else? Did he say his brother wanted to get to know me better?" asked Merjem.

"I don't remember, Merjem. Yes, I'm sure he did. But I'm not really remembering much of anything right now," he replied.

The moon was shining brilliantly and there was no breeze whatsoever. As Merjem was yammering about Tarik, Adi peered over her shoulders and saw something move behind another set of oak trees.

"Merjem. Hush for a second."

"What's the matter?" she said in a slushy whisper.

"There's something over there that just went behind those trees."

"You're just drunk. There's nothing there," she said after gazing in the direction that Adi had pointed to.

"No, I'm telling you. There's something there."

At that moment a huge—what appeared to be a German Shepherd mix—emerged, baring its sharp fangs.

"Oh, God, Adi, what's going on? That is not a happy dog. Worse, he seems unhappy with our presence!"

"Be still. Grab those rocks below you. I've got some here, too. Let's walk to the road, but don't turn your back, and if it comes at us, we'll throw the rocks and yell at it—yell loud."

As they backed up the dog moved warily toward them, growling menacingly.

"I think we better act now, Adi," said Merjem.

"On the count of three, we'll throw the rocks and yell."

At three they screamed while hurling the projectiles at the snarling canine. It suddenly lurched to the side avoiding being hit. But Merjem, displaying bravado instilled by the Czar Lazar, moved toward it with several more rocks she had just picked up. She heaved them with a ferocity that took the dog by surprise. It turned on its haunches and bolted, disappearing deep into the woods.

"Merjem, are you crazy?" asked Adi.

"Adi, my heart is beating very fast, but not from fear. That was wild, actually."

"I believe you're drunk, and crazy, my dear sister. And you would have provided the dog with a lovely meal if he didn't retreat!"

How she missed her brother. She probably was crazy to do what she did. But she also learned that alcohol gave her courage. Of course, it was not natural courage and at times it did little to dissuade any visiting demons. But other times, when she was particularly down, she would sneak a bottle into her bedroom and drink half of it, hiding the rest of it under her bed for another time.

That was when she was a teenager, and before she married Tarik to start her own family. She promised that she would not drink anymore.

As she entered the small grocery store in Karlovac, she had decided that now was a good time for a shot or two of courage.

The smile on her face was slightly askew as she entered the house. With her coat still on, she sat down with the others.

"Please call your brother and cousins down here, I have some good news," she told Halima, who had remained with the adults while the other children were upstairs.

While descending the stairs, Danis excitedly asked, "What good news, Auntie? Halima said you have good news?"

"I have some very good news, Danis. At the UN building I asked who from my list of relatives they had information on, if any. They did."

Halima and Danis edged closer to Merjem.

"I learned that Elvir and Amir are in the camp up on Mount Manjaca. UNHCR said that theirs and the Red Cross list they have tells them this," she said while acutely aware not to slur her words..

"Oh my God," shouted Hajra. "Oh my God!"

"Does this mean we will see them again soon?" an animated Danis asked.

"Let's hope so, my darling," replied Zlata "We must always hope."

"This is truly a miracle!" Hajra exclaimed.

Merjem continued.

"You are here, Hajra, and we know where Elvir and Amir are. I don't know what Manjaca is like, but from what we've heard about it, it is not as awful as the ones in Prijedor. I know it's going to be hard for any of us to rest until we see those two in our midst. We now know they are registered, and alive," said Merjem.

Though it was early and they hadn't eaten dinner yet, Merjem abruptly excused herself saying that she was very tired, and not very hungry. She went upstairs and said that perhaps she would join them later.

"OK, Merjem, thank you for the wonderful news. We'll see you later," said Zlata.

It was a strange exit, but no one seemed to notice that Merjem missed a step at the top of the stairs heading toward the bedroom.

Hajra was momentarily lost in her own thoughts. She was very aware that the condition Elvir and Amir were in could be fragile. But if they were truly alive, she would smother them with a healing love that would be the salve needed for their recovery. If only she could be sure they were going to be reunited.

Before going to bed she thought of Merjem, who had not

returned after going upstairs. There was something not quite right, but she couldn't discern what that was.

The next day, Merjem emerged from her room in an inquisitive mood. She asked Hajra about the camp in Trnopolje as she and Zlata sat down to listen while the children were upstairs playing. Hajra spoke of the conditions of the camp, but skimmed over some of the more sinister details that she was not quite ready to disclose. She knew she would someday, but she was still choosing to bury her encounter with Pavlovic until she felt stronger to do so.

Bringing back stinging memories hit Hajra harder than she thought they would. Knowing that her husband and son were still alive, her own mood was affected by the admixture of hope and grief, leaving her grasping for some measure of equilibrium. It would be the last time Hajra could speak about their time in Trnopolje for a while, but at least she shared most of what had happened, and that was cathartic.

Zlata brought out some burek for lunch, which veered Hajra away from any more thoughts about Trnopolje and Manjaca. The conversation switched to the more mundane—the powers that Bosnian cooking seemed to have to restore anyone's low mood.

Chapter 26
The Snow is Upon Us

The monotony of the camp at Manjaca persisted. But, as time marched on the prisoners were given more freedom of movement. During daylight, they were allowed to be outside, staying within their Wire. However, the first snowfall was happening, and it was not quite mid-November. This was hard for those from Prijedor municipality, as the weather was not typically like this before the winter.

Since most of the prisoners from Prijedor were taken during the summer with little more than light clothing, some even in slippers, there was little protection from the weather. Until early November, that is what continued to pass for their daily wardrobe. However, with the cold arriving, they were given pullovers, socks, shoes, and black wool caps. This made it easier to survive late fall on Mount Manjaca.

The snowfall, though not heavy, settled on the evergreens that proliferated on the mountain. If the prisoners dared to stay outside for too long, they'd return with iced eyebrows and beards, which they tried to brush off inside. But it was not very much warmer in the stall, so one could almost hear the walking skeletons rattling their bones as they attempted to shake themselves free of the cold.

"It is so cold here, Dad. It is not like Kozarac. My teeth chatter every night. And the supposed blanket is flimsy. The new clothing helps, but it is still frigid. It feels like we will never get out of here," Amir said sadly.

"Remember, that German TV news crew that was here last

week will help us to be free soon. I just feel it. It's only a matter of time. I've heard that there are exchanges in the works, too. By now, there are bound to be plenty of Serb prisoners that were captured by the Bosnian Army."

"But there are a few thousand of us here. How many prisoners can possibly be exchanged? Ten, twenty, fifty? That's not all of us by any means," Amir lamented.

"Listen, we're registered with the Red Cross. They seem to be trying to get us out. The snow is already falling. You know those cows in the fields, the ones whose home we are living in? Well, the Serbs don't want to lose all of those heads of cattle. Something has got to give here. To be honest, I'm worried that some of us may not make it through this winter. That concerns me. But I believe there's going to be some movement," said Elvir.

Hasan had been listening in on the conversation. He pulled out a cigarette from the half-a-pack that he had gotten in a trade with another prisoner for a large baked potato and a bag of carrots he had snuck out of the kitchen. He took a long drag on it, and then spoke.

"Amir, how many of their cattle can they exchange for us? If there are not enough prisoners for their so-called exchange, then we may be worth a few hundred cows."

Elvir began to chuckle.

Amir smiled at that, which snapped him out of his melancholy.

"I guess you're right. With all due respect, I'm worth a few more cows than the two of you put together," he joked.

Hasan burst out with a hearty laugh.

"He may have a good point," he added.

Although Manjaca did not resemble Omarska, "the day-to-day nothingness" as one of the prisoners referred to it, was in its own way brutal. The prisoners were definitely being fed better, but the monotony of walking to meals with heads bowed and hands behind, the assignments that bore no consequence for the men, the watchful eyes of the guards who found reasons to beat some of them, made for a different type of torment. And worst of all, they longed for their homes and families. They made bets, usually with cigarettes, when they might be released.

"Never," said some of them.

"When the cows come home," said another with a smirk.

"When the Serbs are overrun by our army," said others.

But the truth was, they didn't know. And that was agonizing enough for the many who had not been free since the plans to cleanse Bosnia of non-Serbs began.

There was some movement, however. It was slow, but movement nonetheless.

One morning, guards rounded up all one hundred Croat prisoners. They lined them up outside for an exchange of prisoners they said they'd arranged with the Croat military, and this was to take place that day.

Elvir and the others were cautiously optimistic for these men. Although the majority of the prisoners in Manjaca were non-combatants, the Serbs tried to convince the world that these were captured soldiers and extremists seeking the annihilation of Serbs. They maintained that they were willing to exchange, however, to save the lives of their brethren from the atrocities that the others intended to rain upon them.

Later that day, the bus returned with the same men. Apparently, the exchange went awry.

Anton, one of the Croats who was housed in Wire Two, had bruises on his face.

"We were in Knin for the exchange," he said, "but it didn't happen. I don't really know why. But the local thugs there were given the go-ahead to beat us. My black eyes and tender cheek bones are courtesy of those devils. The bus ride back here was very quiet. We were so close, but so far."

However, a few days later the Croats were again taken for an exchange. This time, the Croat prisoners included a high-ranking officer in their army, and the deal happened. Still, there were almost 3,000 prisoners cramped into the six stalls for three months, so finding solace in the few that left was not particularly inspirng.

"So," said Elvir to his neighbors in the stall, "people can leave here after all. That's progress. Now, there are only 2,900 to go—give or take a few."

Armin and Karim, two men Elvir had been acquaintances with in Kozarac, and who had been in Manjaca since late June chimed in that Elvir needed to consider trading several packs of cigarettes to the Serbs in exchange for the release of a thousand Muslims.

Elvir laughed and retorted that "the Serbs would probably only take the cigarettes if they were untouched by us Turks."

Winter weather had definitely found its footing deep into late fall. Mount Manjaca was no stranger to being visited by cold, snowy days, and when those appeared, it was all the prisoners could do to keep warm. They were given some heavier clothing and new black shoes, but being significantly underweight, they could not easily warm up. Some were sent to the infirmary with weather-related illnesses.

After the successful prisoner exchange of Croats, there was a slight uptick in the mood of many of the prisoners.

"Dad, the cattle are going to have to be put inside soon, or they'll starve to death. Even the Serbs are not so cruel that they would put us in the pasture," Amir said.

"That's true. I've been thinking about that. Maybe that will be part of the equation that gets us out of here?"

"Besides," Amir said, "since there is no grass left for us prisoners to graze on, the pastures would not be a good place to dine."

They both laughed. They also acknowledged that Elvir was right. Perhaps they were getting closer to leaving, with the hope that it was not to another camp.

The next day, as Elvir left the chilly mess tent after the

afternoon meal, Ajdin joined him as they slowly made their way back to the stall.

"On November 14th, several prisoners are going to Karlovac refugee camps," he said barely in a whisper. "On December 13th, 500 or so deemed military combatants are going to two other camps. But on December 14th, 16th, and 18th the rest of us are also going to Karlovac."

He then split off from Elvir heading to the medical store room to fulfill one of his tasks.

Elvir was taken aback. Not that he wasn't hopeful that some sort of movement for their exit was going to happen. It's just that in a concentration camp one's expectations don't always come to fruition the way one hopes. And by then, there were so many rumors about when the prisoners might be released, it was difficult to know the truth—to know that even what Ajdin had seen was to become reality.

Are we really getting out of here? he thought. *Will the Red Cross be able to get those going to other camps out safely, as well? Will we find Hajra, Halima, and Danis—and the others?*

Elvir so badly wanted to tell Amir, Hasan, and the others. But he knew he would be compromising Ajdin, and even though a few of the prisoners were wary of one or two of the stall commanders, Elvir would never forget Ajdin and his bravery. He knew that all Ajdin wanted was for Elvir to keep a positive mood afloat to prop the prisoners up. Someday, somehow, he would reveal to those he stayed with in Manjaca what a courageous man Ajdin was.

Two days before November 14th arrived, one of the officers announced that in the coming days, those born before 1950 and after 1972 would be headed to Karlovac, and that included Amir. From that point, there was a buzz throughout the camp as freedom was making its introduction.

Amir, of course, did not want to leave his father. Both Elvir and Hasan were staying behind, having been born in the late 1950s. But Elvir promised his son he would be with him again soon. If he trusted Ajdin's information, of which none had been false to-date, then he would, in fact, be joining him in about a month.

After the morning's meal on the 14th, the stall was ablaze with excitement. Not the excitement of watching your favorite soccer club winning a championship; there was no energy for that. But a feeling of anticipation.

Amir packed the few rags-for-clothes he had been allowed to keep in a plastic bag given to those leaving the camp.

"Dad, you know I'd rather stay here with you. But I also have faith that you will join me in Karlovac soon. I'll be on-edge, and I won't rest easily until we are together again. But I'll do my best. Armin said that he will help me when we get there."

"I know, he and I talked about it. He's a good man, and I know he'll help you. Remember, when you get there, I am told, you will check in with the ICRC, the Red Cross at the UN building. They will let you know which family members will take you in. If for some reason there aren't any now, please stay with Armin, and when I get there, we can figure out what to do next. We will be together soon."

Amir threw himself into his father's arms, and as he left a streak of grime-tinged tears appeared to be etched into the lapel of the old coat Elvir was wearing.

Those left behind in the camp beamed as the group departed for Croatia. The Red Cross and UNHCR had finally ensured that the international community knew of this camp, and to facilitate the transfer across the border to relative safety.

My turn next, God willing, my turn next.

Chapter 27
Karlovac

It had been over a month since Hajra and the children reunited with Merjem and her children, and Zlata. Hajra was anxious to speak with her family in Germany. She was curious to learn what life was like for them. The Croatian government seemed to be getting restless about the influx of mostly Muslims to their refugee centers in Karlovac and the few other cities set up to take them in. And they were now entrenched in a war with Serbia to keep their independence. There was also fighting between Bosnia and Croatia in Central Bosnia. It was a confusing time in the Balkans, and those living in the region felt very uneasy.

Hajra finally spoke with her parents and the rest of the family. It was an emotional phone call that involved many tears and tissues. She learned that the German government was welcoming Bosnian refugees, to include apartments, a monthly subsidy, and other support specifically geared toward integrating Bosnians into German society. There was school for the children, even summer camps that provided some sense of normalcy and joy for them. Her family lived in a building with other refugees from the war including another family from Trnopolje that Hajra knew growing up. It wasn't Bosnia, but it was a safe and protected environment of which Hajra knew little about, but was overjoyed to hear. *If only I knew if we'd be reunited with Elvir and Amir. Perhaps we all could go to Germany and leave behind the living nightmares that my beloved Bosnia has been subjected to?*

On a cold mid-November day, the knock on the door startled Hajra. Zlata had gone to the market, and Merjem took the children to the park just across the street after which she joined her mother-in-law in the market. Esma was napping upstairs with the baby, and Ivan was at work. Hajra had just cleaned the house and was sipping steaming hot, sweetened black tea.

She opened the door to find a messenger from UNHCR.

"Are you Hajra Kovacevic?"

"Yes I am," she replied.

"There are some buses with refugees arriving soon. One of the buses has your son, Amir. It should be here within the hour. Sorry for the late notice. There was a slight mix-up with our lists. I can wait until you are ready if you'd like me to escort you to the waiting area. It's the least I can do for telling you so late."

"Amir?" she practically yelled.

"Your son, Amir," he gently replied.

Hajra did not know how to respond. She immediately set the mug down on the floor and leapt into the young man's arms whose face reddened.

"Yes, yes, I'm ready now. Sure. Please take me to the waiting area. I know it will be an hour, you said. Right? That's OK. I'll go now in case it's early. I can't believe it. Amir."

She put on her coat and raced past the man who delivered this most glorious news. He yelled for her to wait up, that he wanted to escort her to the waiting area. Panting, he finally caught up to her at the entrance of the UNHCR building.

He pointed her toward the signs near the bus drop-off across the street.

"You can wait inside our building, if you'd like. It's cold outside. We will let you know a few minutes before the buses pull in."

She could hardly contain herself waiting in the lobby of the UN building. She imagined Amir sitting impatiently aboard the bus anticipating a family reunion.

Even though his dad wasn't completely sure that there would be someone there for him, Amir had a feeling there would be. It was a scene mother and son had both envisioned independently over the past several weeks though it was tainted with the uncertainties of war.

What seemed like hours was actually only forty-five minutes when the buses pulled up to the building.

Hajra bolted for the exit, needing no one to inform her of the their arrival. There were four of them, and she strode along the walkway scanning the smudged windows to see if she could spot her son. The sun's reflection made it more difficult, so she placed a hand above her eyes to screen out the glare. She found herself in the middle of the caravan when she heard her son's voice from the bus she had just passed.

"Mom!" yelled Amir. "Mom!"

"Amir, my son. Amir!"

They raced into each other's arms as Amir flung down his belongings. Hajra couldn't stop hugging him, and Amir had to gently extricate himself from her loving embrace.

"Look at you," she said. "You have grown since I last saw you. You even have facial hair. You are a bit thinner I must say, but I will see to that."

Amir's words came out rapid-fire as he tried to tell his mother about what the bus ride was like, while telling her that he hoped Elvir would be joining them in a month, God willing.

"Slow down my precious one," Hajra said. "I want to take you to the house, get you some food and a shower, and we can talk about whatever you want. Let me just hold onto you and never let go!"

Amir, being taller than his mother, put his arm around her shoulders and leaned his head into hers. Both of them cried while they held on for the few blocks it took to get to the house.

The bus Armin was on just then pulled into the UNHCR drop-off area. He had fully expected to accompany Amir until

Elvir arrived. As he looked out of the bus's window, a big grin came to his face. He noticed Amir and whom he was sure was his mother clinging to each other as they disappeared down an alleyway. He hoped that they would meet again soon.

When Hajra and Amir approached the front of the house, a worried Zlata, who wondered where her daughter-in-law had gone while they were out shopping, stared in disbelief.

"Amir," she yelled. "My Amir!" She threw herself at her grandson with arms outstretched and wails of relief echoing throughout the street.

"Majka, Majka," he practically screamed.

When they entered, Halima and Danis, hearing the commotion at the front door, raced toward their brother and smothered him with hugs and kisses. They were soon followed by Azra and Fatima who pounced on Amir, too, with Merjem waiting with outstretched arms.

After a shower and changing into clothes that Zlata had picked up at the Red Cross, Amir ate a hearty meal of burek that Zlata had prepared the day before. Amir scarfed down several.

After the meal, he seemed peculiarly quiet.

"The food was delicious, Majka, and I'm stuffed. I dreamed of your cooking in the camps, and this was the best food I've ever eaten! I can't tell you how happy I am to be here, but I am so tired I can hardly keep my eyes open. Can I lie down for a few minutes?" he said.

"Of course, Amir," said Hajra. "You go into the bedroom and take a nap."

Three hours later, a groggy Amir appeared in the living room where the others were quietly playing cards.

"I can't believe I'm here," Amir whispered. "Majka, do you have any more burek? I guess I'm still hungry."

Hajra beamed at her older son. *My sefe Amir is with us again.* Her heart was filled with joy. She pushed the thought of Elvir out of her mind for the moment, so that she could simply revel at her son's presence.

Danis asked his brother what had happened to him and Elvir.

Amir replied that he wasn't ready to talk about what had happened just yet. He did say, however, that he and Dad survived Omarska and Manjaca mostly together. He said that it was his greatest worry that Dad make it to Karlovac soon because he had been very battered by the months of confinement, and the cold and snow of Manjaca now made it even more difficult for all of the prisoners.

"One other thing I can say. Dad is the strongest person I've ever known."

There was a loss for words by the others at what Amir had just said. The months of agony that he suffered transformed him into a man even at the age of fifteen. Still, Hajra noticed an underlying angst that had developed, simmering below the surface of her son. Of course, there would be, she surmised, after what he had gone through. She knew from the camp at Trnopolje how vulnerable the prisoners were to the whims of the guards. She knew that Omarska was far worse. When he was ready to speak about it, she'd be there for him. She would not push him knowing that he was a teenager still raw from what he had emerged from. She couldn't imagine how horrible this must have been for him.

***

Amir played cards with his siblings and cousins after dinner. The adults spoke about Germany and when they might be able to go. Hajra had a nagging thought. She didn't want to go without Elvir, if in fact he was to be with them soon as Amir had speculated. The uncharted territory that they continued to sail was unnerving, but they had come this far, and she would not allow them to stop their journey to safety, even if it meant that Elvir was not going to be a part of it. She believed in her heart that they would still find each other wherever they lived.

The card games ended and everyone went to bed. Hajra turned off the lights while the snores of the others reverberated throughout the bedroom that was made a slight bit smaller by the arrival of her precious Amir.

Chapter 28
"Finding My Way"

Amir woke up early the next morning a bit disoriented. He half expected to stand up with his head facing downward and his hands behind his back. He wiped the night-sweat from his face and head. Though he couldn't recall what he had dreamed, he knew what triggered it. It took him a moment to realize that he was no longer a prisoner in Manjaca.

He looked around to see that his mother, sister, and brother were still fast asleep. He squinted as he peered through the small window at the daylight just beginning to peek through the frosted glass. His mouth was dry and he desperately needed water. He quietly got up, found the kitchen sink and grabbed a glass from the cabinet. He refilled it with tap water three times and still couldn't get the dryness out of his throat.

He needed to clear his head. He put on pants, a thick sweater, a heavy jacket, woolen cap, and gloves that his mother had put into a closet for him and his father upon their return. At least that's what she'd prayed for, his mother had told him the previous evening.

He found a piece of paper and pencil, and left a note:

Dear Mom,

I woke up early and decided to take a walk around the city. Don't worry. I won't get lost.

Love,

Amir

Amir found a hard-crusted roll in a basket on the kitchen table that he stuffed into his pocket. He silently exited the house as a chilled wind whipped up into his face. He pulled the hood from his jacket over his head and watched his steamy breath float upward into the cold city air.

He made a mental note of where the house was and told himself to be sure to keep track of his route in order not to get lost. There was little in the way of activity with stores and shops still closed.

He passed the army barracks-turned-refugee camp that Danis told him about. The dull beige façade, with its wire perimeter still present to keep locals out he supposed, brought back a flurry of images from his time at Manjaca. He tried to think of other things—anything to quell the pictures in his head. His mind wandered to his father.

I wonder what Dad is doing right now? Is he keeping warm? Did he eat? Is it lonely for him now that so many of us left? I hope he's well. I want to see him here so badly.

At that moment, a few tears welled up in his eyes and dripped onto his cheeks. He wiped them away with his glove and looked to his right to see a park entrance. He noted his location before proceeding into the park.

He strolled down a pathway that paralleled a sluggish river. Moving closer to the river's edge he saw what looked like Ginkgo Biloba trees. He surprised himself by remembering this type of tree from a science class he had taken in high school in Prijedor.

Strange to remember such trivia. I know that these trees are beautiful, especially with their yellow leaves in the fall, but it is also at that time that the female trees begin to shed their leaves and they smell horribly, like dirty socks or worse. Too cold to stink now.

All of a sudden, the smells of the concentration camps and the bus ride from Omarska to Manjaca flooded his senses. In an instant he felt panicked as images of the past several months crashed into him like ocean waves against coastal rocks. There was a bench back on the path and he struggled to find his way twenty meters to reach it.

Sitting down he was able to settle himself and veer away from the dark thoughts by looking upward at the crystalline blue sky with the bright yellow sun creeping upward through the trees.

Remember, Amir, you are free. You are not a prisoner anymore. You are with mom, Halima, Danis, Majka, Merjem and her kids. Breathe. Breathe deeply. Take in the cold, crisp air.

Amir talked himself back into balance though he felt slightly unsteady. He shook his head to convince himself that he had just rid his mind of those demons, at least for now. He recognized that he would need more than head shaking to take control of the loss he had suffered and been witness to in the camps. He promised himself that he would do whatever he needed to in order to stand solidly on the ground once again.

Slowly, he got up and left the park. Though unsure as to whether he'd made the right decision to leave the house, he was still not ready to go back. He wanted to clear his head some more. It occurred to him that he was walking on his own accord, something he used to take for granted before his imprisonment.

Amir wandered away from the city center and stopped at the foot of a hill. Finding a path at the northern end on Dubovac Street, he strode up past a cemetery and meandered up Zagreb Street, noting the beauty of the hills and medieval buildings.

At the top he came to a square castle with a single tower dominating the small fortress. He walked over to the entrance of what was now a museum and picked up a brochure that was lying on the top steps of the closed building. He read a brief description that noted the castle's importance. Apparently, it was a defensive stronghold against the invading Turks of the Ottoman Empire in the Middle Ages.

So, we Turks attacked this fine city, too, did we? It's a wonder that Croatia has let us come here to find our bearings.

He smiled to himself as the thought of being referred to as Turks by both the guards in the camps and the people of Banja Luka as his bus made its way to Manjaca.

The brochure's text next directed his eyes downward so that he could see the Kupa River and Kozjaca Forest that allowed the defending forces a view of the expanse below to repel the approaching armies.

Right then and there he made a vow to himself that even when he felt down or anxious about what had happened to him and so many others, someday when all this ended, he would be a part of making right what had gone so terribly wrong. He was unsure of how. He was angry. He didn't know how to channel that anger just yet. He was not violent by nature. But, if the opportunity arose for revenge, how would he react? How would he defend himself from what the Serbs had done to him, his father, and so many? He would cross that bridge if confronted with that dilemma. He hoped he would make the right choice.

The cold was biting up on the hill, and he could feel his hunger returning. He pulled out the roll and ate it. He stuffed the brochure into his pocket to show his siblings and cousins. Retracing his steps, he headed back down and found his way to the house.

When he got home his mother and the others seemed to lose their furrowed brows as he entered the house, and with some consternation his worried mother gave him a kiss on the forehead.

"Amir, you can't worry us like this. You just got here yesterday, and you haven't had time to do much more than eat dinner and sleep. And it seems your sleep was restless because you were gone well before any of us got up," said Hajra.

"I'm sorry Mom, but I needed some air. Even if it was cold air, I needed to roam free for a bit to think. I see it's only 9:00. Is breakfast still being served?" asked Amir with an expectant look.

"Of course. There is cheese and eggs that Majka kindly made for us all. Sit down and tell us where you went?" his mother asked.

Amir took off his winter coat and wrapped both hands around the coffee mug filled with steaming, hot Turkish coffee with milk that his mother just gave him. He told them where he went and what he saw, and suggested to the children that he would love to take them there whenever they wanted. He pulled out the brochure and gave it to Halima who seemed excited about seeing it. She shared it with the others who agreed that they loved the idea.

Majka put another cup filled with coffee next to him. Both mugs had no handles like he was used to in his home in Kozarac—*a true Bosnian cup*, he thought.

Amir stared at the cup in front of him before taking a sip. Majka made the traditional Bosnian version of the coffee by toasting grounds in a pan with boiling water poured over them, served with a sugar cube on the side so you could sweeten it yourself, if you chose to.

"Do you remember what Dad used to say about Bosnian coffee? He said that our coffee served in a pretty cup, a *fildzan*, had no handles for a reason. And the extra coffee cup," he paused as he pointed to the other one Majka had placed next to him, "the *fildzan viska*, was always served in case a friend showed up or someone was missing from the table that day. The reason our cups have no handles is because they are more democratic. It gave you options as to where to hold it, unlike other cups with a handle, which only allowed you to drink it one way."

His grandmother and mother stared at Amir with awe. How had he become so wise? It was evident that the camps had drained him. But he also seemed much older than when they last saw him. *Still*, thought Hajra, *I will keep an eye on him to make sure that he doesn't stumble while trying to gain his footing back to some sort of normalcy.*

"I wish Dad was here to drink the *fildzan viska*," Amir said when he finished his first sip.

As Hajra reached her arms around her oldest child, she rested her chin upon his head and closed her eyes, squeezing them tightly so that the forming tears did not betray her emotions.

Amir felt his mother's warmth, and it felt good. Still, there was a numbness of feeling hovering close by—perhaps more a confusion of what to feel. After all, he was contending with having gone through the hell of the camps. As he learned quickly on his outing in Karlovac, there would be struggles that he'd have to overcome if he was to move forward in his life. *Like Dad used to tell me, one step at a time, Amir, one step at a time.*

Chapter 29
Leaving Manjaca

It was December 12th and Ajdin's information did not disappoint. The men were told to expect to be leaving within a few days. The next day, buses that were not UNHCR vehicles transported about 500 men out of the camp. Elvir remembered what Ajdin had said about the perceived military combatants that the Serbs were going to transfer to other camps. Of course, even for the remaining men, there was concern that leaving was a ploy—that they were not to find freedom, that some other fate awaited. On the 16th, however, UNHCR buses arrived, and Elvir, Hasan, and hundreds more were told to board for Karlovac.

Elvir gathered the few belongings he had and the men were told to pick up a bag of food after breakfast as they exited the mess tent.

As he was walking toward the stalls, Ajdin came up next to him.

"Goodbye, my friend. I'm going, too, but I am going to find a way immediately to Zagreb. My wife and I planned this long ago and I hope she is at her uncle's house for our rendezvous," Ajdin said.

"I have kept your information secret, but have used it to bolster the mood of the men as I believe was your intention. You can take solace in knowing that your bravery might have saved a good number of us from going crazy. You're a good man, Ajdin. Thank you," replied Elvir.

Ajdin gave Elvir a squeeze on the shoulder as he sped off

into the stall to get ready for his journey. Elvir stopped for a moment to rub his aching leg while he watched a man he admired greatly disappear into the building, understanding that he would likely never see him again.

Elvir was still walking with a limp courtesy of Milan while at Omarska. His thoughts were lost in anticipation of his own departure to Karovac. He reflected upon a message that he had received from his family.

Many prisoners received messages, which the Red Cross brought to be inspected by the camp censors. For what, Elvir didn't know. Did they think that escape plans would come by message? This always amused him. Two sets of two prisoners did actually escape, but that was in no part related to messages received from family. He thought about the escapees. While the two who stole horses and knew the territory well found freedom, the other two were retrieved and tortured.

The message, which he had received a couple of weeks prior, was from Hajra with each child writing a few words of encouragement, including Amir. Knowing that Amir had made it to Karlovac and that he was with Hajra, Halima, Danis and the others warmed his heart. Though they didn't say, he wondered about his father, brother, and Merjem's relatives. The sentiments were mostly about how much they loved him, and that they couldn't wait to be reunited. Amir mentioned that he was waiting for his father to get to Karlovac before telling the family some of what happened to them, but he was just glad that they were all together, and that he hoped his father would join them soon. Hajra noted that they, too, had been in a camp in Trnopolje for over four months, but she seemed to downplay its significance, calling it a detention and deportation center. This left him with an uneasy feeling that she and the children may have encountered the cruelty that he had at Omarska and even, to a much lesser degree, at Manjaca, but if she said more in her communication, chances are he never would have received it. They managed to squeeze all that on the small piece of paper provided by the Red Cross.

As they boarded the bus to Croatia, a snow squall approached the mountain. *A fitting departure,* thought Elvir. Soon, they would be gone from this place. Soon, the concentration camps he had thought he might never leave would be things of the past. However, he pondered, *How can one bury this past?* He understood that it might haunt him forever. He wouldn't focus on that now. He just wanted to be with his family.

Passing through Banja Luka, Elvir pointed out the window to Hasan, who was sitting next to him. They noted to one another the thin crowd, because others were in their warm homes, still managed to jeer at the passengers on the bus. Elvir imagined that this is what Amir had experienced. But, no matter, this was nothing compared to their tenuous lives in the camps. Being called an Ustasha mother or Turk barely registered for him. That people felt such animus toward Muslims and Croats was no longer shocking, but it was still disturbing. He knew that he wanted to return to Kozarac, but he had learned a while ago that there was nothing to return to after the Bosnian Serb army got through with its murderous rampage and deportations.

Mostly, the bus ride was quiet. Some passengers slept and others stared out of the window. He and Hasan barely spoke as both were clearly lost in their own thoughts.

These were the thoughts that all refugees had. Leaving one's country, the only country either man had known, was like nothing they had ever felt. Their lives, at least before the war, were on a trajectory that was steeped in their communities in Bosnia. Never had there been a time that they would desire to live elsewhere. But the past six months had changed all that. And the future was quite uncertain, likely quite unstable, at least for a while. Their quietude on the bus ride was more representational of an emptiness. Raw were the emotions of the recent past. Hope was what they wanted to feel. They were somewhere in between.

Hajra's message, read back at Manjaca prior to Elvir's exodus, had vaguely mentioned that her family was now in Germany. He had never thought about leaving Bosnia. But with the war continuing to rage and no end in sight, and surviving non-Serbs being expelled and deported, it was not safe.

One step at a time. Let me just hug my wife and my children first. We'll make the rest fall into place. That was his desire. The deep despair still hollowed him out. Trying to make sense of the past six months was impossible. The Serb violence would never make sense, but he wondered what the effects of his and Amir's experiences would do to them? He wondered if Hajra, Halima and Danis had endured similar horrors and how they were managing. More unknowns to be conquered. He would be with them to help his family rise above it. *We have little choice BUT to rise above it.*

Crossing the border from Bosnia had been their moment to finally exhale. They had left Serb-held territory headed to freedom, and changing buses for their next leg to Karlovac felt like walking on air. Elvir noticed the UN peacekeepers maintaining watch over them for the transfer.

Arriving in Karlovac was a dizzying experience. After leaving the conditions of Manjaca, being escorted by police with lights swirling atop their cars, hundreds of people shouting words of encouragement lining the streets, and hundreds more gathering at the UNHCR building, it was quite overwhelming.

They had all been informed that if no family and friends were present, they would go to the canteen, and then the barracks to sleep. But the messages that Elvir and Hasan had received from their loved ones assured them otherwise.

Elvir and Hasan gathered their things and walked down the steps of the bus with their comrades. The shouting from family members and friends awaiting the newly arrived of what seemed like at least a dozen buses, pierced the chilled evening air.

The names of the newcomers wafted amidst the joyous crowd as those awaiting tried to catch the attention of those disembarking from the buses. Elvir heard his name being called by Amir among the cacophony of dizzying sounds. He peered to his right and there, right next to him was Danis, who had detached himself from his mother's hand, followed quickly by the others. They hugged, and cried, and hugged and cried some more. Hajra grabbed her husband's arm and guided him away from the crowd with Halima on his other arm. They made their way to a street corner where Elvir spotted Hasan.

"Hasan, Hasan!" Elvir shouted. "I want you to meet my family. And Amir is here."

Elvir introduced his family, and Hasan did the same. Amir practically knocked Hasan over with a fierce bear hug. As everyone exchanged warm greetings, Hasan slightly pivoted back toward Amir.

"Hana and Kenan, this is Amir. He has become my nephew over the last months and he is now part of our family."

Amir bowed upon meeting his wife. He mussed up the hair of the young boy, who shied away, a little embarrassed.

"My uncle, it is so good to see you!" Amir said.

"The same, my nephew," he said.

"Hasan, you look good. They must have fed you well with their cevapi and burek," Amir teased.

"Of course they did. Just what they gave us when you were there. You look well, my boy. I'm sure it's good to be with your family. And now, you have your father back. We do have some things to be thankful for, don't we?"

Hasan continued, "You should be with your family now. But I'll be in touch, so that we can see each other again. Go. Help your father. The old man needs someone to lean on."

Amir laughed. "OK, Uncle. I'll see you soon. Nice to meet

you, Hana and Kenan."

"Hasan," said Elvir, "I'm staying with my sister-in-law's cousin here in Karlovac. Hajra wrote down the address for you. When you get settled in, you guys should come by. Nice to finally meet you, Hana. Take care, my brother."

"You, too. I'll see you soon, God willing. I'm glad to have met the rest of your family," replied Hasan.

After giving each other warm hugs, the two families departed from the UNHCR compound and headed in separate directions.

The six Kovacevics, which included Zlata, clung to each other as they laughed and cried their way to the house. As he surveyed the scene before him, Elvir's one dominant thought was—*Miracles can happen; yes, they can.*

***

With her family staying behind to allow the others to embrace the special moment of being reunited, Merjem, Azra and Fatima flung themselves into Elvir's arms when he entered the house. Though he tried not to limp too noticeably, Danis asked his father why he dragged his right leg like that.

"No need for Dad to tell you right now, Danis, he's so tired and there will be plenty of time for that," said a protective Amir.

"Alright," said Danis, "I was just wondering."

Elvir was drained. It was as if the past six months literally took the life out of him. He was overwhelmed to be with his family. For most of the time he was in the camps, doubt often crept into his subconscious about ever seeing them again.

They all engaged in some small-talk, unsure of how to tread. Hajra stared at her husband with a glow in her eyes that was visible to the others.

After a couple of burek and tea, Elvir excused himself to take a shower and change into clean clothes that Hajra and the children picked out from the Red Cross donation bin. He emerged from the bathroom with an unfamiliar feeling of cleanliness and warmth, though he mentioned to his family that he believed it would take months to truly be clean.

Hajra cleared away the two couch pillows and beckoned Elvir to sit next to her and Zlata. The others sat just below them on the floor in rapt attention. They understood from Amir that it was a very, very difficult time for the two of them, especially for his father in Omarska. They hesitated to probe too deeply about what he'd experienced.

Elvir spoke.

"The last time I had burek was at my cousin's house when we had the picnic by the river. All that food was so delicious. It was so familiar, so us. It was kind of the calm before the storm that day, I guess. I don't think any of us truly wanted to believe that we'd go through what we did, and it is still happening in our country. We were quite naïve. When I got depressed in the camps, one of the things I thought about was that day. It was beautiful, really. And the food, oh that food. It was what I wanted if I got out. And I wanted it to be on a mild day, at the river, with my precious family safe and sound. That was my fantasy. Anyway, this evening's burek was wonderful. Hvala Mom."

Zlata leaned into her son, as he hugged her tightly. The lump in her throat had to be suppressed. She didn't want to lose it in front of everyone in order that Elvir ease into his new surroundings. The tissue Hajra handed her would have to suffice for now.

Elvir kept his arm around his mother.

"I can't believe that I'm here with you. I am so thankful. The past six months have been the most difficult of my life. Thank God, Amir and I relied upon each other as best we could to get through most of it. He is a most amazing young man."

"Amir told us a little, Dad, but it's just so great to have you here with us. That's all that really matters," said Halima.

"It is great to be together," he replied to his daughter.

"Dad," asked Amir, "I've seen some of our friends from Kozarac here. I ran into Mehmed from my soccer team, believe it or not. He was with his sister. His cousin, Amela met them here recently, and they said they're going to the Netherlands where his mother's brother and family live. I'm happy for them. He didn't tell me where he'd been, and I didn't tell him about the camps. I was just happy to see him."

"That's wonderful. I liked that boy. He was very polite and pretty mature. I could always have an interesting conversation with him, though it was usually about obscure facts he had concerning one European soccer team or another. He'd get so animated."

"Yeah, I remember. It was great to see him, but no talk about soccer this time. I was glad that they are going to the Netherlands. It seems that most of us will have to go somewhere from here. Might as well be to a country with good soccer. Did you get our message when you were at Manjaca?"

"I sure did. It gave me great hope."

"Well, Germany has great soccer, too," he said as he chuckled.

"It certainly does."

Zlata had been silently listening to the banter. But all that was on her mind was to tell her son about his father. She knew he would want to know why he wasn't there. She asked the others to excuse her and Elvir—that she needed to speak with her son. While the others cleaned up, Elvir and his mother went into the downstairs bedroom and closed the door.

She took a deep breath and haltingly told Elvir of his father's fate, including how she got to Karlovac. He listened intently, but then pulled his mother close to him.

"You were so brave, Mom. I'm having trouble digesting how you made it here. And I'm also so sad about what happened to dad. I'm in shock hearing this. On my last phone call with him when we were all still living in our homes..."

Elvir had to gather his composure to resume.

"...I'm so sorry, Mom. I'm just so sorry."

He couldn't believe his father was gone just for being Muslim. This news hit him hard. He wiped the tears from his eyes before he spoke.

"Dad knew many people and they all loved him. He was gregarious and generous, and held no animosity toward anyone. There is no making sense of what they did to him—to us all."

Zlata hugged her son, and suggested they join the others. They exited the bedroom to find the TV on, and the rest of the group quietly talking. They became silent when Zlata and Elvir emerged.

Hajra went over to her husband and mother-in-law and hugged them both.

"Sit down, you two. Come enjoy the warmth of being together," she said.

Elvir needed to know about his brother. He hesitated because he knew how raw he felt, and Merjem and her children might be hesitant to say anything. But on their walk back from the bus drop-off, he briefly asked Hajra if she'd heard about Tarik, and she said that nothing had been known. She also mentioned that Merjem wanted to tell Elvir about him because she knew he'd be anxious to know.

He turned toward Merjem and spoke.

"Hajra said you wanted to tell me about my brother. Do you want to wait for another day? I'm fine with it whenever you are comfortable doing so."

It was Azra who spoke first.

"I know Mom wants to tell you, but I just want to say how great it is to see you, Uncle Elvir. You look a lot like my dad."

This took the group aback a bit, and Zlata grabbed another tissue.

"Azra, I'm glad to be here. And glad that I remind you of your dad. I miss him, too. I want him back with us. Are you and Fatima OK if your mom tells me a little about what she knows?"

"Sure, Uncle," they both responded.

Merjem began. Before she spoke, she gathered her two girls and pulled them close.

"I don't know, Elvir. We ask the Red Cross almost daily, but they have no news to give us. I'm worried sick, we all are, but hopeful that he escaped or was sent elsewhere that didn't have a registry."

"What do you mean escaped?" asked Elvir.

Hajra answered, as she could see that Merjem was clearly distressed.

"The kids and I saw him in the camp in Trnopolje. Often, the guard, Miroslav—you remember him, the mailman—he was one of the few to treat us with some level of dignity. But I'll tell you more about Trnopolje at a later time. Anyway, he would allow the ones who slept in the school to be with those outside, though we still had to be careful not to call attention to ourselves. Most of the people there slept outside, especially those transferred from another camp. We were put in a classroom to sleep. Miroslav didn't mind if we mingled with the men by the fence, as Danis referred to them. About a month or so after our arrival at the camp, we noticed Tarik standing among the group. We couldn't believe it. He told us about Keraterm, the place he was in. For some reason the Serbs transferred a couple of hundred prisoners from that camp to Trnopolje. Tarik had a tough time in Keraterm, to say the least, as I suspect you and Amir did in Omarska. But then, he and several others were not there four days later. They disappeared. Merjem and Esma check in with the Red Cross daily to see if his name comes up on the registry, but nothing so far."

"And I have my own story of how Uncle Tarik took care of me one day when I hid behind a shed," said Danis.

"That was a very difficult day. Danis, can we tell Dad about that a little later?"

"Sure. That's fine, Mom."

Elvir interjected with a deep sigh.

"I want to hear about that. Is it OK if we talk about that later?"

Danis nodded affirmatively.

He turned his attention back to the others and continued.

"I won't speculate what happened to him, but it is definitely concerning. Definitely."

Merjem was staring at the carpet below her; silent.

Hajra changed the subject to the ITN news reports.

"In early August, a team of news reporters from the UK showed up to film and ask questions. I even saw one of Tarik's police colleagues, who apparently had just been transferred from Keraterm, speak to them.

"The British reporters were at Omarska, too. I don't know if Amir told you? But we all suspected that this is why we were transferred to Manjaca."

"I told them, Dad. I also told them about Jusuf, and Hasan, too," Amir said.

"Because of the reports, the camp in Trnopolje changed for the better. Their revelations are definitely why we are all here today," said Hajra.

"These reporters are heroes. I'm grateful that we are together, too. Perhaps someday Tarik will be with us?" said Merjem.

"I'm hopeful too. I miss my brother very much. Let's keep checking with UNHCR. I can do that, too," added Elvir who suddenly found he had to force back a lump in his throat.

"Thank you," said a drained-looking Merjem who went over to hug her brother-in-law.

The conversation had come to an end. Elvir said that he needed to sleep. He was overwhelmed by all that had transpired, and after hugging his family goodnight, he excused himself to the bedroom.

Hajra escorted Elvir as he went to lie on their bed.

"I love you, Elvir. I don't know how you or we survived to this point. But we are together. Sleep well. I'll join you shortly."

Elvir told his wife how much he missed her and loved her. So much had happened to them all. Was he really with his family? Was this a dream? His exhaustion almost made it difficult to fathom this reality.

He laid down, and within thirty seconds, he fell into the deep, dark sleep of the dead.

Chapter 30
Hajra and Merjem

They had been reunited in Karlovac for over a month. It was late January and the typical winter in the Balkans prevailed. Snow, cold, and a steel-gray wintry sky that seemed to never let up. The visits by the adults to the UNHCR office tapered off. It was becoming pointless and futile to perpetually hear no word of Tarik's status other than "Sorry, nothing yet." They got the same response when asking about Merjem's parents and brothers.

The families had settled into a routine of sorts, but it was an economic strain on Ivan, who despite having a reasonably paying job working for the Red Cross, he could not support eleven people even with the generous help for refugees from the Croatian government. Besides, Elvir and Hajra did not want to feel like a burden to people who had gone out of their way to provide them with a safe and loving place to live.

Television news reported about the war and the atrocities that kept mounting in Bosnia, which were unrelenting. In fact, there were definitive reports about the Bosnian Army fighting with and against the Croat Army in Central Bosnia at the same time. It was hard to keep track of the dizzying political realities in the region. Though Karlovac felt safe enough, after the trauma that Elvir's and Merjem's families had survived, the small city was too close to the heart of the new tension. And there were reports that the fighting might get close to the city.

It was about that time that Karlovac was beginning to become overrun with refugees, mostly Muslims. There were many reports of Bosnian Serb atrocities against Muslims and escape, when possible, and deportations were the only out. Even with so-called "safe zones" in Bosnia now being established in certain parts of the country by the UN, the dangers persisted.

In the meantime, Hajra had periodic phone calls with her family in Dusseldorf. Her brothers and parents reported that they felt safe and welcomed. The German government continued to open itself to those fleeing Bosnia.

"Elvir," Hajra said one chilly January morning after speaking with her brother Harun, "Esma and Ivan are wonderful, and they have been so good to us. I don't know how to repay them. But I think we should consider a move to Germany. We have to put in a request with the Red Cross to start the process. Having family in the country will give us a greater possibility of relocating there instead of some other place that Bosnia and Croatia have agreements with. Harun and the others say that it is a special country, and there are many like us living there. He says they walk the streets to parks and stores. The kids go to school, and it is two blocks away, so they can walk. They speak Bosnian in their apartment building to all their neighbors, all of whom are refugees, some of whom they knew from Banja Luka. And they are taking German language classes. It sounds wonderful."

"I've been thinking about the same thing, sweetheart. I've been reading about it. There are other countries that will take us in, too, but being with your family would be a true blessing for all of us. I know that Merjem is reluctant to leave Croatia hoping that Tarik will come here, but my hopes faded a while ago. I'm also not feeling so safe here in Croatia because of the fighting this country is engaged in," Elvir responded, running his hand nervously through his hair.

"Frankly, I'm not either. We need to get our family as far away as possible. I think I can convince Merjem to come with us. We know that Tarik's name is in the Red Cross and UN databases, so if he does show up, we'll know about it," Hajra replied while picking at a nail on her left index finger.

"And with what we fear happened to my brother, I feel it's important for Merjem and the girls to be with us," said Elvir.

"I'll speak with her," said Hajra.

Later that day, Hajra asked Merjem to join her for a walk away from the city center just to get some air. The two bundled up before leaving the house. It was a still day, so the cold did not slice through them as it normally did when the wind picked up.

"Merjem," said Hajra, "you're like a sister to me. Your children are like my own. As you know, I've been speaking with my family in Germany. They say it is wonderful there for Bosnians. They say they don't feel like refugees because the government and the people are so welcoming. And most importantly, it's safe. Safe for our children, which is ultimately what any parent wants for their children."

Merjem replied, "I see where you're going with this. You want to move there. I don't blame you. To be reunited with your family will be wonderful. I encourage you to go. I'd miss you and Elvir, the kids and Zlata very much. But you should go."

"I know that you want to see if Tarik will come back. And when you told me that you now believe your parents and brothers were killed in their home, it sickened me. It stays with me always. When we saw Tarik in the camp, I was hopeful that he had survived the worst. But then he was taken to who knows where after Trnopolje. I know that you want to believe he'll be with us soon, and of course so do I. I guess I'm appealing to you now. Zlata is the closest you have to a mother, and she is your children's majka, and my parents are in Dusseldorf. Your children would have grandparents, cousins, aunts and uncles that would ease the pain of your loss a little. Elvir and I would like you to come to Germany with us. We feel that we live too close to what happened to us, and wars in

Bosnia continue to rage. We are stuck right now, not able to start new lives. My older brother in Germany has written a 'guarantee letter' that will help us get a short-term visa to move there. And many of us are moving there because there are jobs, and we can start rebuilding our lives."

Merjem was not ready for this conversation. She knew that Hajra and Elvir were contemplating leaving Karlovac for Dusseldorf, but she hadn't considered that they would plead for her to go, too. In fact, she had not considered leaving as an option for herself. Tarik may still be out there somewhere, and she wanted to be in Karlovac, giving him access from Bosnia without having to travel to a distant country in Western Europe.

Merjem stopped and faced her sister-in-law.

"I'm so grateful that you would ask us to come with you. But I have mixed emotions. In some ways, I didn't want to think about it actually, even though we've talked about Germany in many conversations at Esma's house. I didn't want to leave until I knew about Tarik, so why entertain the thought? What if Tarik crosses into Croatia? What if he finds us in Karlovac? I don't know. Please let me think about your offer."

"Why would we not ask you? You mean the world to us, and your children and mine, despite the age difference, have a special bond. Azra especially looks up to Halima. She tells me she wants to be like her when she gets older, and we love your children so much."

"One more thing," Hajra continued, "Elvir and I are beside ourselves with grief over not knowing where Tarik is. He was such a brave and loving man. I apologize, is such a brave and loving man. Still, I hesitated to tell you this, but I'm going to do so now."

Resuming their walk, Hajra once again paused at a quiet spot near the city park entrance and spoke.

"Yesterday, I ran into a woman who I was acquainted with

in Kozarac. She and I would exchange small talk in the market. She was pleasant enough, but seemed to always be in a hurry. Anyway, she was in less of a hurry this time. We were glad to see each other, being from the same city. It was even a reminder of the normalcy that used to exist there. I told her about what happened to Elvir, me and the kids. Not too much detail; I just don't have the energy for all that. But she told me about her husband. Apparently, he was in Keraterm. He was also transferred to Trnopolje, she believes, though I wouldn't have known he was there because I'd never met him. What she then told me gave me chills. She'd heard that there were many like her husband who disappeared after Trnopolje. I didn't say anything about Tarik, but this news sent my mind reeling back to when we last saw him. I couldn't speak anymore, I just kept thinking about Tarik. I told her how sorry I was to learn of this, and then went home and told Elvir. He was quite shaken, too, but we both have grave concerns about what's happened to Tarik. It saddens me to tell you this, but I thought it important that you know."

Merjem turned pale. She went very quiet and turned away from Hajra. When she turned back around, she hugged her sister-in-law.

"I know that there is a strong possibility that we may never see my husband again. I must keep up some semblance of hope. He could be fighting with our army, or in prison in Gradiska or some other place awaiting an exchange for Serb soldiers. Though it pains me to hear about your friend, and I'm not saying that her story is untrue at all, I'm just not ready to give up on Tarik."

"Elvir and I are not either. But we want you to come to Germany with us. We can make sure that we check with whatever sources there are in Dusseldorf to see if he shows up on the registries. If he does, since he is your husband, it will be possible to apply for family reunification, so he can join us."

They walked back to the house in silence. Hajra was

unsure if she'd penetrated Merjem's emotional armor. She desperately wanted for her and the children to come with them. She was sure Merjem's ambivalence needed some time to work itself out—either way. She also worried about Merjem's mental health, which Hajra noticed had taken a turn downward in recent weeks.

Hajra assumed that Merjem was understandably feeling anxious about the unknowns surrounding Tarik. After all, everyone was upset about this, particularly Azra and Fatima. She put herself in Merjem's shoes and knew that she would be quite reluctant to leave, too, if Elvir was gone. Still, she would keep a closer eye on her and make sure to be aware of Merjem's fragile psyche.

Chapter 31
Germany

It was late March of 1993, and with a tearful goodbye to Esma, Ivan, and the baby; Elvir, Hajra, Zlata and the children, and Merjem and her children, boarded the train to their new home. The night before happened to be Amir's sixteenth birthday, but it was a bittersweet celebration.

Leaving Croatia for Germany meant being farther removed from Bosnia. Leaving and not knowing the fate of Tarik was even harder. However, Merjem had concluded that if he was alive, he would find them. She would make sure of it.

The train took over seventeen hours to reach its destination at Dusseldorf Central Station. It passed through Zagreb, Vienna, Frankfurt, and Cologne with transfers to connecting trains at all of them.

With each stop, the enormity of the stations was matched equally by the significance of what they were doing. The children were told to stay close to the adults. Their senses were overwhelmed by the architecture, which was quite foreign to them ranging from neoclassical to ultramodern.

Merjem was very quiet most of the trip. Initially, she peered at the seats across the aisle to make sure her girls were doing well, and to inquire about their hunger or thirst, telling them to ask if they needed anything. Zlata, sensing Merjem's melancholy, insisted that her daughter-in-law not worry—that she brought plenty of snacks for them, and would make sure they were taken care of. Beyond that, Merjem mostly stared out of the window or slept.

Danis and Halima pointed out the changing topography of the landscape as they moved further and further away from Croatia. Azra and Fatima were more impressed with the cities and towns they were seeing along the route, noting how different it was in Western Europe.

Hajra and Elvir were preoccupied themselves until Hajra broke the silence about two hours into the trip.

"I'm so excited to be reuniting with my family," Hajra said softly. "But I'm afraid I'm lost in deep thought about what we've been through, and what the future will bring."

"Me too. I see these cities we're passing through, and they are so different from where we lived. And then it triggers thoughts of Kozarac. It's strange, but our city, and Bosnia itself is kind of a blur to me. Being in the camps seemed to blot out the good that we had at home. I can't really explain it."

"I feel this way, too. It's so hard to take all of this in—to take all of how our lives have been upended—and make sense out of any of it. I guess we just need to start with the fact that we're together again, and moving to a safe place, with possibilities that we didn't have not too long ago. As you used to say, one step at a time. That's the best strategy for us right now."

"I miss our lives before all of this."

Hajra put her arm through her husband's and leaned her head on his shoulder. Elvir gave his wife a quick kiss on top of her head before peering out of the window again to wonder what the next step would bring.

The children were especially enamored with the station in Cologne with its ceiling of interwoven metal and glass. They all stepped off the train to get some sodas and chocolate. They had an hour to kill before the last leg of their journey. Danis, Azra, and Fatima had it with sitting on a train. Accompanied by their Majka, who told them to stay close where she could see them, they played tag in an empty area of the station away from other passengers for a much-needed release of pent-up energy. Their excitement was heightened by being only a half hour from their destination.

With fifteen minutes before departure, Elvir went over to his mother and the children to gather them all up.

"Thanks for keeping an eye on the kids. How are you doing?"

"Well, I'm fine I guess. Truth be told, I miss your father. I wish he was here with us. If he had only believed that our lives were in danger, he would be moving to Germany, too. The children have been a good distraction for me. Still, I miss him so much."

Elvir put his arm around his mother as they followed the children who raced back to the train.

When they arrived at Dusseldorf Central train station, they all stood up and gathered their belongings. The children retrieved their backpacks from an overhead bin and slipped them on. The adults ushered the kids through the aisle and down the steps that led to the platform.

They were to be on the lookout for Hajra's brothers, wives, and the children's two cousins. Her parents were waiting for them back at their apartment, getting everything ready for their arrival.

The bright lights and mass of people, both disembarking and waiting to board other trains, was dizzying. Aside from Elvir, none of them had ever taken a train, no less having to navigate a crowded, noisy urban station.

"Stay close," shouted Elvir to the children.

Fatima closed in on her mother, leaning against her with such force that Merjem was briefly knocked off balance. They walked now as if one connected being. The people and sounds overwhelmed their senses as they tried to follow the lines of passengers into the main terminal.

"It's OK," Merjem said to Fatima, "look over there, the station worker is pointing to signs that tell us where to go."

When they arrived at their destination in the center of the terminal, Ahmed and Amina were spotted first behind a roped off area for those awaiting arrivals. Soon, the rest of the family gathered from another nearby waiting area and the celebration began. Within minutes of exiting the train, they were all together.

The reunion was marked by non-stop kissing and hugging. Hajra, especially, was "moved to a thousand tears," as Elvir would later tease her. They left the station to find the number 42 bus for the twenty-minute ride to the family's apartment building.

"Mom made a fantastic meal for all of us to celebrate your moving here. She was so nervous wanting to make sure everything was perfect. You know Mom," said Ahmed.

The children were ogling over the sights of the city on the ride pointing out a park, a huge McDonald's Hamburgers, and the well-known department store, Galeria kaufhof Konigsallee.

"I want a Big Mac," screamed Danis.

"In time," said Hajra. "Let's have some of our own delicious Bosnian food that awaits you, first," she replied.

The bus arrived at their stop and they quickly lowered themselves down the steps onto the street.

"Just a one block walk," said Amina to the children, now practically running as Ahmed pointed them in the right direction.

Ahmed yelled for the children to stop—that they were in front of the apartment. As the adults caught up, they all entered the four-story brick building. The aromas inside were that of wonderful Bosnian food, and the language of their native country echoed up and down the hallways. The city was certainly different from what they were used to, including their recent stay in Karlovac, but inside the apartment building they were met with a familiarity that put everyone at ease.

They walked up to the third floor. Hajra's parents had

heard the commotion as the group came upstairs, and they were waiting at the open door.

"Praised be God," shouted Safija as she wrapped the children up in her arms. They could hardly get inside the apartment with all of the hugging and kissing and crying going on. They were met with the smells of Safija's scrumptious meal of dolmas, Begova Corba, and Cevapi, which Safija remembered was Amir's favorite.

"Please put your bags in our bedroom," said Nedim.

"Babo, I need to go to the bathroom badly. Where is it please?" a squirmy Danis said to his grandfather.

"Right over there," he chuckled. "Please, all of you feel free to freshen up before we eat Nana's delicious food."

Nedim was scrambling around making sure that everyone was taken care of.

"Water? There's a container and glasses over there. Bathroom? Just follow Danis. Here's a closet to put your jackets in. Please put your belongings in our bedroom for now."

Hajra grabbed her mother around the waist and kissed the back of her neck several times. She then hugged her father, who was still directing traffic in the apartment.

"It's a miracle, Mom," she said. "I've been counting the minutes until we were actually in the same place together again. Germany. Who would ever have thought this is where 'together' would be?"

As the chatter, hugs, and kisses continued to permeate the reunion, Safija called everyone to the table.

"You must be hungry. Please. I've been cooking all morning"

Dinner was delicious. It was made better because they were together. The banter and laughter were infectious. There was a notable release of whatever worry the journey brought to both those from Karlovac, and those in Dusseldorf.

After the dessert of some sweets and coffee, Safija, Amina

and her daughter, Jasmina cleaned up, insisting that the others relax after their arduous trip. The children gathered in their grandparents' bedroom. There were now seven of them ranging in age, practically spilling out of the small room. Sweet laughter emerged, and Jasmina shared the few stuffed animals with her younger cousins that she had brought from her family's apartment on the fourth floor.

The three older teenagers, including Amir, huddled near each other awkwardly. Halima, soon to turn thirteen, toggled between her younger cousins and Danis, and the older ones. Hamza was now eighteen and Jasmina was sixteen, same as Amir. They spoke Bosnian, but the two siblings occasionally tried out their German. They told their younger cousins all about school, the neighborhood, and the building they lived in, which had only refugees from Bosnia.

While the children were becoming reacquainted, the adults sat in the living room, which was next to the kitchen, drinking coffee and talking about life in Germany. Harun described where they all lived in the building. Ahmed and Amina, and their teenagers Hamza and Jasmina lived on the fourth floor, while he and his wife, Asla lived in this apartment with Safija and Nedim. Amina was the first to move the conversation to a more personal level.

"We are so happy that you're here. We want you to know that we'll do anything to help you settle in. In fact, it's been agreed upon by all of us that Ahmed and I will take you to the government office to help you complete the process of applying for a permanent visa. But we are all here for you. Soon, we'll caravan over to your apartment and get you set up there.".

"Thank you," said Elvir, "Our lives have not been settled for what feels like an eternity. I'll be nice to have our own place again."

"I know that you've heard some of it, but needless to say, our lives had been, well...upended until we got to Karlovac," said Hajra.

"That's an understatement," Elvir responded..

"We're so saddened about Besim, and...the others," Nedim said, staring at a small stain on the carpet below him.

Merjem replied, "Nedim, please don't feel cautious when you're speaking with us. You all were so wise to get out before Banja Luka became the nightmare that we experienced in Prijedor. Tarik and I considered leaving, too, but it was too late. The decision for me to leave Karlovac with Hajra and Elvir was so difficult, but in the end, I had to do what was best for the girls. I still hope that my husband will show up one day, but I am realistic, too. Each day that passes is a day that distances me from that hope. The girls miss him terribly, and Fatima cries herself to sleep many nights. All I can do is be strong for them. I'm grateful to be able to be here with everyone. And I recognize that I am not the only one who has suffered."

As she said those words, Merjem wondered if she sounded more like her strong sister-in-law, Hajra. *Who am I kidding?* she thought. Yes, she moved to Germany for the children. And yes, being surrounded by family, even if they were not blood relatives, was good, but she still ached at leaving Tarik. She could sometimes tamp it down, but her heart was often drenched in an almost immobilizing sadness. And when the kids were asleep, she would occasionally binge on red wine.

Zlata moved over to where Merjem was seated and placed her warm, comforting hands over her daughter-in-law's.

After a brief moment of silence Danis came bounding out of the bedroom.

"Hamza said that there is a park near us, and that we can go ice skating on a pond!"

The adults were thankful for the boy's enthusiastic interruption during a solemn moment, and Harun beckoned the newly-arrived to gather themselves and the kids to head over to their apartments.

"Babo and Nana," Halima, who just emerged from the bedroom, asked her grandparents, "are you coming?"

"I'm going to stay to clean up some more, and Babo is probably tired from all the excitement. But I think the rest of you are walking the three short blocks to your new home. Bundle up, though, it's cold here in Dusseldorf."

"Not much different than in Bosnia," Halima replied.

Hajra told the children to retrieve their suitcases and backpacks to bring to their new place. As the families exited the door, Hajra lingered for just a moment.

"Mom and Dad, I am so happy to be here. We've had the most difficult time in our lives, which goes without saying, I guess. But to be here with you, even if in an unfamiliar place, is something I couldn't have fathomed just a couple of months ago."

Misty-eyed, the three hugged goodbye knowing that they could see each other freely and as often as they wanted.

Chapter 32
New Lives

The apartment building was a lot like the one Hajra's family lived in. The German government made them feel welcomed, it was true. It was a four-floor walk-up with two types of apartments: the one for Elvir and family on the second floor had a common area, two bedrooms, one bathroom, and a kitchen. They were on the second floor. Amir and Danis shared the smaller bedroom. An accordion divider was placed in the common area separating Halima's "room." It had a rolling cot and a small chest of drawers. Halima was always accommodating, so she was fine with this set-up, especially knowing that her parents said they hoped to move to a larger place at some point. Zlata insisted on a single bed in the same room with her granddaughter.

Merjem, Fatima, and Azra were on the fourth floor, and their place had three rooms with one bedroom that they shared.

The government provided vouchers for food, clothing and a monthly stipend for incidentals. The children were to go to school, including having a tutor to teach them to speak German. The language lessons were in an after-school program with mostly Bosnian refugees, though there were a few others from Turkey, and one each from the Congo and Senegal.

Late one night when the children were sleeping, Elvir turned to a wide awake Hajra.

"I miss making love with you, but we have not only not

had the opportunity, but I'm afraid."

"Afraid. Why?"

Elvir took a deep breath.

"I know what you told me about Trnopolje and you being...being assaulted."

It was clear Elvir struggled to find a word that wouldn't sound so awful, though it may have been as much for his own protection as Hajra's. And, disturbing images of what he knew happened to the women in Omarska crept into his consciousness.

"I don't know how to approach you, to make you feel loved, not violated. I don't know how to put it into words, but I don't want you to feel you have to do anything here if it makes you uncomfortable."

"My love, you're my husband. You're my rock. We were both tortured, in different ways, but nonetheless both dehumanized as you've rightfully referred to our treatment. I miss your touch. I miss you holding me close. I miss us. I miss feeling loved."

It was dark and still, but Hajra could sense Elvir's tenuous smile. He moved closer and began to caress her body with his hands. As she responded, the two became one, quietly, gently, yet intensely, finding their way back to the complete beings that had been missing for so long.

***

It was three years from the day they stepped onto German soil. The children all spoke fairly fluent German, but since their apartment building was inhabited by only Bosniaks, the Bosnian language was still the tongue of choice while there. This fact made German quite difficult for the adults when they went into the city. The children and their cousins chose to speak mostly German, much to the chagrin of their parents and grandparents, but they had gone from being Bosnian to

Bosnian-German, they said. Still, at home they spoke mostly Bosnian with their parents.

Much had happened.

The U.S.-brokered Dayton Accords found some measure of peace in the Balkans, though it was understood by all parties that no one was particularly satisfied. The three sides: Serbs, Croats, and Bosniaks a now-used more historically accurate name for Bosnian Muslims, reached an agreement to stop the killing, but the distribution of the land, which included the new Republika Srpska carved out in Bosnia, with a shared central government in Sarajevo, was cause for angst on all sides. Prijedor municipality was now part of the new Republic. It was estimated that over 100,000 Bosnians were killed, 80% of whom were Bosniaks. Equally chilling was that some estimates revealed that up to 50,000 Bosnian women and girls were raped and sexually assaulted. Millions of people were displaced from their homes in Bosnia resulting in many going to live in countries that welcomed them. The Kovacevics, and Hajra's parents and siblings just got a head start.

Elvir had found a job in a local textile's factory on the assembly line. The money was not good, but it was something, and it kept him busy. Hajra got a part time job in housekeeping at a hotel in their neighborhood. Since the stipend from the German government had ended requiring refugees to find work to support themselves, the money she brought in helped somewhat. They had moved to a bigger apartment not far from Merjem, who had remained in their original dwelling.

Amir was attending his last year of gymnasium, a university preparatory high school program for those students with the highest marks, providing a well-rounded education to bright students who tested into it. He also continued to take English classes and was becoming quite proficient, practicing with his dad, too. Halima and Danis attended the middle levels in the gymnasium. Their cousins Azra and Fatima were well on their way to the same program, as both excelled academically.

Merjem struggled.

She bounced around to a few jobs at nursing facilities as an aide. She was very good with older people, but showing up to work on-time was her challenge. Babo and Nana, as they were now called by Azra and Fatima, took care of the children after school while Merjem was at work. They were delighted to do so. But numerous times they expressed their concerns about Merjem to Hajra and Elvir. Merjem stated to her brother-in-law and sister-in-law that she was fine, just a little tired. Privately, the two worried deeply about her, but were at a loss for what to do except to be available when the girls called upon them.

Merjem had still not given up on Tarik being alive. It was difficult for anyone to discuss otherwise with her. This clearly had an impact on her life and those close to her. Hajra implored Merjem to seek professional help. However, denial runs deep.

One morning, the children couldn't wake their mother. She smelled of alcohol and was unresponsive. Azra called 112, and an ambulance was dispatched to their apartment. She then called Hajra who was getting ready for work.

"Aunt Hajra," she screamed into the phone, "please come here, Mom won't wake up. She's breathing, but she smells of alcohol. I called 112 and the ambulance is on its way."

Hajra shouted for Elvir to tell him what just happened. He called his boss to say that he would not be coming in that day.

The two ran out of their apartment just a few blocks to where Merjem and the kids lived. Their arrival coincided with the emergency medical van.

"Come with us," said a panting Hajra. "It's my sister-in-law you've been called for."

The paramedics brought medical equipment up the four flights of stairs to Merjem where they found the children frantically hovering around their mother, who was still not moving.

The paramedics asked about medications in the apartment. Fatima showed them what their mom was taking. One of the pill bottles, the one with anti-anxiety medications, was empty when it had been half full a few days before. There was an empty bottle of German wine that was on the floor just under the bed.

Merjem was placed on a gurney and into the ambulance. Hajra and Elvir followed in the used Volkswagen Jetta they had purchased six months before. Safija and Nedim arrived at the apartment soon thereafter to be with the girls who were too shaken to go to school.

In the ER, Merjem's stomach was pumped and she was now sleeping. She was alive, and according to the doctors would recover physically if she stayed away from alcohol and pills. It was the psychological issues that needed to be addressed.

Merjem was placed in a medical ward, and when she woke up the next day Hajra, Elvir, and Merjem's daughters were there to visit.

"Mom, what happened to you?" Azra asked.

Merjem whispered. "I don't really remember."

"No matter right now, Merjem," said Elvir. "We're here for you, and we'll help you get better."

"I know I've been avoiding you all lately, but I've been having nightmares about Tarik, and I just felt so hopeless.".

"We all miss him. Let's give you a chance to take better care of yourself. We've spoken with some people here at the hospital, and they have some good resources for you," Hajra said.

"Mom," said Azra, "you almost died. I don't know what we would have done if that happened? Please get help. Please, Mom."

Merjem took hold of her daughter's hand, and sighed.

"I know, my darling. I have to figure this out, so I don't do anything that will hurt you both—you all, really. I am very tired right now, and can't think very clearly. We'll talk more later."

The nurse entered the room and asked everyone to leave. Azra and Fatima gently hugged their mother goodbye, whose eyes were half closed as she groggily said goodbye. Hajra reassured Merjem that she would be staying in their apartment with the girls and help get them off to school. She promised to help Merjem arrange for any of the services provided to individuals and families that the hospital recommended. But she wasn't sure her sister-in-law heard her.

During the three days in the hospital, Merjem had time to reflect upon her life. She didn't want to die, she told herself. What would that do to her children? For years, she had relied on being a "sneaky drinker," as she thought of herself. But her children were not stupid. They knew she was not right. They covered for her, but in recent weeks they had no more energy to enable their mother's drinking. And Hajra's parents likely were telling of their concerns to their daughter and husband. It was time for her to take care of herself. There was no other choice.

In the subsequent months, Merjem did what she had to do to begin her recovery, and to stay sober. Nothing she needed to do was familiar or comfortable. She would never have done this in Bosnia. But she understood that because of the limited services there, she might have killed herself instead. Hajra helped her with an outpatient plan discussed with a discharge planner in the hospital.

There was an Alcoholics Anonymous group that met in a local church basement near her apartment. Her AA sponsor, a woman named Bettina, made sure to touch base with her by phone a few times a week. When Merjem felt weak with the thoughts of Tarik overwhelming her, she knew to call Bettina to help overcome the panic she felt. Little by little, she took control. She learned in AA that it was important to talk openly with her children who marveled at their mother's progress. In Bosnia, except maybe in the big city of Sarajevo, there was often the stigma that her children would have to live with, that their mother was a drunk. In Germany, there was a greater understanding of how trauma can affect people. Not that they spoke about what their mother was going through to anyone, except for their aunt and uncle, but this was new to everyone involved. And monthly, they attended a group with their mother specifically for children of alcoholics and substance users.

Merjem's boss said that her job was waiting for her when she was ready to return, which turned out to be two months after the event. Her supervisor's support and compassion was unequal to anything she could imagine.

She was piecing her life back together again stronger than she had been in a long time.

One evening while the children were with their cousins visiting Babo and Nana with Zlata, Elvir and Hajra were over for dinner at Merjem's, which was a salad and dolma from the local Bosnian delicatessen. For the first time, Merjem spoke as honestly to them as she ever had.

"I'm learning that until I can know for certain about Tarik, even where his remains are, I must be super vigilant of my moods. I don't want to hurt my children by leaving them with no mother. But I got so caught up in the pills and alcohol that I lost all perspective. And the girls were trying to take care of me, but for the longest time they didn't want to say anything to you hoping that I would be better soon. I am still a bit fragile sometimes, but I'm getting stronger. I'm sorry that I withdrew from you for a while. I know you tried to reach out to me, and I pulled away. You and all the others here are my family, and I am so thankful to have you in our lives.".

"Listen, Merjem," Elvir said, "we've lost Tarik and so many fellow Bosnians. I miss Kozarac. I miss Bosnia. We are always here for you. I don't know if this is a good time to talk about this, but now that you're on much more solid ground, we want to discuss this with you."

"Of course. I'm open to anything you'd like to say," she responded. "I have changed my perspective on life, and believe that I am on the right path now. Please, speak freely."

"Thanks. I will broach this delicately, but forthrightly. Hajra and I have been discussing this for a while, but wanted to wait until you were ready to hear it. We are overjoyed at the changes you've made in such a short time."

Elvir was testing the waters to make sure Merjem was, in fact, ready to hear what he had to say.

"Go on. You've piqued my interest," Merjem interjected.

"OK. Well, we feel like foreigners here despite how well we have adapted. We've been thinking lately about having us all move to the U.S. The government here has been making noises about wanting Bosnians to return to their homes or move to a new country. Too many bitter memories in Bosnia. And now that Prijedor is part of the Republika Srpska, it is probably not too welcoming for Muslims. But I have a cousin who lives in a small city in central New York State called Utica. He says there are lots of us there. And lots of opportunities. He even knows a man in the import/export business from Sarajevo who lives there and is willing to consider having me join him."

Hajra interjected.

"Actually, Elvir's cousin just started the sponsorship paperwork. It is quite complicated and the vetting process to get us to the U.S. is a challenge, to say the least. But we'd like for you and the children to join us. Zlata wants to, as does my brother Harun and his wife. I'm trying to convince the others, but they say they'll wait and might come to America later on."

Merjem was taken aback.

"The U.S.? That means starting over again. I feel like we've been refugees for a few years, and now we'll have to resettle again."

"I've started to develop a support network here that I don't want to lose. They help to keep me grounded. I would like to research what support they have in the States. But I don't know what to say. Let me think about it. I'll speak with my girls, too. They've made friends here, and know this place very well."

"Our kids have, too. They are ambivalent, although Halima is quite adventurous and is in love with America, at least her idea of what America is. And Danis still thinks Pennsylvania must be the greatest place on Earth. Amir is less committed. He is wanting to go to the university here in Dusseldorf for pharmacy at the end of this school year. But his English is pretty good and they have excellent colleges in America."

"Still, this is a huge decision. True, I am feeling much stronger. I guess I'm not sure I want to test out my new-found strength to that degree. I'm not saying no. I just want to think it over and speak with my girls," Merjem said.

"Of course," said Elvir. "We wouldn't expect otherwise. Hajra has said she will help locate resources for you in Utica. My cousin tells me that there is a wonderful Cultural Center for Bosniaks there as well. We are family, and we'd love for you to come with us."

For Elvir and Hajra, they planted the seed, and hoped that Merjem would join them. They understood what a transition this would be. Many Bosnians were beginning to move out of Germany. Some city governments, like in Berlin, were strongly encouraging their refugees to leave. Hajra and Elvir were ambivalent about moving, too. They understood that it might take Merjem some time before wrapping her head around such a monumental change. But they learned all too well that adaptation is the key to survival. And they believed that their best opportunity to adapt and succeed would be in Utica.

***

Amir was home one afternoon after school. He was studying more quickly than usual because he had a soccer game with his club. He'd lost some of his enthusiasm for the game since moving to Dusseldorf. He knew why, too. His time in the camps were so unpredictable that he only wanted to put himself in situations that didn't rely on others so much. School was one way to do that. He was an excellent student. In Kozarac it was the opposite. Though he was a decent student, soccer was his life.

He was the only one in the apartment at that time when someone rang the buzzer downstairs.

He absentmindedly pushed the button to open the big, glass door in the lobby without asking who it was.

Two minutes later there was a knock at the door.

Amir opened it and stared at the young man standing in front of him.

"Greetings from the dead, my friend," said the visitor.

"JUSUF! Am I dreaming? Is that really you?"

"Are you going to let me in or should we visit here in the hallway?" chided Jusuf.

"Come in, come in. I am so confused. But I am beyond happy to see you. I can't believe it!" said Amir as he scooped Jusuf up in a big hug.

"Please sit down at the table. Let me get you some coffee." Amir used the automatic coffee maker, which made it easier than making it the traditional way that Zlata still did.

"Amir. Let me look at you. Last time I saw you, you were headed to Manjaca. You've grown and look more like a man," said Jusuf.

"And last time I saw you was before I went to my new home at Manjaca, but you were taken away and I thought you were...you know..."

"Killed?" interjected Jusuf.

"Yes. I was in such despair," continued Amir. "I figured that your bravery in speaking to the reporter cost you your life. It took me a long time to get over what I feared was your death. I never really got over it to be honest."

"None of us knew at the time, but there were about fifty of us sent to Croatia. We were exchanged for Serb soldiers captured and imprisoned by the Bosnian army. We were dumped at the border by a UN-escorted Serb truck and given the Serb national salute as a send-off. It was surreal. Talk about confusion. All of us thought that it must have been a trick—that we were going to be executed. But, how could we? We were in a UNHCR building being processed. We were then transferred to the UK as 'guests' is what they called us. They have been very welcoming, actually. I have a job working as a caseworker with disabled people, driving them places, and supporting their independence. I guess living in Omarska looked good on my resume.. I'm here for a conference on disabilities that my organization sent me to. And I checked an online UNHCR registry for your names, something I do now and then. This time, bingo."

"That's amazing. It really is. My dad will be so happy to see you, and to know you're alive and well."

"Well? Are any of us truly well? I still have nightmares, especially when I hear of people from my village who didn't make it. Or that their remains cannot be found. That is what's happened to my family. My father and his two brothers were murdered by his Serb neighbors that were fed the lies by Karadzic and Milosevic, and we're still waiting to know where they're buried. I live with my mother in London where there are other Bosnians like us. London is a busy city and I yearn to live in nature away from everyone. In fact, it would be the best to move back to Hambarine, but there is nothing to move back to, and the Serbs pretty much have taken over with their damned republic."

"I miss Kozarac, too. My parents are now considering

moving even further from Bosnia. My dad has a cousin living in the States, and he says how wonderful it is there. He says that there are lots of Bosnians, and he even has a job waiting if he wants. But still, it's not home. We are kind of homeless, Jusuf, don't you think?"

"I agree. But we're alive. How many of us didn't make it? And we know what happened to so many of our mothers and sisters, cousins and friends. I've spoken with Adina, a cousin of mine who lives in the Netherlands. She's the one who lived in Visegrad with her family. The Serb paramilitaries were brutal there. Her younger brother, Arif, was only twelve, but they threw off a bridge into the Drina River, and shot him on the way down. Her parents were burned alive in a house where the criminal Lukic locked many families in before he set it on fire. And she is very open about what happened to her and her sister at the hands of the Serbs. They were imprisoned for several months in that Vilina Vlas Spa, and raped nightly. Her sister didn't make it, and Adina was only one of ten to leave alive. Her story is always a part of my nightmares. She misses home, too, but she can never go back. Too many horrible memories, she says. I am sorry to be so frank with you, but all of what happened to us, to our families and friends, still haunts me. As for Adina, she lives in Amsterdam. She's married to a Dutch man, a very kind man, and they have an infant. But she will forever be haunted. How can she ever truly heal from what she went through? Maybe the U.S. is a great place for us? England has been good to me, so I will stay there."

It was the end of the workday. Amir missed his soccer game, but that was secondary to being with Jusuf: an alive and thriving Jusuf. When the front door opened the rest of Amir's family entered with Elvir almost bursting out in tears, and the others wondering who the young man was.

"My God," he exclaimed, "But...but..."

"I know," said Jusuf, "you look as if you've seen a ghost."

The three men laughed as Elvir tightly hugged the young man.

They talked about Bosnia before the war, and how much they missed its sweetness. There was little talk of Omarska. Jusuf stayed for dinner, but needed to head back to the hotel for tomorrow's final day of the conference, he said. They exchanged contact information, and Jusuf promised that if they did go to the States, he would someday visit them.

As Amir walked back upstairs after accompanying Jusuf down to the lobby, an odd thought occurred to him. *Life is a strange affliction.* He smiled and shook his head at the idea of comparing life to a disease. But he felt no need to dissuade himself of believing otherwise.

Chapter 33
America: 1996

The vetting process was complicated. Between the UN resettlement program and the various U.S. government agencies, the only easy entity to deal with was the German government, which seemed relieved to have many of its Bosnian refugees find other homes. Not that they were unwelcoming when the families came from Croatia. In fact, Dusseldorf was still a wonderful city for its refugees. But, the restlessness from some in Germany, showing signs of discontent and lobbying for the local governments to legislate for Bosnians to either go back to Bosnia or another country to live in, was unsettling. This somewhat nationalist sentiment garnered particular attention by its intended recipients. Having family in Utica, New York, made it an easier transcontinental jump.

Elvir, Hajra and all three children; Zlata, Merjem and the girls; Harun and Asla all made the trek. Hajra's parents, and other brother and family stayed in Germany. Nedim had a heart condition that would not allow him to fly. It was best for him to stay put. He was not that adventurous anymore and told the grandchildren that moving to Germany was adventure enough.

Their separation from one another was a difficult choice, and painful, but America sounded like a perfect place. There would be no moving after this. They all promised to see each other after the "Americans," as Nedim teased them, settled into their new home. The travelers simply had to put one foot ahead of the other, and get on the plane, as bittersweet as it was.

They were headed for Utica where a strong Bosnian community was beginning to take root. Elvir's cousin, Jasmin, on his father's side, along with his children, picked them up at Syracuse Airport. His two children appeared to be the same age as Halima, who was sixteen. Jasmin's friends, Ismar and Dzan were there as well, in order to have enough cars to drive all of them. It did not go unnoticed by Danis and Halima how big American cars are.

It was a windy day as dusk settled in. There was a slight chill in the air, not unusual for the local climate in early spring.

As they drove down a city street called "the Parkway," Danis noticed that the traffic lights were swaying rapidly on their wires, and worried that they might get caught under one if it fell. In Germany, traffic lights were on poles and remained steady.

"Dad, why are the traffic lights swaying? Will they fall down?" he asked.

Jasmin responded.

"No, Danis, that is just how they are here. I remember when we moved before the war, my son, Ibrahim had the same concerns. It is different here than Bosnia or Germany, that's for sure. But I think you'll like it."

Ibrahim added.

"I remember that. I was scared, too. In Bosnia, the lights were probably more like in Germany, although I've never been there. In fact, there are lots of new things for you guys to check out."

"Yeah," said his sister Dragana, "we'll show you around. And we'll help Halima out at our high school"

That seemed to put Danis at ease. He would remember to tell his sister, who was in another car with their mom. *These are nice kids,* thought Elvir. *Well-adjusted and nice kids.*

They arrived at his cousin's house to the sounds and smells

of their home in Bosnia. Bosanski Lonac was simmering in the large pot on the stove with its aromas of beef and vegetables permeating every room in the house. Jasmin's wife, Aida, greeted them warmly and showed them to their rooms complete with towels for showering after the long journey.

After a sumptuous meal and light conversation, the visitors' exhaustion took hold, and they all exchanged one last hug before trudging off to bed. Zlata also stayed in Jasmin's house, while Hajra's brother and wife, Merjem and the girls went to Ismar's house.

Over the next several days the adults were introduced to the Imam of the Bosnian Islamic Association of Utica; the Islamic Cultural Center, as it was also referred to. Roughly Elvir's age, the Imam was quite welcoming. In fact, his parents were originally from Donji Vakuf in central Bosnia, and had arrived in Utica not too long before the war to join their son and his family. He invited the newcomers to join them for an event that the Association was having for newly arrived Bosniak refugees being held in the next few weeks.

Elvir and Hajra soon found a two-story house on Bacon Street in East Utica. It was a bit run-down, but it was suitable enough for theirs and Merjem's family to live. Elvir knew that he could ask the Imam to find local Bosniaks to help do some repairs on the house, in exchange for him helping them with any home projects they may have. Harun and Asla found their own place a few blocks away.

Catholic Charities was the local non-profit designated to help in the resettlement process including transitioning the children into school. Amir decided to go to Mohawk Valley Community College to get familiar with colleges in the U.S. and test out his proficiency in academic English, which was much different from conversational English. He also needed time to decide whether he truly wanted to pursue a career in pharmacy. He told his parents that he was considering another direction for his life's work, but he needed time to let the "seeds germinate." Everyone took English classes, but Bosnian was still the language of choice at home.

During the first months in Utica, there was a focus on orienting themselves to a very different place than Europe.

One day, Danis came home with a bruised right eye.

"What happened, my love?" asked Hajra.

"A boy in my school called me a dirty Muslim," he responded.

"What? We're in America. There are all sorts of religions here. Why would he do such a thing?"

"I don't know, Mom, my first reaction was to hit him. I told him he had no idea what me and my family went through because of our religion, and I was not going to let anyone do that again."

"Did you get into trouble from the school?"

"No, it happened when I was walking home from the bus stop. Fatima saw it and actually stopped the fight from going further. I'll just avoid that kid. Besides, you should have seen what he looked like after I hit him."

"I don't want to know. What I do want to know is that you will not do this type of thing again. We are guests in this country. I know we want to be citizens, and I don't know enough to say whether we will be someday. We have to be models for what strengths Bosnians bring here, not give them reasons to send us away. Please promise you'll think about that next time."

"OK, Mom, I will," Danis said reluctantly.

Hajra was not happy with Danis' actions, but they had only been in Utica for a couple of months, and she often had a feeling of being between worlds herself. Germany always seemed temporary for some reason. She often had a yearning to return to Kozarac, as did Elvir for that matter. But the Balkans were still a powder keg. And, besides, there were too many unknowns there. They had no idea where their missing or, likely dead, relatives were. She and Elvir had occasionally spoken of at least giving a proper burial for his father and brother. But this was 1996, and there was no word on their whereabouts or remains.

Hajra also realized that the previous year, after the massacre of over 8,000 men and boys in Srebrenica by the Serbs, followed by the Dayton Peace Accords brokered by the U.S. a new Serbian Republic emerged within Bosnia and Herzegovina. This area included Prijedor, Banja Luka and other municipalities. So, their own cities and towns were given up to the Serbs, which is mostly what the nationalists wanted in the first place. That fact was hard for any Bosniak to accept.

On second thought, pondered Hajra, what would we be going back to anyway? Utica, as they had said prior to leaving Germany, was to be their new home forever, and she and Danis would have to deal with it. Yet, there was often a nagging feeling that the two of them had not quite slayed their demons. She tucked that concern away for another day.

***

A year after their arrival, they were more settled into their new lives. Not that it went without challenges. But, characteristic of most Bosniaks, they worked hard to adjust to their new surroundings. New arrivals still came to Utica, and now it was Elvir and Hajra who were part of the welcoming committee with the Islamic Association.

Elvir was working in the import/export business in downtown Utica, and Hajra was working part-time at a florist.

Merjem, took English classes. She got a temporary job at the local nursing home as an aide. She was told that if she proved herself, she would likely get a permanent position there. One concern that the family had was that she stopped her connection with Alcoholics Anonymous. She had promised Bettina, her sponsor in Dusseldorf, and her family that she would attend a local meeting.

On a blustery winter's evening, Hajra went upstairs, to bring some spinach and feta pie she had just made to Merjem. Since Merjem's apartment had a separate entryway, it was not evident when they were there other than when footsteps could be heard down below. But even that was softened by the insulation that Elvir had installed.

Hajra knocked on the door. No answer.

She knew that the girls were having a sleepover with Zlata who continued to live with Jasmin and his family having her own separate room and entryway. But Merjem said nothing about being away that night. And besides, it was beginning to snow.

She went back down to their apartment where her children were studying and watching TV. Elvir was studying in their bedroom from his English book.

"Did Merjem say anything about going out somewhere tonight?"

"I don't think so. I know that her kids are with my mom for a sleepover, but that's all."

"I'm a bit concerned. She said nothing to me either. And she's not home. It's getting a bit nasty outside. Should we be worried?"

"Hmmm...maybe. She's been a bit more distant from us lately. And she keeps promising to attend a meeting, but I don't think that's happened yet. Of course, her shifts at the nursing home vary. Have you spoken with her lately about AA?"

"I try. But she tells me that she is just trying to adapt to the U.S., but that she'll get to it soon."

Elvir put his book down. He looked at his wife and said he'd call his mother to see if she was there.

"Mom, how's it going with the girls?"

"Fine. They're enjoying being with Ibrahim and Dragana. I'm so glad they have such good relations here."

"Me too. Have you heard from Merjem?"

"No. I haven't seen her in a few days. Why?"

"Hajra went upstairs to bring some food, but she wasn't home. I was just wondering if you knew anything?"

"Fatima told me that she's been acting strange again. The girls are making dinner because Merjem says she's too tired to cook. They're doing laundry, too. I know that Hajra takes her to Price Chopper for groceries, so they have food. But Fatima also said that she goes out for walks in the evening sometimes when she's not working. Even in the cold weather. Were you aware of this?"

"Hmmm...no. I wonder why the girls haven't said anything to us?"

"Should I ask them where they think their mother is now?"

"Maybe not. If she's been taking walks then probably that's what she's doing. We'll keep an eye out for when she gets home and go upstairs to see what's going on."

"OK, Elvir. Let me know, please," said Zlata as she hung up.

Elvir told his wife what his mother had said. Hajra had no idea that Merjem was going out for walks, or that she was not cooking or doing the laundry for that matter.

"I'm concerned. I wonder if she's drinking again? Lately, she's been more withdrawn, and when I ask her if anything is wrong, she denies it."

"Let's watch for when she comes home and head up there."

It was 10:00 at night when they heard the door slam in Merjem's place.

Elvir put his slippers on and followed Hajra upstairs.

Hajra knocked on the door.

"Who is it?" she asked.

"It's us, Merjem," said Hajra.

"Just a minute," she yelled through the door.

Merjem took some time to open the door. Her brother- and sister-in-law were met with a distinct odor of toothpaste and alcohol.

"We just came up to see how you're doing. We haven't seen you so much lately," said Hajra.

"Come in, come in. Let me get you some coffee. How about tea? Water?"

As she moved backward to let them in, Merjem tripped over a throw rug and fell on the floor near her couch.

"MERJEM!" yelled Hajra.

Elvir quickly got down on the floor while Hajra got a pillow from the couch to put under her head.

"I'm sorry," Merjem slurred. "I don't know who put that rug there. I'll have to get Azra to move it when I see her tomorrow."

Elvir saw blood trickling from the back of his sister-in-law's head. Hajra was already next to her with a damp washcloth gently swabbing the cut.

"We've got a problem here, Elvir," said Hajra. "I suspected as much."

"Merjem, I'm going to get you some water. It's good for you to drink some water, OK?" said Elvir.

"OK, Tarik, whatever you say. Did I say Tarik? I meant Elvir."

It was nearly midnight and Hajra cleaned Merjem up and put her in pajamas. She was beginning to sober up.

Merjem wept inconsolably about not having Tarik anymore. There was no use in either Elvir or Hajra doing anything but trying to calm her, knowing full-well that Merjem would only have a hazy memory the next day. They guided her to her bed where she immediately fell asleep snoring with an almost staccato rhythm. Hajra told Elvir that she would stay the night and sleep on one of the girls' beds. They kissed goodnight knowing that the next day would be rather difficult.

***

Counseling itself was still a foreign concept for Bosnians. Typically, raw feelings had to be buried. Family and community often provided the soft-landing needed to counter the demons that visited many Bosniaks. Still, there were some that needed more than just a landing spot. The idea of receiving counseling was more acceptable in America, though it still came with a stigma in some circles of society.

When Merjem awoke the next morning she immediately went to the bathroom to vomit. Elvir had returned before this to talk with Hajra about what to do. When Merjem came back from the bathroom she apologized profusely.

"What happened last night? Why are you guys here now? What the hell did I do that I'm feeling so nauseous now?"

Hajra had already brewed the coffee and she brought steaming, hot cups to the kitchen table for the three of them.

"Merjem, we need to have a serious talk," said Hajra.

"Your kids were at Jasmin's for a sleepover and you apparently went out for a walk, which they said you've been doing lately. We heard you come in around 10:00, so we came up here to check on you. You were quite drunk, fell, and hit your head," said Elvir.

Merjem rubbed the back of her head and gently caressed the bump she felt.

"I guess you're right about my head. That's sore."

Merjem sighed deeply.

"You're right that I was drunk. I've been drinking again. I have also been encouraging the girls to have sleepovers with Zlata. As hard as I try, I just keep getting into these ruts of thinking non-stop about Tarik. I know that this is very bad for me. And very bad for the kids. In Germany, I had a better handle on it."

"You also had AA and Bettina," said Hajra.

"I know. I know. I guess I need to find a local group here."

"Listen. I never told you this, but I will now, and I'd like you to consider the same for you," said Hajra.

"Since we came to the States, I have been ruminating about what happened to me in the camp. Elvir is always incredibly supportive, but there is just so much he can do. And he can get withdrawn from his own time being imprisoned. He has found some friends and they meet up for coffee regularly just to talk about what happened to them. That seems to help him.

Elvir interjected.

"We talk about other things, too, but it's a good release."

Hajra continued.

But for me, I felt I needed to speak with someone: a professional. Not very Bosnian of me, I know. I should be able to handle this on my own, right? But I had to admit that it was getting me down and affecting my life."

"I don't understand. You seem fine to me," said Merjem. "I'm the one who's not so fine."

"I first spoke to Elvir about it. He knows me so well. He agreed that I haven't been myself lately. It's not easy to speak with anyone about this, even to my husband. I've been having flashbacks to Trnopolje and being...being raped. So, a few weeks ago, I began counseling with a woman at Catholic Charities who specializes in violence against women, who herself is from Sarajevo and has been in America since 1987. She is a lovely woman."

"I'm glad to hear you're doing that, I truly am. But my situation is different."

"Is it?" asked Hajra. "You were violated in a different way. The Serbs took your husband's life. And the lives of your parents and brothers. They had no right to do that to them or any of us."

Merjem pondered this for a minute.

"I need help. I fool myself into thinking I can stop drinking anytime—that this is just temporary and eases my burdens until the demons pass. But after a few months or so, they return. It just never seems to end."

Merjem had been holding in her tears for what seemed like an eternity to her, but she now let them go. Both Hajra and Elvir put their arms around her and said that they wanted to help her.

"I know you know how to find the nearest AA group. I'll give you the name of the counselor and can even call to make the appointment if you'd like. If she's open to it, I'll attend the first session if that will ease your anxieties about going?"

Merjem's tears slowed.

"You two—I don't know what I would do without you. I am a mess, as they say in America. But I have another chance to reclaim my life. I don't know how many more I will have. I'll find the AA group. Hajra, if you would please call the counselor for me, I'd appreciate it. And can we keep the part about counseling quiet for now? I'm not ready to tell the girls. Telling them about AA is fine. I'm sure they're worried about me, too, so getting a handle on the drinking will be a relief to them. I am so grateful to you both."

"Let me speak to the counselor," said Hajra.

Elvir and Hajra straightened out the apartment and Hajra made her sister-in-law some eggs and toast. Back in their apartment they acknowledged that Merjem was on the brink of heading into the darkest of places, and they hoped that their intervention was not too late.

***

The next morning there was a knock on their door. It was Merjem.

"May I come in?"

"Of course," Hajra replied. "Of course."

"Please call the counselor to see about us going together, at least to the first session. I'll need to lean on you, I think."

"That's great. In fact, the office opens in a little while. Let's sit down and have some coffee, and then you can be here when I call. I'm pretty sure Amila goes in at 9:00 with her first client at 10:00.

Merjem sat at the table tapping on the outside of her coffee mug while Hajra called Catholic Charities. Amila was able to take the call right away. Hajra briefly explained the nature of her call.

"You have a 4:00 appointment for this Thursday. You're not working that afternoon, are you?"

"No, no. Thursday is my early day. That's good. Thank you, Hajra. I'm nervous, but I've got to do this. And you being there will be so helpful."

"You know, we all need to acknowledge when we just can't do something on our own. In America, people like to be independent, and usually not told what to do. But I believe we need each other, especially during the hard times. I figured that out a long time ago. I'm happy to have you lean on me, on us, whenever you need to."

***

Merjem was unfamiliar with what counseling entailed, so she awkwardly circled around the issues she was facing. Amila was a soft-spoken woman who just allowed Merjem to speak. She then gently asked if it was alright for Hajra to share a bit more of what she'd observed.

Hajra gave a brief description of what Merjem and her children had been through. Of course, this included what happened to Tarik. Amila nodded and took some notes. She looked over at Merjem and handed her some tissues.

In not so many details, Amila told her that her father was killed by a sniper in the Siege of Sarajevo in 1993 while trying to get some food for him and her mother. She told the two women how difficult it was, and still is at times, to reconcile such a senseless act. But she also said that she wants to help other Bosnians to grieve as she did, and she wished that they were as willing and open as Hajra and Merjem were to do so.

This set Merjem at ease. There was a sense that this woman, this counselor, knew exactly what she was going through.

After that initial session, Merjem told Hajra that she was ready to continue. Hajra breathed a sigh of relief knowing that this was a giant step for her sister-in-law.

The following week, Merjem went on her own. The evening before, she went to her first AA meeting in America. The comfort she had left during the meetings in Dusseldorf quickly returned. It gave her the strength to enter the counseling session with more determination.

She sat down with Amila, and after greeting each other in Bosnian, she began.

"My children, and family are going to lose me if I continue on the path I've been taking. I know I can never get my husband back, but his loss visits me all too often. So, please help me find the strength and wisdom to do so much better than I have. I'm ready to create a different story from the one that awaits me if I don't make some very significant changes."

"You're so brave to be open to making changes. Understand that this may be a rough road for you. But you've already decided that the road you've been traveling has only worked sometimes. Meaning, that you have the ability to make it work. So, if you are open to it, let's have you agree that it's there inside you, and you have other supports like AA and family, but that you'll commit to finding ways to manage the sadness that visits you periodically, and spirals you downward."

Merjem took a deep breath. She'd thought that she'd managed things in the past, but this woman saw right through her. She understood that Merjem had the will, but not always the way. If she wanted to take control, she needed to acknowledge that she didn't have it together like she thought, but fooled herself into thinking she did.

"You get me, don't you, Amila? I like the idea of managing my life better when I get sad. Alcohol and pills are not good ways to manage anything. I learned that in AA a long time ago. So, yes, I like this approach. I'm not crazy, but sometimes I think I am."

When the session ended, Merjem drove over to the local Bosnian bakery and grabbed some bundevara for the kids. She had a lot to think about—a lot to do if she wanted to be there for her children, to be a much healthier version of herself.

As she left the bakery, she could smell the just-baked pastries as the aroma wafted toward her from the box. Images of her childhood—of her mother teaching her how to cook and to bake surfaced.

Why have I never thought to teach Azra and Fatima what my mother taught me? It's not too late. Maybe that's a good place to start putting my life back together?

Turning the key in the ignition, she reiterated to herself. *Just maybe.*

Chapter 34
Danis' Reckoning

It had been three years since they arrived in America. Many more Bosnians had moved there in the years since. Elvir, Hajra and Merjem became de facto ambassadors for the newly arrived. Merjem was doing well. The import/export business that Elvir continued to work in was well-respected. And Hajra got a part-time job in a large nursery where she had become quite an expert in exotic plants and flowers.

The children did not go unscathed from what they experienced in Bosnia. Danis especially, had become distant and moody. His grades in school were marginal although he was considered an underachiever. He struggled as a teenager, which meant his parents struggled along with him.

Amir was going to Syracuse University to study journalism, so he wasn't around much. Even though the school was an hour away from Utica, he was often busy, so coming home on weekends had become less frequent. He and his sister were just built differently than their younger brother. They had a strong network of Bosnian and non-Bosnian friends, and were open about sharing their experiences in the camps. Amir was always concerned for his brother and was usually a good influence. Still, as Amir told his parents, Danis is like a "wild horse" sometimes. "Even I can't tame him."

Halima was an excellent student and she was away at college in Pennsylvania. She was an activist at school, working in communities of color in Philadelphia. She told her parents that she long-ago lost her patience with Danis, and no longer had an influence on him.

Elvir took Danis into his work occasionally and tried to get him to focus on tasks there. They would get into arguments as Danis seemed uninterested. This caused further tension at home. Elvir and Hajra were quite worried about their youngest child.

The school counselor at Proctor High called Danis' home to set up a meeting in the middle of his freshmen year. His grades were not good, and he and a boy named Edward had cut school more than once. Danis told them that he only left at lunch to grab some pizza at Rosario's, but the counselor stated that all students know that going off campus was not allowed. They were even caught smoking cigarettes on the football field. Edward, Elvir and Hajra realized, was the friend that Danis spent many Friday nights with probably partying.

The school meeting had minimal impact, although Danis was made aware that he was being tracked by the school, and his parents.

Elvir and Hajra made Danis come home from school every day, grab a snack, and do his homework. They checked to see that he'd completed his tasks, but because they were unfamiliar with the subject matter, all they could do was to see that he had finished. Danis assured them that the work quality was excellent.

They forbade him to have contact with Edward, although at school they were unable to monitor this. More times than not, they invited Merjem, Azra and Fatima, or Jasmin and his family to visit on weekends. Their hope was that Danis would interact more with his Bosnian family. He was not allowed to go out without his parents knowing who he was going with, and where they were going. He had to check in by phone at prescribed times, and if he didn't, he lost the privilege of going out the following weekend. When he came home at the 10:00 curfew, they smelled his breath and clothing for smoke and alcohol.

It was tough love, they knew, but their worry warranted this approach to rein him in.

Danis told no one about the dreams. They had started to ramp up at the beginning of high school, and with only a brief hiatus here and there, they continued to haunt him.

Smoking pot occasionally with Edward, and drinking vodka didn't quell the nightmares. They always revolved around the same images:

He is in Trnopolje hiding behind a shed. He spins around as he hears loud gurgling coming from the woods adjacent to the goal at the far end of the school soccer field. He is horrified to see that it's his Uncle Tarik getting his throat slashed while a soldier is shooting a baby that he's holding. He screams for them to stop, but nothing comes out. He's mute. No one can hear him. And now, the murderous guards are coming for him brandishing a knife dripping with his uncle's blood. Just as they reach him, he wakes up in a cold sweat.

He'd heard of PTSD, but thought that only happened to soldiers coming home from a war zone. He loved Sylvester Stallone movies and especially the Rambo series. "First Blood" introduced him to the idea of PTSD, but he'd never really thought much about it until recently. He wondered if he had it, too.

Danis went to the local library after school to read up on it. He hated to read, but this sounded so much like what he was going through. And it disturbed him. His moods and behavior were clearly impacting his family. But he had no idea what to do.

It was his sophomore year, and he needed to address it. It was consuming him now. So, he got up the courage to speak with the school counselor, Mr. Graziano.

Mr. Graziano's office was welcoming. On three of the walls he had framed posters of Derek Jeter, Muhammed Ali, and Gandhi. The sofa was a soft brown leather, and the window behind his modest wooden desk illuminated the room with natural light.

Mr. Graziano was a well-built man with slightly unkempt brown hair who always wore jeans, a button-down shirt, and a colorful tie.

"Come in Danis. It's good to see you again. What's going on?"

Danis noticed his palms were sweaty, and his heart was racing. Lately, these were not unfamiliar physiological reactions to the anxiety he'd felt more acutely. He looked down at his knock-off Adidas shoes as he began to speak.

"I've been a jerk, I know. I don't care about school very much. But...I think I need some help. When we met last year with my parents, I wasn't so cool with you, was I?"

"I'm just glad you've come in now. What's going on, Danis?"

"I have these horrible dreams about my uncle. I don't know how much you know about what a lot of us went through in Bosnia, but my whole family was in concentration camps."

"Oh Jeez. No, I didn't know that. That sounds awful."

"Well, it was. I've tried to block it out for a lot of years, but lately I can't. I even tried to block out that I'm Bosnian. A lot of times I tell kids I'm from Germany, and that's it."

"Sure. Please, tell me why you're here now to see me? Something has prompted you to come here today. That tells me it's really important that we talk."

"Yeah, I think it is. I had these scary dreams when I was younger, but I usually didn't remember what they were about. The past year, though, I do. I kind of don't want to tell you the details, but it's pretty bad. I think it's why I've been such a...butthead, if it's alright to put it that way. Actually, I've been not behaving well, to put it mildly. So, I've been doing a lot of reading about PTSD, and I think I have it."

"Hmm...I've read some about PTSD, but I'm no expert. Still, it sounds like you may be onto something. It's very insightful and brave of you to want to deal with this. Very brave."

"I've been thinking about coming in here. I've heard that you're nice, and very understanding. And mostly kids say you're pretty cool. I didn't give you a chance last time. Thanks for making it easier for me to talk about this stuff. What do you think I should do?"

Mr. Graziano was surprised at the forthrightness of Danis. He could pick up right away that the boy was in trouble. And to come in and want to speak with him was very hopeful. Many times, high school kids clammed up. That was the challenge he faced as a counselor. But once kids started to open up, he was ready. Danis clearly had been mulling this over, and was ready to talk right away.

"Well, here are my thoughts. As I said, I'm no expert in PTSD. But there's a guy I know, a counselor, who helps vets coming home from wars like in Afghanistan. He's pretty cool. He was a war veteran himself. Now, he'd need to assess you to make sure that's what's happening in order to work with you, but if it's not, he'll get you to someone who can help no matter what it is. The only thing is, I think it's important that you say something to your parents. If anyone will understand, it'll be them."

Danis took a deep breath and exhaled slowly.

"I don't know. They've been through a lot themselves. My mother and sister were with me in the camp, but my father and older brother were in much worse places than we were. They're pretty open about what happened, but...I don't know."

"Then, why don't you think about it. In the meantime, I'll reach out to my friend. I won't give him your name just yet, but I'll give him a heads up in case you want to see him. Is that OK?"

"Sure, Mr. Graziano. That's OK. I'll think about it."

The counselor told Danis to come back if he wanted to see his friend—that he'd make an official referral. But before he headed out the door, Danis turned around to face the counselor.

"Thank you, Mr. Graziano," he said, looking directly into the counselor's eyes.

Danis left the office feeling like a weight had been lifted from him. His mind was racing in many different directions. It was the last period of the day, and he had study hall. He sat at his desk and pretended to read his science book. He read the same paragraph several times.

After school, he went home and straight to his room. His parents were not back from work yet, so he brought the portable phone with him as he sat on the bed fiddling with the buttons. He called his brother.

"Amir, it's me. Do you have a couple of minutes?"

"Sure, buddy, I don't have class until tonight. What's up?"

"I went to Mr. Graziano today. You know, the school counselor."

"Cool. Why? Is something wrong at home?"

"Well. I'm what's wrong at home. I know you've been mad at me for being a butthead for a while. And...I think I have a problem."

"Ok...can you tell me what's up?"

"Well, I've been having really bad dreams for the past year or so. I mean, really bad. I don't know if I want to tell you because it might upset you."

"Try me. I've had my share of nightmares, believe me. And I guarantee Halima, and even Mom and Dad have had them."

"It's about Uncle Tarik. I think Mom may have told you guys what I saw in the camp—you know like the baby getting shot? I mean, I saw beatings and other stuff, too, and that guy getting shot from the minaret, but the baby getting killed was the worst. And you know, Uncle Tarik found me when I was hiding near the shed at the soccer field. Anyway, in my dream, it's Uncle Tarik holding the baby, but he's getting murdered, too, and when I scream nothing comes out. And then, the guards come at me. I wake up just as they're about to slit my throat."

"Wow. That sucks. That really sucks. So, did you tell this to Mr. Graziano today?"

"I told him that I've been reading about PTSD, and that I think I have it. I didn't want to go into what I'd actually been dreaming. I was worried he'd think I was nuts, although he's a good guy and was really understanding. You're the only one I've ever talked to about the actual dream though."

"Wow, little brother. That's kind of heavy. But, no, you're not nuts. I never told you, but I've had dreams, especially about Omarska. That place was awful. Of course, you know that. But somehow, talking about some of what went on there with Dad and Mom, and a few buddies I made at the Cultural Center, seemed to help. I haven't seen a counselor, but I think it's cool that you do. It's important to talk about what we went through. I truly believe that. And, you're right, I'll bet it's what's been causing you to be such a butthead. For you that's definitely a proper noun, by the way," he said, trying to lighten the mood a little.

"That's for sure. Anyway, Mr. Graziano has a friend who's a counselor, and the guy specializes in PTSD. I guess he was an army veteran in some war himself. Do you think I should go?"

"What do you think, buddy? That's the most important. If you believe you should, then you should. And it sounds like you're hurting. So, I ask you, what do you want to do?"

"I want to get help, Amir. I don't like what's happening. I feel anxious and sometimes even depressed. I'm gonna talk to Mom and Dad tonight, and then to Mr. Graziano tomorrow to see about going to his friend for some help."

"That sounds good. You know, I'm damn proud of you. Damn proud. Keep me posted. OK? One more thing, I know I'm not big on saying this much, but know that I love you, little brother, and I'm glad you called me. Really glad."

Danis told his parents all about the dreams, his meeting with the counselor, and his call with Amir. They echoed Amir's sentiments of how proud they were of the courage he was showing.

***

In his junior year, there seemed to be a further burgeoning of his maturity. He could still be moody at times, but he took more of an interest in visiting with his extended family. His grades even improved. He started to talk about being interested in going into business of some sort someday. The school year went without incident. Danis was making a comeback. He had made a couple of new friends: guys who he played pick-up basketball with, and this exposed him to other kids, as well. Edward was mostly out of the picture. He even got a job for eight to twelve hours a week at the Tasty Creme serving up ice cream when it was open during the warmer months.

It was his senior year that cemented the fact that he had morphed into a young man with a conscience. A person who both his family, and more importantly, he could find respect for.

Danis knew some of the Bosnian kids from the Cultural Center, but he didn't hang out with them at school. It was still somewhat difficult for him to talk about his time in the camp except sometimes with his family, and the counselor who specialized in PTSD that he saw for a whole year. He usually kept it light with the other Bosniaks though.

Every once in a while he'd sit down for lunch with Edward. But it was different than it used to be. Edward was a little calmer. Still, he could be a jerk sometimes, and Danis wondered why he'd bothered.

Early in his last school year, he noticed a boy limping in the halls of the high school. He hadn't paid much attention to anyone other than in his social circle, so for him this was different.

"Edward, did you see that kid? What's up with him?" asked Danis.

"No clue. He's just a gimp, I guess."

"Yeah, I guess."

But that didn't sit well with him. He knew the boy was Bosnian and he'd only arrived at school at the end of the previous year as a junior.

When he got home, he called his cousin, Azra, who was a sophomore. Azra was involved in the Bosnia Club, a group at school that met regularly and shared news about their homeland, but mostly held events in tandem with the Cultural Center's activities.

"Hey cuz, how you doing?" asked Danis.

"Good, good Danis, how are you?"

"Well, I was wondering if you could help me with something?"

"Sure."

"Do you know that Bosnian boy who has a limp? The one who showed up at school at the end of last year? He's super quiet and avoids other kids."

"Yeah. I think his name is Haris. But when he first got to school last year, I tried to talk with him and tell him about our club, he didn't seem interested."

"Sorry, but I guess I haven't been interested either. OK. I was just wondering. I've seen some kids give him a hard time because he limps pretty badly."

"Not cool. Maybe I'll approach him again. I'm sure he could use some friends."

"I think I will, too."

Danis told his mother about Haris. She was impressed that he even noticed.

The next time he saw Haris dragging his leg through the halls he stopped him. Haris stiffened as if to be ready to repel more bullying.

"Hey, what's up?" Danis asked in Bosnian.

"Umm...nothing. Just headed to my class," replied Haris.

"Can I walk with you?"

"Sure."

"I was wondering if it would be OK for us to sit together at lunch. I'm from Kozarac, and I just wanted to talk with you."

"Ok, how about tomorrow? I have an English language class at lunch three days a week, and today is one of those times."

"Cool" I'm Danis, by the way, and you're Haris, I've been told."

"Nice to meet you," Haris said as he hobbled down the hallway to his next class.

When he got home Danis wondered why he was so interested in this kid. He felt sorry for him. But upon meeting him he thought Haris to be fairly confident. He looked Danis directly in his eyes.

The next day, the two met up for lunch. Edward mocked Danis for wanting to eat lunch with a gimp instead of him. Danis told himself that he was finally done with Edward.

"Hey Haris, what's up?" asked Danis.

"Nothing really. How are you?"

"All good."

After some small talk, Danis got to his concern.

"Hey, I noticed some kids giving you a hard time because of, you know, the way you walk."

"I'm used to it. They don't bother me. I pretty much ignore them. They don't know what I went through to get this way."

"Are you OK telling me?" Danis said, surprising himself that he was that direct.

"Well, sure. Most people don't ask."

"I live here with my aunt and uncle. They moved here a few years ago, and then last year I came. I was living with an older cousin in Bosnia."

Danis trained his gaze at Haris sensing that this was going to be heavy. He was truly interested in what happened. Danis still had occasional nightmares about his time in Trnopolje, but it had been difficult for him to tell most people about them. He just avoided many things Bosnian until last year when he started to reconnect with his cousins. His past was something that he was truly just coming to grips with.

"I was only nine-years-old in Mostar when the trouble began. I lived with my parents and sister in the eastern suburbs. My sister, Mirela, was two years older than me, but we were very close. It was crazy. All of a sudden it seemed, there was so much bombing of my city. At first, we thought that the Croat army was with us to fight the Serbs. Then, they turned on us, too. My father joined the Bosnian Army. I never saw him again."

Haris paused for a brief moment.

"I miss him all the time. After he left, it was just the three of us, and we knew that we needed to leave because of the shelling. We had no time to even grab our clothing. My mom said we had to run for safety. Me and my sister didn't know where we were going, but Mom led us through the woods to get to my cousin's house. He was quite a bit older and more like an uncle."

"Wow, that kind of sounds like what we went through in Kozarac. But I can tell you more about that if you want to know someday."

"I do. I think we Bosnians have a lot in common, but don't talk about it enough."

"Please finish your story. I didn't mean to interrupt."

"Well, this is the tough part. As we fled with lots of others, my mother stepped on a land mine. She was holding my sister's hand and they were both killed. I can't remember much more than that. Except when I woke up in a hospital my cousin was by my side in the recovery room. I lost my leg in that blast."

"Oh shit."

"Yeah, oh shit. But somehow, I got to Sarajevo and a prosthetic was grafted to my hip by a surgeon in the big hospital there. My cousin stayed with me the whole time and took me home with him, which is where I lived until last year."

"Why didn't you stay with him?"

"Another sad story, I'm afraid."

"He and his wife were killed in a car accident. I know, it's one tragedy after another. Needless to say, I was very depressed. But an aunt in Utica reached out and here I am. It all is shit, as you said, but I am happy here. My aunt and uncle are great people, and they make me feel like I am their kid. They have two older children who live in the area that are married, and have small kids themselves. It's as good as it can be, I guess. I do miss my family still. I'll never get over that. I miss my leg, too. But I deal with this prosthetic fine enough. Actually, an orthopedic surgeon in Syracuse is willing to replace this one with a more advanced version. That'll probably happen this summer. So, you see, when somebody at school mocks me for how I walk, I don't really care. They haven't a clue."

When he finished his story Danis was quiet.

"Lunch is almost over, but I want you to know that I'm your friend. Let's hang out again tomorrow. My mom made some dolma for me, so I'll bring some extra for you, too."

"I love dolma. Thanks. And I'd like to hear what happened to you if you're up for talking about it?"

"Sure. I'll see you tomorrow. Hvala, my friend."

It was a profound moment for Danis. He had avoided many things Bosnian, especially the first couple of years in high school. But this brought back a flood of memories. And he realized that there were so many tragic stories from his country.

He also understood that Haris didn't shy away from telling his. He just had to be asked. He was in deep thought the rest of the day. When he came home after school neither parent was there. He went into his bedroom, but couldn't focus on his homework.

He called Azra.

"Cuz, I just want to tell you that you're the best."

"What? Usually, you act like I'm not there when we see each other in the hallway."

"I know. I'm an ass. I'm sorry. Yo, does the Bosnia Club take dummies like me at this point in school?"

"Of course, Danis, we take all sorts of dummies any time!" she teased.

"Thanks, I'll be at the next meeting. I don't know how much I'll say, but I'll be there for sure."

"One more thing," he said before hanging up. "I spoke with Haris today. You know, the kid I told you about yesterday?"

"OK..."

"What an amazing dude."

"Cool. I'm glad you spoke with him. He probably needs a friend. I wonder if he'll reconsider joining our group?"

"I think he will. And I'll let him know that I'm joining. That'll help."

"Thanks, Danis. Oh, by the way, I think you're pretty cool, too," she said just before she hung up.

Chapter 35
A Somber Return

It was a cold winter day on the second Saturday in early January, 2005 when Hajra answered the door.

"Merjem, what is it? You look like you just saw a ghost."

"In a way, I have."

Elvir emerged from the kitchen.

Stepping into the apartment, and with no hesitation, Merjem spoke.

"An organization in Tuzla called the International Commission on Missing Persons, the representative referred to them as ICMP, found some remains of Tarik. He was found buried in a mass grave with several others near Prijedor, and they wanted to confirm it was him. They said the skeletal remains had a thin gold chain around the neck with faded letters M-e-r-j, on it. I...I gave him that when we were first dating and he never took it off."

She put both hands over her face and began to cry.

Both Hajra and Elvir came over to her as they guided her onto their sofa.

"My God, Merjem, my brother has been found," said Elvir.

"Yes, they believe so, but they need further evidence. And, they only found partial remains. As we are learning, the Serbs dug up the original graves and moved those buried to other sites around Bosnia and Herzegovina to try to conceal what they did. I know we've been hearing about things over the past couple of years. I'm still shocked at hearing this news. I am also happy that we know where he is. But it is all so difficult to process right now. By moving Tarik and the others to other parts of Bosnia, as well, what was the word they used, yes, they 'disarticulated' the bodies so they were no longer intact. I am kind of numb right now."

"It's likely then that the same thing happened to your parents and brothers," Hajra said.

"Likely. I need to take this all in. I need to stay seated for a minute."

"Have you told the children?" Hajra quietly asked.

"Not yet. I wanted to come here first."

Elvir was stone silent.

Merjem continued.

"I'm grateful that we can now have a proper burial, but the strange thought that maybe he had amnesia or was in a prison somewhere—or another country—that he would someday return, is no longer a possibility. I know it was irrational for me to think that he could return, but I wanted to have hope that we'd someday, somehow see him alive. Of course, the help Amila gave me to grieve was immense. Weird to still have those thoughts, though."

"One more thing, Elvir, they asked that you, as his brother, give them a sample of your DNA."

"Of course I'll do it. Of course."

Hajra brought out the box of tissues, and the three of them cried on and off for the next hour huddling together on the sofa.

Elvir was instructed by the ICMP that they would have a team in Syracuse shortly for him to give a blood sample. They wanted one from Zlata, too, but she was in a nursing home now with mild dementia, and somewhat frail, so travel was too difficult for her.

The DNA sample came back as a positive match. It was confirmed that the remains were those of Tarik. Merjem was working that day. She told her supervisor that she needed to go home—that she suddenly felt quite ill. She sat in her car in the parking lot and wept. She then drove home, and later that evening told Hajra and Elvir she had garnered the strength to tell her children, who, she said, immediately hugged her without letting go.

The Islamic Association organized a ceremony for family and friends at their rented building's auditorium. Ceremonies for those relatives found in the mass graves had begun to be a familiar event these days. Zlata was in attendance in the front row with other family members. It turned out to be an overflow crowd that had come to honor Elvir and Merjem, and the rest of the family. The Imam presided over the gathering. He asked Elvir to give a eulogy.

"My family and friends, as some of you have, or God willing, will experience, our journey to find my missing brother, Merjem's husband, and Azra and Fatima's father has ended. It has been thirteen years of not knowing. And, like many of you, though we understood the great odds against it, we always had hope that somehow, he would find us. In a way, he has. The sadness we feel is profound. But the closure of this chapter in our lives can now begin. Tarik was a great man. He and I were very close when we were growing up, and as adults in Bosnia. He will always inspire me to be a better person, a better father and husband, and a better man. Soon, we will go to bury him in Kozarac. We have not been there since that horrible day in May 1992, when our lives took a path that ultimately led us here. It is days like this that I am reminded of the angst that lurks below the surface; the pain that we try to push back down in order to live our lives as best we can, though I guess it never truly leaves us. I am not here to make any political statements. I am here to honor my brother, and to welcome him home."

As tears flowed from many in the room, Elvir stepped down from the riser and hugged his family. He was surprised he didn't cry while speaking, but he accepted the tissue that Hajra offered him to wipe the building moisture from his eyes.

A week later Merjem got a letter from ICMP saying that on July 20th, the remains of the more than 100 found along with Tarik would be buried in ceremonies at various Muslim cemeteries around Bosnia. Tarik would be buried in the only Muslim cemetery in Prijedor Municipality, which was in Kozarac, with thirty-two others.

The discovery of Tarik's remains hit Merjem hard. She always had a sliver of hope that somehow, he would show up. But, of course, realistically she knew that this was the curse that survivors had to contend with, believing that their relative was still alive. It also triggered the simmering grief that punctuated her life for her parents and brothers. She told this to the counselor, Amila, whom she had been seeing on and off for the past number of years, and who she needed now. The counselor suggested she continue to hope that her parents and brothers would be found, so that she could honor them as well.

As the time came closer to go back to Bosnia for the ceremony and burial, Merjem became more sullen.

Hajra saw this and made sure that she and Elvir didn't allow Merjem to go astray emotionally as she had done in Germany or in Utica. She had gotten very strong since then, but this opened a deep wound within her.

"Merjem, I'll make flight and hotel reservations for you and the girls. Our children want to go, too. With none of us having been back since the war began, this will be an especially tough time. But like we've been doing for years now, we have to lean on each other for strength," Hajra said.

"I know. I'm going back to the counselor, and she said the same. I'll be strong even if I feel weak. I want to be there for Azra and Fatima—and for Zlata, too, who I know won't be able to join us."

"Next month, when we're all there, let's not expect too much of each other. It will be very difficult, but it will bring some kind of closure to our pain. At least knowing that Tarik is buried in Kozarac will be some consolation, I pray," Hajra replied.

***

They flew first to Germany to see Hajra's family. It was an emotional reunion with the pain of what they were to do in Bosnia set aside for the few days they visited. Hajra's parents looked older, as her father's heart condition seemed to take a bigger toll on his health than her mother let on during their phone calls. Leaving them for Tarik's burial left everyone in a swirl of emotions.

They arrived two days before the ceremony. Returning to the place that held so many wonderful, yet so many bitter memories was the first thing they all contended with.

Everything was the same, yet nothing actually was. The rebuilt houses of Prijedor and Kozarac mostly looked like what they had left before the shelling. At least it appeared that those who rebuilt them attempted to maintain the original structures. But there was an unfamiliar air present.

Kozarac had been slowly reinfused with Bosniaks. A grocery store, butcher shop, bakery, and a mosque now dotted the small community. The cemetery, which was where the ceremony and burial were to take place, contained relatives buried there years before the war. Visiting their graves offered such a contrast to what was to take place for the thirty-three people to be buried there in a couple of days. None of this was lost on the visitors from Utica.

"My business was right over there," pointed out Elvir to the others while walking around Kozarac. "It doesn't look as good now that it's a feed shop for livestock," he mused.

"The grocery store looks so much smaller than I remember," said Hajra.

"That's because I believe it is," said Halima. "The old one was bigger. But of course, Kozarac was destroyed and had to be rebuilt."

"Danis, do you remember the last soccer match I played in, the one where we celebrated by the river with Nikola?" asked Amir.

"I sure do. It seems like a dream. Like it never happened. So much has gone by. So much to get a handle on being back here."

"Even though we knew that things were getting worse, I still wanted to believe that we would be fine. Soccer was the most important thing to me. It is such a simple game, really. And it brought us all together: Serbs, Croats, and Bosniaks. And Nikola. We just lost track of each other. Funny. I've never tried to find him. I guess I'm afraid of how he turned out," said Amir.

Merjem put her arms around both Amir's and Danis' waists and brought them close to her as they slowly walked down a quiet, tree-lined street.

"It is overwhelming. When we saw your house earlier today, or what used to be your house, I could sense in your family's silence how shocking it is to be back here," she said to them.

Azra strode over and inserted herself in between Danis and her mother. Danis put his arm around his cousin.

"Mom," said Azra, "I'm scared to go to the ceremony. I'm worried that I'm going to lose it. I want to remember Dad when he was alive with us."

"We are all very emotional, and I don't think that will subside for a while."

"Azra, let's make a pact that we sit as close as possible during the ceremony. We can lean on each other," said Fatima.

"We all will, my darlings, we all will," Merjem responded.

"And we'll be right there with you," said Halima.

Halima and Danis moved over to where their parents and Amir were.

With Halima now in the middle, Elvir and Hajra each held

a hand like they had done so many times when the children were little. Looking over at the two women in his family, Elvir tilted his head toward the sky and then back at them. All he could do was to think about how grateful he was for what he had despite the loss that they all continued to grieve, and probably would for a lifetime.

The ceremony and burial were a blur to the families attending. Tears made it hard to focus on anything but the pain they all were releasing. It was also a reunion of sorts, as many of the attendees knew each other from before the genocide. This was an unexpected benefit. They were able to catch up at the gathering held afterwards. There was food and drinks. And, of course, coffee. No one seemed to want to speak about what they had just participated in that day. It was understood that the rawness of the ceremony would provide some sort of closure along with hope for finding others who were still missing.

Two days later they boarded a flight back to the States having navigated one of the most difficult tasks they'd done since leaving Bosnia many years before. As the jet touched down at the airport in Syracuse, bright sunshine reflected off of the runway where rain had recently fallen, and the clouds had drifted away, exposing a deep blue Central New York sky. They had made it. In their hearts they knew that the pain would always be there. They were also well aware that hope was the eternal flame that would guide them going forward. They would surely have their highs and lows, as is wont in the ebb and flow of life, but they had arisen from the ash heap of a genocide, scarred as they were, but nonetheless triumphant. Their own free will could never be taken from them. Their successes were theirs alone, as were their failures, flaws, joys, sadness and dreams. That was their victory over the oppressors. They knew the truth. They lived it. Their lives could no longer be beaten down. It was theirs to share with the world if they so choose. Or not. They were alive and representing the legacy of those who were violated and murdered; they survived and now thrived. And if the revisionists wish to say it didn't happen that way, well, just ask one of them. Sit down over a strong cup of Bosnian coffee, and listen, and learn what truths sound like. Listen with your own heart as you hear of the struggles that still go on, of the stain on both Bosnia and humanity as a whole, explained in the stories of survivors of genocide. And know that they triumphed.

Just listen.

Epilogue

Dear Mom,

I know we speak by phone often, but sometimes writing is a better way of expressing all that is inside. I am moved to do so as I reflect upon time now that I am sixty-three.

I can't believe it's been seven years since Zlata died. Or ten years since Dad died. I miss them both. I am always thankful that I got to see Dad when we went back to Bosnia to bury Tarik. I know that it is still difficult for you without him even after all these years. Ahmed and his family have been an amazing support for you and Dad, and I am so appreciative for that.

I don't know why, but lately I've been feeling very nostalgic for the old days. Not the days of suffering, of course, but for the days well before the war, well before we became pariahs in our own land.

I can recall you standing by the stove cooking the wonderful meals you created, always with love. That was so evident. We'd all laugh at the silliest things, like when Harun impersonated Elvis Presley's "You Ain't Nothin' but a Hound Dog." He didn't know the words in English and tried to dance like Elvis. Actually, who even paid attention to who Elvis was? But that was our Harun. In America, they say he was an original. There are even people who impersonate him for a living, and I tease Harun now that he missed his calling. It's funny, but I remember when Danis did the same type of thing when he was young. I guess he must have seen his uncle do his impressions.

I also miss the beauty of Bosnia. The mountains, the rivers, the villages and cities like ours. The warmth we all felt for one another in Prijedor among Bosniaks, Serbs and Croats. I have nightmares sometimes about the camps. I told you though, the counseling I got from a Bosnian woman here in Utica was so helpful. And it got me to start that informal group of women a few years ago who were violated in the camps. There are ten of us that meet once a month to talk and share. We often just talk about our lives and benefit from the comradery, the commonality of what we experienced. Sometimes we read a book, usually about Bosnia, but not always, and discuss it. I wish there were more groups like that for others like us, but it's a hard thing to convince women to speak of such trauma. Some of the women in the group say that their husbands can't talk about what happened to them: too painful. I get it, but for me I've learned that we need a sense of community, of belonging in order to mourn and heal.

When we were growing up, if someone mentioned that they were depressed and thought about getting psychological help he or she would be called crazy. That's what worried Merjem many years ago, but thankfully she got help, and got so much stronger because of it. It has occurred to me over the years that thinking about sharing our pain with others is not a weakness, but seeing it that way is detrimental to us survivors and our children. In the past several years, it seems to be changing a lot. I know that more of us are speaking publicly about our experiences, which is another way to heal. We are not immune to depression and anxiety. I still get jumpy when I hear shouting, even if it erupts at a soccer match.

Are we to bury our sadness? Are we to pretend that nothing happened to us? Are we to forget the horrors we experienced and let them go, especially with what's happening now in Republika Srpska, on land that used to be ours? Am I to forget that I was violated at the hands of a monster?

I have spoken with many people who have been back, even a friend of mine here who went to Kozarac to stay for a month. She said that most of the Serbs living in Republika Srpska don't accept that a genocide happened. They act like Milosevic, Karadzic, Mladic and others are heroes—that they fought to preserve the Greater Serbia that they deserved to have, and that we Muslims were the invaders. That's called revisionist history: genocide denial. All anyone has to do is to hear our stories, to know our truths. And yet, my friend says, most of the Serbs act oblivious to what actually happened. There are some who get it, of course, but they are fighting an uphill battle. So, we have to tell our stories to anyone who will listen. We who witnessed the genocide must leave our experiences as testimony to what occurred. Elvir and I have given some talks at local schools to teach students about what happened. They don't teach this in American schools. Our Imam here once said that we are a forgiving people, but we have not been asked for forgiveness. That sums it up for me. I miss my Bosnia. But sadly, I can never feel safe there again.

It's interesting, but as I reflect on this letter to you, I realize that each of my children are fighting injustices in their own way.

Of course, Amir and his wife Lejla love Munich, and it warms my heart that you get to visit with each other. How I miss him. But his work as a journalist with *Balkan Insight* is very fulfilling. He is very busy doing what he loves. And Lejla's career has taken off with *Der Spiegel* as a reporter in Munich. We are so proud of them both. But I guess I'm preaching to the choir, aren't I?

I am always in awe of Halima. Do you remember when she was young, she always said she wanted to be a lawyer? I am sure she never thought back then what she'd be fighting for. When she graduated from Law School in international law, she was determined to find her path in human rights. She loves her job with Amnesty International in New York City.

She comes up to Utica now and again, but she is so busy with her work. Too busy to ever marry, which makes me sad, but she is very content with her life. She has lots of friends. Many are "committed singles" as she likes to say to me.

And Danis—my Danis. He and Nadija, and their three kids bring me such joy. Living nearby, we get to see them a lot. Those kids are so cute and growing fast. I love being their majka and taking care of them. Danis is a hard worker like his dad. He loves the import/export business and will soon take it over when Elvir retires. Although, I don't know if Elvir will ever actually retire. Somehow, he'll keep his hands in the business. He and Danis are very close. They continue to do so much for our Bosnian community here.

They love to host events at the new Cultural Center. Last month, they had a fundraiser for food banks in Bosnia. We had traditional dancers, a band from Bosnia, and a local professor, who Amir loved as an instructor when he went to the community college, and who herself is from Donji Vakuf. She, too, survived the genocide with her family. They even lived in a refugee camp in Pakistan. Imagine that. She gave an impassioned speech that spoke to those of us who survived the war, and to those who lost so many to the Serbs. It made me cry. I could see Elvir tear up, as well. We didn't need to talk about it because he and I practically read each other's minds. He is always so supportive of me and me of him.

You may not know the American musician Bruce Springsteen, but he has a song that speaks to our marriage. His message is about two people who love each other, and their commitment is that when one falls behind emotionally or spiritually, the other will wait and be there to lean on. That's like Elvir and me. I feel so blessed.

Last September, we commemorated 9/11 here in the States. It's been nineteen years since the attacks by the terrorists. I remember that we had been here only five years when that happened. I was so depressed. It brought back the helpless feeling that I had during the war. I felt quite distraught at the loss of life and property. I felt a deep sense of sorrow for this country, my new country. And then Muslims got targeted. I was worried that we would be among the hate that too many Americans had for people who had nothing to do with the attacks. Strangely, we were not in their line of fire. I believe because we are white-passing. I tell you this because it is a sad state of affairs that skin color or religion or any other characteristic that make up us humans should even be an issue, but it still is, even in 2021. The insurrection at our Capitol in January was a stark reminder that leaders like Trump play off of people's fears. I remember all too well the relentless propaganda that Milosevic and Karadzic spewed to their minions about non-Serbs. They always acted like the victims, when it was their hate that victimized others. I see many parallels here. It is a divisive time in America, and fear is the driving force. I continue to wonder: why does this continue to happen all over the world? Fortunately, we have elected Joe Biden as our new president. I am hoping that he can bridge the deep rift that exists here. And I am in awe that our vice-president is a woman, Kamala Harris, whose father is Black from Jamaica, and whose mother is South Asian from India. This country still never ceases to amaze me, despite the disappointments.

So, with everything I shared in this letter, I am still never sure how I get through a whole day without thinking about the war. It may not even be a conscious image. It might just be that something happened which triggered an almost imperceptible chill quietly making its way down my spine. But life must be lived, regardless.

Finally, Mom, we will be coming to visit you all when COVID-19 is under control. It has been a scary thing, for sure. But Elvir and I have gotten our vaccinations. I am anxious to see you. We are all getting older and our time to be together is finite.

Please give my love to everyone there. When you see my Amir tell him I have a special memory for him that I will bring when we see each other. I won't give it away, but I found something that was his when he was a kid, and that I had patched and cleaned up. Hint: it was always dirty and caked with sweat. I can't wait to hug you again, my dear mother. We'll speak by phone very soon.

Your loving daughter,
Hajra

<u>Data from ICTY on genocide in Prijedor</u>

(Slide presented by prosecution team at the Hague during Mladic trial)

	1991 Muslim population	1993 Muslim population
Bišćani	1421	0
Čarakovo	2324	2
Hambarine	2768	2
Kamičani	3014	0
Kozarac	3740	3
Kozaruša	2853	0
Rakovčani	1406	1
Rizvanovići	1551	1
Trnopolje	2667	2
Kevljani	1893	0
Zecovi	701	0

Resources

This list only represents a fraction of what one can find on the internet. I encourage you to seek the truth. -JSS

Balkan Transitional Justice Programme/Balkan Insight for up-to-date news articles out of the Balkans
Balkaninsight.com

Holocaust and Genocide Lecture Series (Sonoma State University)-April 16, 2019
Irfan Mirza: "Voices of the Bosnian Genocide" (YouTube)

Srebrenica Memorial
Srebrenicamemorial.org/en (in English)

"Omarska's Survivors: Bosnia 1992 (YouTube)
Al-Jazeera English; May, 2017

"The Horrors of a Camp called Omarska and the Serb Strategy"- article by Mark Danner
pbs.org-Frontline

"The Trial of Ratko Mladic" PBS Frontline documentary
2019 Season; episode 18

Arnesa Buljusmic-Kutura interview with survivor of Omarska and Manjaca, Satko Mujagic
YouTube-June, 2020

International Criminal Tribunal for the former Yugoslavia (ICTY)
icty.org

International Commissions for Missing Persons (ICMP)
icmp.int

Prijedor: Fields of Death (four parts)
YouTube Modern History

"More Lasting than Bronze," Touring the Architecture of Revisionism by Jack Hitt
vqronline.org

People to search:

Ed Vulliamy (UK), journalist, author.

Hikmet Karcic, Genocide scholar at Institute for Islamic Tradition of Bosniaks and Center for Global Policy in Washington D.C.

David Pettigrew, professor at University of Southern Connecticut

Elvira Hasecic, activist and founder of the "Association of Women Victims of War" (Bosnia)

Kemal Pervanic, founder of Most Mira (Bosnia)

Ajna-Jusic, Activist and founder of "Forgotten Children of War Association" (Bosnia)

BOOKS

Peter Maass: Love Thy Neighbor

Kemal Pervanic: The Killing Days

Rezak Husanovic: The Tenth Circle of Hell

Jasmina Dervisevic-Cesic: The River Runs Salt, Runs Sweet

Arnesa Buljusmic-Kustura: Letters from Diaspora

Bosnian Alphabet	English Sound	Pronunciation Example
A	/a/	a as in **car**
B	/b/	b as in **bat**
C	/ts/	c as in **cats**
Č	/tʃ/	č as in **chalk**
Ć	/tɕ/	ć as in **church**
D	/d/	d as in **dig**
Dž	/dʒ/	dž as in **gin**
Đ	/dʑ/	đ as in **jack**
E	/e/	e as in **let**
F	/f/	f as in **fit**
G	/g/	g as in **game**
H	/x/	h as in **heaven**
I	/i/	i as in **east**
J	/j/	j as in **year**
K	/k/	k as in **cut**
L	/l/	l as in **love**
Lj	/ʎ/	lj as in **million**
M	/m/	m as in **mice**
N	/n/	n as in **nice**
Nj	/ɲ/	nj as in **onion**
O	/o/	o as in **autmn**
P	/p/	p as in **pick**
R	/r/	r as in **Fritz**
S	/s/	s as in **sound**
Š	/ʃ/	š as in **shut**
T	/t/	t as in **time**
U	/u/	u as in **shoot**
V	/ʋ/	v as in **verb**
Z	/z/	z as in **zest**
Ž	/ʒ/	ž as in **pleasure**

Acknowledgements

I met with Satko Mujagic several times via Zoom, and we often corresponded by email as he enlightened me with his own experiences in Omarska and Manjaca. He graciously gave his time to provide for me feedback to enhance the veracity of the story during the revision process. Satko's foreword is especially poignant, and I am grateful from the bottom of my heart to call him my friend. I would also like to thank Dr. David Pettigrew, professor of philosophy at Southern Connecticut State University, for giving me insight into both the genocide and current political situation in BiH. He is a member of the Steering Committee of the Yale University Genocide Studies Program. He also serves as an International Expert Team Council Member of the Institute for the Research of Genocide Canada. I am grateful to have him as my friend and ally. Special thanks to Dr. Adis Maksic, political science researcher and Associate Professor at International Burch University in Sarajevo, for his help in understanding the political situation in Prijedor and BiH. Finally, I appreciate Dr. Hikmet Karcic, genocide scholar at the Institute for Islamic Tradition of Bosniaks in Sarajevo and Senior Fellow for Global Policy in Washington, DC, for his contribution to this book by introducing readers to the etiology of the Bosnian genocide.

On a more personal level, my wife Pina is always inspirational and supportive of my work. Her passion as a cancer researcher always humbles me. I also am grateful to my daughter, Rebecca, who was my first beta reader and provided me with excellent and usable feedback. Her forthrightness and honesty, especially coming from such a well-read and insightful woman, means the world to me, as does she. And to my son, Aaron, who makes me laugh even when the topic is sobering, and who never ceases to amaze me.

Lastly, and perhaps most importantly, I am thankful for the many survivors who I have spoken with over the past couple of years for generously sharing their stories; their pain; their resilience. For them, it is critical that we shed light on the truth, and tamp down the darkness that is the denial which continues to hold back the justice that must be served in order to have their murdered, wounded, violated, and displaced loved ones truly find peace.

About Atmosphere Press

Atmosphere Press is an independent, full-service publisher for excellent books in all genres and for all audiences. Learn more about what we do at atmospherepress.com.

We encourage you to check out some of Atmosphere's latest releases, which are available at Amazon.com and via order from your local bookstore:

Twisted Silver Spoons, a novel by Karen M. Wicks
Queen of Crows, a novel by S.L. Wilton
The Summer Festival is Murder, a novel by Jill M. Lyon
The Past We Step Into, stories by Richard Scharine
The Museum of an Extinct Race, a novel by Jonathan Hale Rosen
Swimming with the Angels, a novel by Colin Kersey
Island of Dead Gods, a novel by Verena Mahlow
Cloakers, a novel by Alexandra Lapointe
Twins Daze, a novel by Jerry Petersen
Embargo on Hope, a novel by Justin Doyle
Abaddon Illusion, a novel by Lindsey Bakken
Blackland: A Utopian Novel, by Richard A. Jones
The Jesus Nut, a novel by John Prather
The Embers of Tradition, a novel by Chukwudum Okeke
Saints and Martyrs: A Novel, by Aaron Roe
When I Am Ashes, a novel by Amber Rose
Melancholy Vision: A Revolution Series Novel, by L.C. Hamilton
The Recoleta Stories, by Bryon Esmond Butler
Voodoo Hideaway, a novel by Vance Cariaga

About the Author

Jordan Steven Sher's first book, Our Neighbors, Their Voices: True Stories of Immigrant Exodus, chronicling the stories of immigrants to the U.S., was published in 2019. Inspired by two survivors of the genocide Sher met during the writing of this book, his subsequent work has focused on the genocide in Bosnia and its aftermath for survivors. He lives with his wife, Pina Cardarelli in Northern California, and has two wonderful adult children, Aaron and Rebecca, making their own mark on the world.

Jordanstevensher.com